Praise for Lucy Parker
and *Act Like It*

"This story made me tremendously happy. I liked this book so much, I read it twice."
—*Smart Bitches, Trashy Books*

"This was a book that made me feel safe. It made me feel safe in the author's hands, safe in the characters' hands, safe in the story's hands."
—*Dear Author*

"Well written, with very human characters and an entertaining plot, this debut novel is highly recommended for romance lovers."
—*Library Journal*

"Ms. Parker has a deft hand with dialogue, making it feel both current and witty. I found myself smiling while reading this, and frequently laughing out loud."
—*All About Romance*

"An engaging book, so much fun and so well written."
—*Fiction Vixen*

"A fun, sexy, laugh out loud romance.... Well written with a delightful pace, witty dialogue, and dynamic full-bodied characters. I will definitely be looking for more from Ms. Parker in the future."
—*Smexy Books*

"As soon as I started reading, I fell in love with the writing. With its feisty heroine, grouchy-but-loveable hero, and unlikely love story, this was a winner!"
—*Aestas Book Blog*

act like it

LUCY PARKER

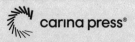

carina press®

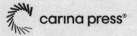 carina press®

Recycling programs
for this product may
not exist in your area.

ISBN-13: 978-0-373-00411-9

Act Like It

www.CarinaPress.com

Printed in U.S.A.

For my parents and my nana,
for their unfailing love and support.

act
like
it

ONE

ALMOST EVERY NIGHT, between nine and ten past, Lainie Graham passionately kissed her ex-boyfriend. She was then gruesomely dead by ten o'clock, stabbed through the neck by a jealous rival. If she was scheduled to perform in the weekend matinee, that was a minimum of six uncomfortable kisses a week. More, if the director called an extra rehearsal or the alternate actor was ill. Or if Will was being a prat backstage and she was slow to duck.

It was an odd situation, being paid to publicly snog the man who, offstage, had discarded her like a stray sock. From the perspective of a broken relationship, the theatre came up trumps in the awkward stakes. A television or film actor might have to make stage love to someone they despised, but they didn't have to play the same scene on repeat for an eight-month run.

From her position in the wings, Lainie watched Will and Chloe Wayne run through the penultimate scene. Chloe was practically vibrating with sexual tension, which wasn't so much in character as it was her default setting. Will was breathing in the wrong places during his monologue; it was throwing off his pacing. She waited, and—

"*Farmer!*" boomed the director from his seat in the front row. Alexander Bennett's balding head was gleaming with sweat under the houselights. He'd been lounging in his chair but now dropped any pretence of indifference, jerking forward to glare at the stage. "You're blocking a scene, not swimming the bloody breaststroke. Stop bobbing your head about and breathe through your damn nose."

A familiar sulky expression transformed Will's even features. He looked like a spoilt, genetically blessed schoolboy. He was professional enough to smooth out the instinctive scowl and resume his speech, but with an air of resentment that didn't improve his performance. This was the moment of triumph for his character and right now the conquering knight sounded as if he would rather put down his sword and go for a pint.

Will had been off his game since the previous night, when he'd flubbed a line in the opening act. He was a gifted actor. An unfaithful toerag, but a talented actor. He rarely made mistakes—and could cover them better than most—but from the moment he'd stumbled over his cue, the additional rehearsal had been inevitable. Bennett sought perfection in every arena of his life, which was why he was on to his fifth marriage and all the principals had been dragged out of bed on their morning off.

Most of the principals, Lainie amended silently. Their brooding Byron had, as usual, done as he pleased. Bennett had looked almost apoplectic when Richard Troy had sauntered in twenty minutes late, so that explosion was still coming. If possible, he preferred to roar in his private office, where his Tony Award was prominently displayed on the desk. It was a sort of visual aid on the journey from stripped ego to abject apology.

Although a repentant Richard Troy was about as likely as a winged pig, and he could match Bennett's prized trophy and raise him two more.

Onstage, Chloe collapsed into a graceful swoon, which was Richard's cue for the final act. He pushed off the wall on the opposite side of the wings and flicked an invisible speck from his spotless shirt. Then he entered from stage left and whisked the spotlight from Will and Chloe with insulting ease, taking control of the scene with barely a twitch of his eyelid.

Four months into the run of *The Cavalier's Tribute*, it was still an undeniable privilege to watch him act.

Unfortunately, Richard's stage charisma was comparable to the interior of the historic Metronome Theatre. At night, under the houselights, the Metronome was pure magic, a charged atmosphere of class and old-world glamour. In the unforgiving light of day, it looked tired and a bit sordid, like an aging diva caught without her war paint and glitter.

And when the curtain came down and the skin of the character was shed, Richard Troy was an intolerable prick.

Will was halfway through the most long-winded of his speeches. It was Lainie's least favourite moment in an otherwise excellent play. Will's character, theoretically the protagonist, became momentarily far less sympathetic than Richard's undeniable villain. She still couldn't tell if it was an intentional ambiguity on the part of the playwright, perhaps a reflection that humanity is never cast in shades of black and white, or if it was just poor writing. The critic in the *Guardian* had thought the latter.

Richard was taunting Will now, baiting him with both words and snide glances, and looking as if he was enjoying himself a little too much. Will drew himself up, and his face took on an expression of intense self-righteousness.

Lainie winced. It was, down to the half sneer, the exact same face he made in bed.

She really wished she didn't know that.

"Ever worry it's going to create some sort of cosmic imbalance?" asked a voice at her elbow, and she turned to smile at Meghan Hanley, her dresser. "Having both of them in one building? If you toss in most of the management, I think we may be exceeding the recommended bastard quota." Meghan raised a silvery eyebrow as she watched the denouement of the play. "They both have swords, and neither of them takes the opportunity for a quick jab. What a waste."

"Please. A pair of blind, arthritic nuns would do better in a swordfight. Richard has probably never charged anything heavier than a credit card, and Will has the hand-eye coordination of an earthworm."

She was admittedly still a little bitter. Although not in the least heartbroken. Only a very silly schoolgirl would consider Will Farmer to be the love of her life, and that delusion would only last until she'd actually met him. But Lainie had not relished being dumped by the trashiest section of *London Celebrity.* The tabloid had taken great pleasure in informing her, and the rest of the rag-reading world, that Will was now seeing the estranged wife of a footballer—who in turn had been cheated on by her husband with a former *Big Brother* contestant. It was an endless sordid cycle.

The article had helpfully included a paparazzi shot of her from about three months ago, when she'd left the theatre and been caught midsneeze. *Farmer's costar and ousted lover Elaine Graham dissolves into angry tears outside the Metronome.*

Brilliant.

The journo, to use the term loosely, had also complimented her on retaining her appetite in the face of such humiliation—insert shot of her eating chips at Glastonbury—with a cunning little system of arrows to indicate a possible baby bump.

Her dad had phoned her, offering to deliver Will's balls on a platter.

Margaret Ward, the assistant stage manager, paused to join the unofficial critics' circle. She pushed back her ponytail with a paint-splattered hand and watched Richard. His voice was pure, plummy Eton and Oxford—not so much as a stumbled syllable in his case. Will looked sour.

Richard drew his sword, striding forward to stand under the false proscenium. Margaret glanced up at the wooden arch. "Do you ever wish it would just accidentally drop on his head?"

Yes.

"He hasn't *quite* driven me to homicidal impulses yet." Lainie recalled the Tuesday night performance, when she'd bumped into Richard outside his dressing room. She had apologised. He had made a misogynistic remark at a volume totally out of proportion to a minor elbow jostle.

The media constantly speculated as to why he was still single. Mind-boggling.

"*Yet*," she repeated grimly.

"By the way," Margaret said, as she glanced at her clipboard and flagged a lighting change, "Bob wants to see you in his office in about ten minutes."

Lainie turned in surprise. "Bob does? Why?"

Her mind instantly went into panic mode, flicking back over the past week. With the exception of touching His Majesty's sacred arm for about two seconds—and she wouldn't put it past Richard to lay a complaint about that—she couldn't think of any reason for a summons to the stage manager's office. As a rule, Robert Carson viewed his actors as so many figureheads. They were useful for pulling out at cocktail parties and generating social media buzz, but operated beneath his general notice unless they did something wrong. Bob preferred to concentrate on the bottom line, and the bottom line in question was located at the end of his bank statement.

Margaret shrugged. "He didn't say. He's been in a bad mood all day, though," she warned, and Lainie sighed.

"I could have been in bed right now," she mused wistfully. "With a cream cheese bagel and a completely trashy book. Bloody Will."

On the flip side, she could also still have been in bed *with* Will, enjoying the taste of his morning breath and a lecture on her questionable tastes in literature. From the man who still thought *To Kill a Mockingbird* was a nonfiction guide for the huntin', shootin' and fishin' set.

Life could really only improve.

On that cheering thought, she made her way out of the wings and backstage into the rabbit's warren of tunnelling hallways that led to the staff offices. The floors and walls creaked as she went, as if the theatre were quietly grumbling under its breath. Despite the occasional sticking door handle and an insidious smell of damp, she liked the decrepit old lady. The Metronome was one of the oldest theatres in the West End. They might not have decent seating and fancy automated loos, but they had history. Legendary actors had walked these halls.

"And Edmund Kean probably thought the place was an absolute dump as well," had been Meghan's opinion on that subject.

Historical opinion was divided on the original seventeenth-century use of the Metronome. Debate raged in textbooks as to whether it had been a parliamentary annex or a high-class brothel. Lainie couldn't see that it really mattered. It would likely have been frequented by the same men in either instance.

Personally, she voted for the brothel. It would add a bit of spice to the inevitable haunting rumours. Much more interesting to have a randy ghost who had succumbed midcoitus than an overworked civil servant who had died of boredom midpaperwork.

Aware that Bob's idea of "in ten minutes" could be loosely translated as "right now," she headed straight for his office, which was one of the few rooms at the front of the theatre and had a view looking out over the busy road. Her memories of the room were associated with foot shuffling, mild sweating and a fervent wish to be outside amid an anonymous throng of shoppers and tourists heading for Oxford Street.

"Enter," called a voice at her knock, and she took the opportunity to roll her eyes before she opened the door. Her most convincing fake smile was firmly in place by the time she walked inside, but it faltered when she saw the two women standing with Bob.

"Good. Elaine," Bob said briskly. He was wearing his usual incorrectly buttoned shirt. Every day it was a different button. Same shirt, apparently, but different button. He *had* to be doing it on purpose. "You remember Lynette Stern and Patricia Bligh."

Naturally, Lainie remembered Lynette and Pat. She saw them every week, usually from a safe distance. An uneasy prickling sensation was beginning to uncurl at the base of her neck. She greeted Pat with a mild unconcern she didn't feel, and returned Lynette's nod. She couldn't imagine why the tall sharp-nosed blonde was here for this obviously less-than-impromptu meeting. She would have thought her more likely to be passed out in a mental health spa. Or just sobbing in a remote corner. Lynette Stern was Richard Troy's agent, and she had Lainie's sincere sympathies. Every time she saw the woman, there was a new line on her forehead.

It was Pat Bligh's presence that gave Lainie serious pause. Pat was the Metronome's PR manager. She ruled over their collective public image with an iron hand and very little sense of humour. And woe betide anyone who was trending for unfortunate reasons on Twitter.

What the hell had she done?

She was biting on her thumbnail. It was a habit she had successfully kicked at school, and she forced herself to stop now, clasping her hands tightly together. She had been in a running panic this morning to get to the Tube on time, and now she wished she'd taken time to check her Google alerts.

Nude photos? Not unless someone had wired her

shower. Even as an infant, she had disliked being naked. She usually broke speed records in changing her clothes.

She blanched. *Unless Will had taken…*

In which case she was going to hit the stage and make short work of borrowing Richard's sword, and Will was going to find himself minus two of his favourite accessories.

"Sit down, Elaine," Bob said, his expression unreadable. Reluctantly, she obeyed the order—Bob didn't do invitations—and chose the most uncomfortable chair in the room, as if in a preemptive admittance of guilt.

Get a grip.

"I'll come right to the point." Bob sat on the edge of the wide mahogany desk and gestured the other women to sit down with an impatient wiggle of his index finger. Reaching for the iPad on his blotter, he flipped it open and keyed in the password. "I presume you've seen this."

He held the iPad in front of Lainie's face and she blinked, trying to bring the screen into focus. She could feel the heavy pulse of her heartbeat, but dread dwindled into confusion when she saw the news item. *London Celebrity* had struck again, but she wasn't the latest offering for the sacrificial pit after all.

It appeared that Richard had dined out last night. The fact that he'd entered into a shouting match with a notable chef and decided to launch a full-scale offensive on the tableware seemed about right. She took a closer look at the lead photograph. Of *course* his paparazzi shots were that flattering. No piggy-looking eyes and double chins for Richard Troy. He probably didn't *have* a bad angle.

God, he was irritating.

She shrugged, and three sets of pursed lips tightened. "Well," she said hastily, trying to recover her ground, "it's unfortunate, but…"

"But Richard does this kind of shit all the time," was probably not the answer they were looking for.

And what exactly did this have to do with her? Surely they weren't expecting her to cough up for his damages bill. The spoon in baby Richard Troy's mouth had been diamond-encrusted platinum. He was old family money, a millionaire multiple times over. He could pay for his own damn broken Meissen. If he had a propensity for throwing public temper tantrums and hurling objects about the room, his management team should have restricted him to eating at McDonald's. There was only so much damage he could do with paper wrappers and plastic forks.

"It's getting to be more than *unfortunate*," Lynette said, in such an ominous tone that Lainie decided to keep her opinions to herself on that score.

Pat at last broke her simmering silence. "There have been eight separate incidents in this month alone." Three strands of blond hair had come loose from her exquisitely arranged chignon. For most women, that would be a barely noticeable dishevelment. Lainie's own hair tended to collapse with a resigned sigh the moment she turned away from the mirror. For Pat, three unpinned locks was a shocking state of disarray. "It's only the second week of October."

Lainie thought that even Richard should fear that particular tone of voice from this woman. She flinched on his behalf.

"Any publicity is good publicity. Isn't that the idea?" She glanced warily from one mutinous face to the next.

It was an identical expression, replicated thrice over. A sort of incredulous outrage, as if the whole class were being punished for the sins of one naughty child.

Apt, really. If one considered the personalities involved.

"To a point." Bob's nostrils flared. She couldn't help noticing that a trim wouldn't go astray there. "Which Troy has now exceeded." He gave her a filthy look that suggested she was personally responsible for Richard's behaviour. God forbid.

"Men in particular," he went on, stating the loathsome truth, "are given a fair amount of leeway in the public eye. A certain reputation for devilry, a habit of thumbing one's nose at the establishment, sowing one's wild oats…" He paused, looking hard at her, and Lainie hoped that her facial expression read "listening." As opposed to "nauseated." He sounded like a 1950s summary of the ideal man's man. Which had been despicably sexist sixty years ago and had not improved since.

"However," Bob continued, and the word came down like a sledgehammer, "there is a line at which a likable bad boy becomes a nasty entitled bastard whom the public would rather see hung out to dry in the street than pay to watch prance about a stage in his bloomers. And when somebody starts abusing their fans, making an absolute arse of themselves in public places, and alienating the people who paid for their bloody Ferrari, they may consider that line *crossed*."

Lainie wondered if an actual "Hallelujah" chorus had appeared in the doorway, or if it was just the sound of her own glee.

She still had no idea why she was the privileged audience to this character assassination, but she warmly appreciated it. Surely, though, they weren't...

"Are you *firing* him?" Her voice squeaked as if she had uttered the most outrageous profanity. Voiced the great unspoken. The mere suggestion of firing Richard Troy was the theatrical equivalent of hollering "Voldemort!" in the halls of Hogwarts. He-Who-Shall-Not-Be-Missed.

Still...

She wondered if it would be mean-spirited to cross her fingers.

Bob's return look was disappointingly exasperated. "Of course we're not firing him. It would cost an absolute bloody fortune to break his contract."

"And I suggest you don't attempt it." Lynette sounded steely.

"Besides," Bob said grudgingly, "nobody is denying that he's a decent actor, when he confines his histrionics to the script."

That was a typical Bob-ism. Pure understatement. Richard Troy had made the cover of *Time* magazine the previous year. The extravagantly handsome headshot had been accompanied by an article lauding him as a talent surpassing Olivier, and only two critics had been appalled.

"And if he conducted his outbursts with a bit of discretion," Bob said, as if they were discussing a string of irregular liaisons, "then we wouldn't be having this discussion. But Troy's deplorable public image is beginning to affect ticket sales. The management is not pleased."

Lainie couldn't match his awe of a bunch of walking wallets in suits, but she echoed the general feeling of dismay. If the management weren't pleased, Bob would make everyone else's life an utter misery until their mood improved.

"I'm not sure what this has to do with me," she said warily.

"If ticket sales are down, it's everybody's problem," Lynette said pompously, and Pat looked at her impatiently.

"We need some good publicity for Richard." She folded her arms and subjected Lainie to an intense scrutiny, which wavered into scepticism. "The general consensus is so overwhelmingly negative that he's in danger of falling victim to a hate campaign in the press. People might flock to see a subject of scandal, but they won't fork over hard-earned cash to watch someone they wholeheartedly despise. Not in this competitive market. At least not since it became socially unacceptable to heave rotten vegetables at the stage," she added with a brief, taut smile.

Lainie allowed herself three seconds to fantasize about that.

"How badly have sales dropped?" she asked, wondering if she ought to be contacting her agent. She had a third audition lined up for a period drama that was due to begin shooting early next year, but if there was a chance the play might actually fold…

An internationally acclaimed West End production, brought down by Richard Troy's foot-stamping sulks. Unbelievable.

"We're down fourteen percent on last month," Bob said, and she bit her lip. "We're not going bust." He sounded a bit put out at having to lessen his grievance. "It would take a pipe bomb as well as Richard's presence onstage before there was any real threat of that. But we've had to paper the house four nights running this month, and we opened to a six-week waiting list. This play has another four months to run, and we want to end on a high. Not in a damp fizzle of insulted fans and critics."

Lainie was silent for a moment. It was news to her that management were giving out free tickets in order to fill empty seats. "Well, excuse the stupidity, but I'm still not sure what you expect me to do about it. Ask him nicely to be a good boy and pull up his socks? Three guesses as to the outcome."

The tension zapped back into her spine when Bob and Pat exchanged a glance.

Pat seemed to be debating her approach. Eventually, she commented almost casually, "Ticket sales at the Palladium have gone up ten percent in the last three months."

Lainie snorted. "I know. Since Jack Trenton lost his last remaining brain cell after rehab and hooked up with Sadie Foster."

Or, as she was affectionately known in the world of musical theatre, the She-Devil of Soho. Lainie had known Sadie since they were in their late teens. They had been at drama school together. She had been short-listed against her for a role in a community theatre production of *42nd Street*, and had found shards of broken glass in the toes of her tap shoes. Fortunately before she'd put them on.

She was so preoccupied with a short-lived trip down a murky memory lane that she missed the implication.

"Quite." Pat's left eyebrow rose behind the lens of her glasses. She was now leaning on the edge of Bob's desk, her blunt, fuchsia-painted nails tapping a jaunty little medley on the surface. "And the only genuine buzz of excitement Richard has generated in the past month was when *London Celebrity* printed photos of the two of you attending the Bollinger party together." She again stared at Lainie, as if she was examining her limb by limb in an attempt to discover her appeal, and was coming up short.

The penny had dropped. With the clattering, appalling clamour of an anvil.

"You," Pat confirmed, horrifyingly, "are a publicist's dream. Probably about as interesting as a shrivelled balloon to the worst of the paps, but Joe and Jane Average think you're a doll. Blogger commentary was wavering between speculation you're headed for a breakdown and reluctant fascination. Theatre's favourite bastard and a reigning sweetheart of the London stage. For five minutes, Richard had never been so popular. But nothing came of it." This last was uttered accusingly.

Lainie's mouth opened. And closed. And opened again. "Nothing *came* of it—" she managed to find her voice to retort "—because nothing *happened.* We didn't even speak at that party. We happened to leave at the same time, and not only did Richard pretend he didn't see me—" her voice was rising in remembered annoyance "—but he failed to notice when his cuff link caught on my dress and tore it. Which meant that I felt obliged to *buy* the bloody thing. It was custom Jenny Packham, and I didn't even like it."

It was a gorgeous, gaspingly expensive dress that not been designed for a redhead with breasts. Countless fashion bloggers had agreed with her. It was now the priciest dust-catcher in her wardrobe and probably felt miserably out of place among the high street sale bargains.

Pat ignored her. "If you and Richard were seen out together for a while, if the public believed you were a couple…"

"Let's just get this straight, shall we?" Lainie looked from one face to the next. She could feel her cheeks burning red and wasn't sure whether the embarrassment or the fury had top billing. If people thought they could make this kind of…of…*shoddy* suggestion, things had apparently not changed that much since the good old days when the word *actress* was synonymous with the word *whore*. "Are you seriously suggesting I conduct some sort of faux-mance with Richard Troy in the tabloids, for the sole purpose of getting a few more bums in seats?"

Go from genuinely dating Will Farmer to fake-shagging Richard Troy? It seemed like a lateral move.

"Considering that most of the people who would care are well aware I was recently seeing Will," she pointed out crossly, "I hardly think that jumping into bed with another of my castmates is going to maintain this alleged 'sweetheart' image. I can imagine several more likely comments."

"Well, they would still be more flattering than what's already being hurled at Troy." Bob grimaced. "I believe the old epithet 'Byron' has been substituted with a simple 'Dickhead.'"

Lainie couldn't help snorting again. She'd always suspected that Richard had coined the Byronic comparison himself. He played a little too closely to the stereotype.

"You've handled the Will situation like a pro," Pat

cut in, and she sounded warm with approval. Lainie half expected a proud pat on the head. "Public sympathies are entirely in your corner. He helped, of course, by immediately taking up with that inflated tart."

"Yes, that *was* fortunate," Lainie said dryly.

"People want to see you move on—and trade up."

"Therefore, in a fun twist, I get naked with the most despised actor in London?"

"Nobody is asking you to sleep with him," Bob said, annoyed, before Pat could reply. He made an impatient gesture. "God forbid. It might put him in a good mood for once. All that brooding method acting completely undone by a fatuous smile." He tried a placatory smile himself. It was not endearing. "It's not simply a matter of sales. Everyone's professional reputation will take the hit of even a minor failure." He raised both hands, palms up. "All we're asking is that you salt the mine a bit. Attend a few parties together. Actually speak to one another. Perhaps really push the boat out and hold hands in public. Gossip stirs. Ticket sales rise. Everyone's happy."

"*I'm* not happy."

"No, but you are employed, and presumably wish to remain so."

"You can't threaten my contract because I won't agree to be pimped out for your profit margins. That's completely unethical."

Bob scowled. "I've already said that the sex aspect doesn't come into it. Nobody is 'pimping' you out anywhere."

"No," she said sweetly. "But that will be the resounding implication when I farm out the story of my unfair dismissal to the media."

After a moment, Bob said, "I feel almost proud. Our Elaine, all grown up and indulging in a spot of reciprocal blackmail. You were such a sweet little thing when you auditioned for us."

"And she'll remain so from the perspective of the public and their disposable income." Pat looked at Lainie. "You know perfectly well how little it takes to generate a romance rumour. I could do half the work with a simple tip-off. All we're asking is that you let Richard accompany you to a few select parties and participate in some of your charitable activities. For which I've meant to commend you."

Lainie suspected she wasn't being congratulated from a humanitarian angle. She choked. "Take *Richard* along on fund-raising events? I can just imagine it. Richard Troy making chitchat with little old ladies at the village. Standing outside Sainsbury's with a donation box. Taking part in the 5k Fun Run."

"He'll do it," Lynette spoke up, and Lainie shook her head, totally unconvinced.

"Will he?" she asked ironically. "Because you haven't mentioned his cooperation in this little scheme, and it sounds about as likely as an ice cream van in hell to me."

"He'll do it," Lynette repeated firmly.

"Well, I won't." Lainie cast Bob a scathing glance. "This was *your* idea, wasn't it? A load of bollocks with an unsavoury hint of lechery. It has your handiwork all over it."

"It's a solid plan," Bob said, unoffended. "The public loves a mismatch. The bad boy redeemed by the company ingénue."

"I am *not* the company ingénue," she snapped.

"Well, the role of femme fatale has been adequately filled by Chloe, poppet." Bob managed a decent leer. "*More* than adequately, I should say."

"Why don't you rope *her* in, then?"

"Don't think I didn't consider it. But Chloe's rep isn't exactly spotless at the moment either. And she's too old for him."

"She's thirty-nine."

"Might as well be fifty-nine in this industry. We're trying to clean up Richard's image, not add toy boy to his list of sins."

"I don't know how you sleep at night."

"Usually on top of a nubile blonde," Bob fired back, but the words were more wistful than lascivious.

"Endeavour not to become a *complete* stereotype of a stage manager. I'm not doing it. I have a huge family and at least a handful of friends, most of whom read the gossip sites. What on earth would they think if they saw me 'holding hands' with Richard Troy at a launch party?"

"If you're an actress worth the moderately high salary we pay you, they'll think you're having a mild flirtation with an eligible bachelor."

"*Eligible bachelor.* Insert derisive laugh here. My brothers would probably stage an intervention."

Giving her up as a hopeless hysteric, Bob turned to vent his frustration on Lynette. "Where the hell is Troy? The run-through must have finished at least five minutes ago."

Lynette's expensively made-up face assumed a pseudo-apologetic "boys will be boys" expression. She probably pasted it on out of sheer habit by now. Before she had time to offer an unconvincing excuse, Richard himself opened the door and came in without knocking.

"My God," Lainie murmured. "Perfectly on cue and he's not even being paid for it."

Richard spared her one unamused glance before he directed his attention to Bob. The piercing intensity of his blue eyes was entirely due to their depth of colour. The look within was lethargic and bored; Richard appeared as astonished as anyone else that he was actually awake and functional. "Yes?"

"Troy, do come in." The thinning hairs across Bob's scalp almost bristled with indignant static. Lainie wouldn't be surprised if his comb-over rose in the air like an enraged rooster. "Take a seat. Make yourself at home."

"*Yes?*" Richard repeated, unimpressed. He took in the presence of Lynette and Pat, and a brief grimace twisted his mouth. Lainie, he continued to ignore.

"Sit down, Richard." Pat used a tone that Lainie suspected was usually reserved for her cocker spaniels. After a tense few seconds, Richard hitched his trousers—seriously, who wore Tom Ford to a morning rehearsal, anyway?—and did sit. Naturally, in the most comfortable chair. It was a beautiful fluid motion that ended in the casual propping of one ankle over the opposite knee. She could whip out her iPhone camera and sell the resulting image to *Vogue*.

"You rang, sire." Richard's voice was sardonic. It wasn't entirely clear whom he was addressing, which underlined the insult. In the glare of natural light, his short black curls were struck through with tinges of blue. A few locks lay in careful disarray on his bony forehead. Lainie wondered if he followed in Byron's footsteps and slept in curlers.

"You're about three decades too old for that tone of voice," Pat told him in deflating accents. "Zip it."

Lainie hid a smile and encountered a dangerous flash of blue.

"Apologies," Richard drawled. "Do tell why I've been summoned into the great presence." He quirked a brow at Bob, and the stage manager glowered, his cheeks flushing an angry crimson. Richard looked directly at Lainie for the first time. "And why, if one might ask, is the scorned lover here also?"

It was clear he was not referring to her role in the play.

Pillock.

Lynette glanced from one to the other of them. "I'm not sure their acting skills are up to it," she said frankly to Pat.

The other woman's lips tightened in a thin line. "If you don't keep a civil tongue in your head, Richard, you're going to find yourself booked for joint interviews with Will every week for the next two months. Keep your mouth shut for five minutes and listen."

The threat must be appalling. Richard obeyed.

Pat outlined their scheme far more succinctly than Bob had managed with Lainie, but by the time she had finished speaking, the look on Richard's face registered somewhere between scorn and black amusement. He twisted in his chair to stare at Lainie.

She glared back. "I hope you don't think this is my idea. I've seen what happens when you leave the house. I might as well paste on a few feathers, slap a target on my forehead and take a stroll during duck season."

"And I hope you don't think I want to be publicly associated with a woman who—presumably in a state of complete sobriety—took her clothes off for Will Farmer."

Lainie's fingers closed into fists in her lap.

"A hit, a very palpable hit," Pat quoted under her breath. Then, louder: "And…back to your corners, ladies and gents. That's quite enough of that, thank you." She actually waved a finger at them. Lainie was beginning to think she had missed her calling as a primary school teacher. Or a prison guard. She imagined that much of the same skill set was required in either occupation.

"Richard…" Lynette began.

"Not a chance in hell," came the blunt, chilly response.

Pat folded her arms and leaned back against Bob's desk as she surveyed him. "I'm aware that you seem to take a perverse pleasure in rendering yourself as obnoxious as is humanly possible."

A flicker passed over Richard's face, and Pat went on relentlessly, "But I'm also given to understand that you're aiming to take over the presidency of the RSPA in the December by-elections. And frankly," she said, with the distinct air of a poker player producing an unexpected ace, "if you don't make some small effort to improve your PR profile, 'not a chance in hell' would be an equal description of your shot at the chair."

Richard sat in complete silence. His face was set in grim lines. He, in his turn, was the player who had rested in smug confidence on a hand of two pairs and now found it wasn't enough to take the round.

Lainie eyed him with some curiosity. So, Richard

had his sights set on the Royal Society of the Performing Arts. In her experience, the RSPA was the most
stodgy, entitled and ineffectual of the national arts bu-
reaucracies. They seemed to spend most of their time
congratulating themselves on their existence, turning
down grant applications and generally doing sod-all.

...Seems about right, then.

To her horror, Richard's gaze on her was turning
faintly—and very reluctantly—speculative.

"Forget it," she said bluntly. "I endorse the first instinct. Not a chance in hell."

"One month." Bob was watching her as well, and his
own eyes were calculating. "Keep up appearances for
at least the next four weeks—"

"*False* appearances," Lainie interrupted.

"And I'll see that half the profits from two evening
shows in November are donated to that kiddie cancer
charity of yours. What's it called? Shine a Light?"

"Shining Lights UK," Lainie corrected automatically. She bit down hard on her lip.

Bugger.

West End ticket prices were daylight robbery. That
was thousands and thousands of pounds.

In a last valiant attempt at defiance, she said rather
nastily, "You've already told me takings are down and
you're having to paper the house."

Bob pursed his lips and seemed to come to a decision that caused him actual physical pain. "Saturday
nights," he managed to get out. "Cling to Troy like a
bloody limpet in public for the next month, and half the
profits from the first two Saturday night performances
in November go to the sick kids. It'll look good on the
books," he added reprehensibly.

Lainie's hand slipped into her pocket and closed tightly around her phone. She knew the photograph on her screen background down to the last freckle on her sister's nose.

Hannah, my pet.

You can still make me do the most insane things.

"*All* the profits," she said, and Bob blanched.

There was a long, fraught pause, broken only by the faint sound of Richard's nails tapping against the sole of his leather boot.

"All the profits," Bob finally agreed, and he sounded strangled. He looked from her to Richard. "And you'd better be *bloody* convincing."

TWO

London Celebrity @LondonCelebrity. 35m
Hot new couple alert!
West Enders Richard Troy and Elaine Graham cuddle
up at Pink Ribbon benefit...goo.gl/Ep2m03

IT WAS THE noise that was so overwhelming. More so even than the cluster of camera flashes, which left her temporarily reeling and blinded, circles of light pulsing in her vision. The chattering sound as the cameras got their shots, snapping one after another like rapid-fire machine guns. It seemed to run through the crowd of paparazzi in the rhythm of a Mexican wave, each click of a button echoed by its neighbour. And the competing human voices shouting demands—"Richard! To your left, Richard! Richard, to your right! Elaine! Over here, Elaine!"

Trying to bait or cajole or provoke with their commentary: "Looking gorgeous, Elaine! Who are you wearing, Elaine? Are you two dating? Richard, how long have you been together? How does Will Farmer feel about it? Did it start before the breakup?"

Hammering away at them. Rude. Relentless.

Usually, it was a minor barrage. Theatre actors tended to get only the surface interest from the paps, who congregated outside overexposed celebrity events. They ranked somewhere between minor reality stars and radio personalities on the saleable news scale. The increased harassment was one of the reasons she had thought twice about pursuing roles in television.

Thanks to her escort, she was getting her first taste tonight of what it meant to be prime real estate in the banner news headlines. And she was not enjoying it. Nor, she had to admit, was Richard, to judge by the grimness of his face as they pushed forward from the car. The valet whisked the Ferrari away, and he followed its progress as if he suspected an illicit joyride might take place. His fingers were iron-tight around hers, the skin of his hand surprisingly rough and calloused. She couldn't imagine him doing manual labour. Or even the dishes. He growled a warning in the back of his throat when a heavily built photographer advanced close enough that she felt his moist breath against her ear.

Her feelings of empathy were limited. It was not lost on her that if Richard didn't make the paps' job so easy by losing his temper left, right and centre, they wouldn't flock around him like starving seagulls.

With her free hand, Lainie held down her skirt against the brisk wind. She had read somewhere that the Duchess of Cambridge had weights sewn into the hems of her dresses, which seemed like sound common sense. The last thing Lainie needed was a wardrobe malfunction. She was wearing her lucky knickers with the hole over her left bum cheek. The evening ahead had seemed a miserable enough prospect without adding Spanx into the mix.

"Would you keep up?" Richard muttered in her direction, and she barely resisted the urge to pull a face in response. There was something horribly provocative about the knowledge that one irresponsible gesture would set off a rippling wave of flashes, like blowing into a pool of water and causing a tidal wave. It perversely made her want to misbehave.

A teenage YouTube star arrived to pandemonium from young fans, which diverted most of the camera attention. Lainie let out a deep breath and released her skirt to catch her handbag before it dropped from her arm. It contained her phone, and her favourite sister-in-law had strict instructions to call with a fake emergency if prompted by text. She had promised to *appear* at the Pink Ribbon benefit with Richard; she had no intention of remaining by his side for the entire evening if he proved his usual intolerable self.

At least it was for a good cause, she thought gloomily, as Richard gave another impatient pull on her arm.

"Stop it," she hissed, and then smiled at the bouncers as she handed over her pass. "You're not hauling around a bag of golf clubs."

Richard also produced his pass but dispensed with the smile. A muscle flexed in his jaw, but he said nothing until they were inside the hotel foyer. "I don't carry my golf clubs," he eventually remarked. "That's what a caddy is for."

First eye roll of the night.

The hub of voices in the room was almost as loud as the throngs of paparazzi outside, only here the shouted demands were replaced by shrieks of recognition and social giggles. Lainie was an adamant city girl, but for a second she thought wistfully of a quiet spot in the countryside, where the only noise came from birds and trickling water.

And probably wasps, heavy machinery, meatworks and cattle trucks, she acknowledged a moment later with a faint smile. The peaceful haven of her imagination had more in common with *Lark Rise to Candleford* than the twenty-first century. Occupational hazard: too much time spent amongst artificial sets, slight loss of grip on reality.

Richard handed her a cocktail glass from a waiter's passing tray, and then ruined the polite gesture by frowning in the direction of her breasts and asking, "Did your stylist choose that?"

She took a very large gulp of fruit-laced vodka. "I don't have a stylist," she said grimly, resisting the urge to make self-conscious tugs and adjustments to her dress. Which was *fine*. It was a perfectly simple LBD with a classy amount of cleavage.

Richard sipped gingerly from his own glass, looking into it as if he suspected lacings of cyanide. He must have been quite good in *Hamlet*, she noted absently.

"Have you considered hiring one?" he asked, in tones of friendly interest.

Thousands.

Thousands of pounds for Shining Lights.

She put a mental heel on her growing irritation and ground it into the very fancy parquet floor.

She tried not to imagine Richard's face was under there also.

"Darlings!" Greta French arrived in a wash of air kisses and perfume. The chat show matriarch was the only three-dimensional human Lainie had ever met who actually addressed people she had neither slept with nor conceived as "darling."

Greta beamed at them. Her nose was all but twitching as she scented material for her five-past-two gossip slot. Lainie felt Richard's biceps shifting against her shoulder. She told herself it was an impatient fidget. He probably wouldn't clock the woman. However tempting it might be.

"I had *no* idea," Greta went on, looking from one to the other of them. "Elaine, you sly thing. You didn't utter a peep when we had our little chat about Will last week." Her voice was hushed and confidential. An eavesdropper—and there were at least four in Lainie's direct line of sight—could be forgiven for thinking that she made a habit of phoning Auntie Greta in tears after every romantic disaster.

The "little chat" in question had consisted of Greta ambushing her in the yoghurt section of Waitrose and making snide digs about Will's obvious preference for silicone.

Richard smiled back at Greta. It was a completely manufactured, calculated movement that had nothing whatsoever to do with genuine feeling. That didn't lessen the impact. Eyes became more blue, interesting lines and dimples appeared around firm lips, and a face that could be overly severe in repose became almost mythically handsome. Even Lainie's heart gave an extra thump in response, and she still wanted to upend her cocktail over his smug, shapely head.

"No idea about what?" Richard asked, his words blandly curious. He took another sip from his own glass and managed to skip the aftertaste blench this time. It *was* a fairly horrible drink.

Greta looked slightly discomposed. She blinked under the dual threat of the smile and the purring lack of response. "Well…" she said, tearing her eyes from Richard's mouth with some difficulty. Her gaze kept drifting back like a fly unable to pull its feet from sticky spider webbing. She looked meaningfully at Lainie. "I couldn't help noticing you come in," she said, with a revolting comradely nudge. "*Holding hands*."

The undertone of "Scandal!" was so heavy that one would think Lainie had walked into the room with her hand thrust down Richard's pants.

"Oh, you know me, Greta." Richard was still smiling. "Always a gentleman." He ignored Lainie's muffled cough and patted her on the shoulder. "She was a bit unsteady on her feet. Light-headedness is fairly common with that particular strain of the virus, I believe. I assume you've had your vaccination?" he added with concern. "It's running rampant in the theatre at the moment."

Greta tried an uncertain smile, obviously prepared to humour the joke, but at Richard's persistent look of bland enquiry, she grew restless. With a wary glance at Lainie, perhaps checking for a flush of fever or sprouting pox, she developed an intense need to greet another acquaintance.

Lainie watched her departing back. "I'm speechless," she said. "I am without speech."

"If I thought that was remotely true, I would feel considerably more optimistic about my evening." Richard glanced at his watch. "Christ, we've only been here for five minutes. It's like being stuck in the TARDIS. Time has lost all meaning."

He turned away to ditch his cocktail glass, thus missing Lainie's gobsmacked expression. A *Doctor Who* reference from her second-least-favourite person? Wonders never ceased. How potent *were* these drinks?

She followed his example and got rid of hers on a side table, watching Richard from between lowered lashes. She could not, for the life of her, imagine him going home after a performance and crashing in front of the TV. She actually couldn't imagine him existing in a room by himself. It was as if he flashed into being inside the doors of the theatre and disappeared again when he left. With occasional sightings of the poltergeist reported on Twitter when he threw plates at people's heads.

"So, is it solely my presence that offends," she asked when he returned with obvious reluctance to her side, "or do you just despise people in general?"

He seemed about to resort to sarcasm, but changed his mind and considered her question. A faint frown appeared between his arching black eyebrows. "I do find the majority of people somewhat lacking in intelligence," he admitted. Eye roll number two. "But they're more tolerable in isolated groups. En masse, with the addition of alcohol, these occasions tend to be a social experiment in pushing the absolute boundaries of insipidity and vanity." He looked around the filling room with disdain. "Three-quarters of these people are a walking waste of oxygen. And that's a conservative estimate."

"Well, it's nice to see that success hasn't gone to your head." Lainie gave him an exasperated look. "If you hate people and parties so much, why do you bother coming? You could go home and get to bed at a reasonably decent hour. I bet you're a chronic insomniac," she said thoughtfully. "It might explain part of the grouchiness. And the dark rings."

He instinctively touched under his eye with the pad of his thumb, and then looked furious with himself for the gesture. He glared at her. "My success has not gone

to my head." He ignored the rest of her insults in favour
of the first observation, which seemed to truly offend
him. "My personality has not once altered under outside influence."

"Then I'm genuinely appalled, and your childhood
nannies have my intense sympathy. You've got a bit of
a nerve, don't you think, accusing *other* people of vanity? You make Mr. Darcy look like the poster child for
low self-esteem."

"There is a difference between *vanity* and having a
clear idea of your own abilities and potential."

She grimaced, lifting her hands to her cheeks. "Oh
my God. I have never had such a sisterly feeling for
Elizabeth Bennet." She looked at him with both brows
raised. "Please tell me that you were misquoted in *Time*
when you referred to theatre as the only true forum for
the craft. And that you did *not* call screen actors 'fame-
mongering puppets with as much understanding of the
complexities of drama as Kim Kardashian has of nuclear physics.'"

"The journalist exaggerated, as usual. Although my
opinion of the comparative status of theatre against film
and television is fairly well-known, I believe," Richard
said, a bit stiffly.

"Yet you obviously watch TV." She was suddenly
feeling defensive about her miniseries ambitions, and
was correspondingly cross with herself. Who bloody
cared about Richard Troy's out-of-date elitism? "And
I'm frankly amazed that you even know who Kim Kardashian is."

"I'm not denying the entertainment value of screen
productions, nor the importance of their documentary
and educational role. But I maintain that the roots and

truest expression of drama is in live theatre. With the odd exception, most of the programmes produced for British television are absolute rubbish. And I was once unfortunate enough to share an interview slot with Kim Kardashian." After a moment, he said grimly, "Don't even get me started on reality TV."

She possibly agreed with him on that score. Still—

"You're going to be perfectly suited for the RSPA," she said, and it was not intended as a compliment.

"Yes, I am," he agreed coolly. He looked behind her. "Speaking of which…"

Lainie turned and saw a florid sixtyish man in a suit approaching. He couldn't have declared his status any more clearly if he'd pulled out his wallet and offered them a tenner to do a skit. If he wasn't on some sort of committee, and in it for the tax benefits, she would eat her bargain-price handbag.

"Eric Westfield. Current vice president of the Society," Richard said close to her ear. He put his hand on her upper arm and gently moved her about six inches away from him. "Could you just…"

"I'm sorry," Lainie said, "did you just *move* me? You do realise I'm not actually contagious?" She nodded at a point on the far side of the room. "Would you like me to go and stand over there? Because I think he may still guess that we're together."

"We aren't—"

"*I didn't mean romantically.*"

"Richard." Eric Westfield beamed at them both. The bunched-up cheeks were rather sweet but didn't go at all with the jaded expression in his eyes.

Richard wiped his face free of impatience and returned the other man's handshake. "Eric. Good to see you."

Westfield turned to Lainie. "And I believe this young lady has something to do with the theatre?" He accompanied the question with a roguish twinkle that made her take an instinctive step back.

"Elaine Graham. I'm currently appearing in *The Cavalier's Tribute* with Richard." Shaking his hand, she added sweetly, "When I'm not spreading the plague."

"I beg your pardon?"

"I was going to get in touch this week," Richard cut in, shooting her a warning look. *Well, aren't we just all politeness when we want something?*

"We should meet up for a drink sometime. Perhaps Thursday evening if you're free."

Thursday was the night his alternate took over the role of Bandero and the rest of the cast breathed a sigh of relief.

"We'll do that." Westfield looked chuffed. Not so jaded after all, if he could still be gratified by the prospect of socialising with notoriety. Unless it was the snob value of Richard's blue blood. Lainie remembered reading that he was seven hundred thirty-second or something in line for the throne.

God help them all in the event of an actual plague. If Harley Street succumbed and the royal family was forced to rely on the aid of the NHS, they would probably drop like flies. Whereas Richard would likely crawl unharmed from the rubble of a nuclear disaster. Like a cockroach.

She tuned out the rest of the conversation going on above her head. It reeked of the stale cigar smoke and ego-bolstering of an old boys' club. She was vaguely disappointed in Richard. Pandering to the conventions of the Boodles set was almost worse than acting like an ill-mannered, temperamental diva. At least the latter side of his personality seemed honest. In this industry, she could have a certain amount of respect for someone who didn't paste a fake cover over an obnoxious book, even if she wished she could swap that book for a lighter read.

Richard finally finished his schmoozing, and Westfield kissed her hand before he disappeared into the crowd. She wrinkled her nose. There had been a definite suggestion of tongue against her knuckle.

"You want to be careful," she said. "One more pump of hot air and his self-importance would have exploded all over the room. Imagine the size of your damages bill then."

"It's called regrettable but necessary networking." Richard took another long-suffering glance at his watch. "I'm sure you occasionally have to employ some of it yourself."

"No. I generally just employ good manners, no matter whom I'm speaking to."

"I can't say I'd noticed."

"I'm polite, not a saint." Lainie returned the smile and wave of a former castmate, and hoped he wouldn't come over. It had been a very long run of a very bad play. "Do you really want a stodgy bureaucratic role?" she asked with genuine curiosity. "I would have thought you would have enough to do."

"I have no pressing desire to wrangle committee meetings and have my portrait painted for the presidency wall. But I want to see a certain amount of change instituted in arts funding and education, and this is the first step toward achieving that."

Oh, God. He was going to end up as their Minister of Culture someday.

She hesitated. "Do you really think you're the political type?" she ventured, trying to think of a way to put it tactfully.

"Meaning?" The enquiry was frosty.

Screw it. "Meaning you have the diplomatic abilities of a tea bag, and a tendency to go off like a rocket at the slightest provocation."

"I'm aware I'll have to work on controlling my temper," he said even more stiffly.

"And the playpen behaviour?"

He looked seriously annoyed now. "Such as?"

"Such as chucking expensive china at irate chefs. If the food was that bad, why didn't you just ask for a new plate?"

He made a sound of intense irritation in his throat. "I may have a quick fuse, but I do have *some* idea of how to conduct myself in a public place. I have never thrown a plate or any other object at anyone. The closest I've come is hurling a truly appalling script at the wall, and I don't recall any material damage to either. Unfortunately, in the case of the script."

"Then what happened at the Ivy?"

"Randolph Gearing has held a grudge since I gave his first restaurant in Primrose Hill a bad review. It was a throwaway remark on the radio, and he needs to learn how to accept criticism. Nor was it my choice to dine at the Ivy the other night. My companion thought it was the place to be seen," he added with a slight sneer. "Gearing picked a fight, *he* threw a plate and I merely responded. With *words*, not actions, violent or otherwise."

"I see." Lainie studied him. "I hate to imagine the task of the police if somebody eventually snaps and has better aim with a platter. Your list of enemies must be reaching to the floor by now. Have you tried counting to ten?"

"I wouldn't have to lose my temper if people weren't such morons."

"I would suggest going with a different quote when you open your campaign speech."

Richard suddenly swore under his breath, and Lainie saw Lynette weaving toward them through the crowd. She was also wearing a little black dress, but it was decidedly *littler* than Lainie's. And her shoes were fabulous. Lainie eyed them covetously. Evidently, even a commission from Richard's salary was more profitable than her own earnings.

"A photographer from *Tatler* is circling." The theatrical agent looked them up and down critically, exactly as if she were a parent grooming her children for their school pictures. She looked about three seconds away from licking her thumb and smoothing back Richard's errant curl. "In a moment, I want you to put your arm around Lainie, Richard, and say something into her ear. Lainie, you look up at him and laugh. Then kiss her. A peck. Playful. Affectionate."

"This is not a sitcom," Lainie snapped. "I am not going to mindlessly giggle and pucker up on cue. We agreed to attend events and hold hands. Done and done."

"No," Lynette said with barely leashed temper. Maybe Richard was rubbing off on her. "You agreed to foster a certain impression." She looked around at a few interested faces and lowered her voice. "Which is not being fulfilled by the two of you standing three feet apart, glowering at one another. Only the most diehard romantic and the clinically brain-dead would be seeing hearts and flowers."

A camera flash went off nearby and Lainie spotted the photographer turning in their direction.

With a sigh that almost parted her hair, Richard lifted his arm and slid it around her waist. Pulling her up against him, he smiled down at her and the creases reappeared around his sardonic blue eyes. His warm breath gently fanned her ear when he ducked his head and whispered, "You're habitually overplaying the death scene."

Her own eyes sparking retribution, she returned his smile. And laughed, light and tinkling, like an absolute idiot. She could feel herself tensing, knowing what was coming next, and had to steel herself not to physically lean back from his mouth.

It was the most sexless, unexciting kiss she'd had since primary school, when a seven-year-old boy had kissed her on a dare and then run off screaming to stick his face in the drinking fountain. Eric Westfield had used more tongue on the back of her hand. After a couple of seconds, there was another camera flash, and Richard removed his lips from her person, looking equally bored.

"There," said their proud surrogate mother. "That wasn't so hard, was it?" She smiled cajolingly at an unimpressed Lainie. "And you look great. Love the dress." Which was not exactly convincing, when her own was clearly nicer. "Doesn't she look nice, Richard?" Lynette prompted him, again with the parental nagging.

Richard spared Lainie's dress another brief glance. "Hmm," he said, and Lynette looked as if a few silent prayers for patience were taking place behind her bland expression.

"It's fortunate you're so attractive," she said to Lainie, with a certain amount of relief.

It would obviously be too much to expect the great actor to lower his lips to a plain face.

This whole evening was beginning to feel exhausting.

"Don't you think Lainie's pretty?" Lynette had turned into a stuck record.

Richard was eyeing Lynette's neck, and Lainie wondered if he was valuing her diamonds or indulging in a strangulation fantasy. "I hadn't really thought about it," he said, and she scowled at him.

That was no less flattering than her opinions of him, but *really*.

"Have you ever actually spoken to a woman before? Because with charm like that, I can't *imagine* where your new nickname came from."

His lips tightened. Evidently that one was rankling a little.

"Play nice, kiddies. Remember, you're smitten," Lynette warned, and then thankfully took herself off before either one of them could give in to a murderous impulse.

Another camera flashed and people turned to look their way, whispering to one another. A few partygoers entirely gave up on manners and just openly pointed. Richard's affectionate smile looked more like a grimace from where she was standing. "You can hold my hand," he said, as if he were the Queen bestowing a knighthood.

She ignored his raised palm. "No, thank you."

His smile became even more horrifying. "Just take my damn hand. Two more circles of the room, a donation at the door, and we can get the hell out of here."

It was the prospect of going home to her bed, kettle and chocolate stash that sealed the deal. Suppressing a sigh, she held the tips of his fingers. He rolled his eyes and wrapped a warm, rough hand around hers.

"Why, *hello*. Fancy seeing you two here. Together."

They turned to greet the newcomers with identical fixed smiles.

"Two more circles of the room" was easier said than accomplished when they were stopped by friends, colleagues and nosey parkers every two steps, but they finally made it to the exit, where they each made a pledge to the cause. Lainie was impressed against her will by the size of Richard's donation. He was many things—few of them complimentary—but he wasn't mean.

In the financial sense. In terms of attitude, half a dozen stage assistants reduced to tears would disagree with her.

They left by the side entrance of the hotel, where only a handful of photographers lay in wait. A valet brought Richard's car around and received a generous tip but no verbal acknowledgment. Richard didn't even look at the friendly young man.

When the valet had moved away to take another guest's keys, she shook her head. "You could have at least said thank you."

"To whom?"

"The valet."

Richard shrugged. "I thank people when they do me a favour. He's paid to do a job. For which I gave him additional compensation."

"Because it would kill you to just say a quick 'thanks' when people work hard to make your life easier?"

Under her steady regard, his high cheekbones took on a very faint tinge of red. He said nothing in response, but when the valet walked back past them, he held up the keys. "Appreciate it," he said, and the kid blinked and grinned.

"No worries, sir."

Richard looked at her with a raised brow. "Satisfied?"

She was, oddly. For the first time—ever, possibly—she gave him a genuine smile.

It was also the first time she had ever seen him genuinely disconcerted. His eyes flickered to her mouth and then up to her eyes, and he hesitated before opening the car door to let her climb inside.

The journey to her flat in Bayswater was quiet and almost peaceful. It was a stark contrast to the constant bickering earlier in the evening when they'd left the theatre. Lainie, her gaze fastened dreamily on the lights and nightlife out the darkened window, put it down to mutual tiredness. She said very little beyond giving the odd street direction. Richard brought the Ferrari to a stop outside her building, an old Victorian terrace house, and deposited her on her doorstep with a curt "Good night." She nodded, and watched thoughtfully from the open door as he returned to the car. About thirty seconds later, he stared at her impatiently through the window, and she realised he was waiting for her to go inside so he could leave. With a spark of mischief, she offered a cheerful wave, and his scowl deepened. It was tempting to blow a kiss, for the sheer novelty of seeing his head explode, but she did have her limits.

Grinning, she closed and locked the door, and made her way up the creaking stairs. It was a tidy, warm house, but as comfortably decrepit in its small way as the Metronome was on a grand scale. The carpets definitely needed replacing. Her flat was on the top floor, which was a bugger when she had shopping to carry up, but at least meant she got enough exercise to justify skipping a gym membership.

That was her story, and she was sticking to it.

Her landlady's fat ginger cat was asleep outside her door and she stopped to stroke his soft fur. He was also called Richard, which had afforded her considerable amusement over the past couple of months, particularly since he had one of those adorably squished, chronically grumpy faces. Human Richard, for all his good looks, was afflicted with a similarly epic case of resting bitch face. He had the elastic features of a natural-born actor, but at the close of a scene, he tended to return to his factory setting of grouch.

Turning on lights and pulling curtains as she went, she set the kettle boiling in the kitchen and hunted out a bag of Yorkshire tea. As she played with the spoon, pressing the bag against the side of the cup in an attempt to speed up the steeping process, she idly wondered what human Richard was going home to. Not a wife and four hopeful children, unless he kept secrets locked tighter than the vaults of MI5. She found it hard to believe any woman would voluntarily cohabit with him. There wasn't enough money in the world to put up with that level of stress.

She was imagining chandeliers and staff. Perhaps a Jeeves-style butler to murmur approvingly over his choice of evening clothes and help him put his jammies on. Although ten to one, he slept naked.

Her mind temporarily shorted out at that point.

Her clutch vibrated on the table and she went to retrieve her phone, taking her cup along for a sustaining gulp of too-hot tea. Flicking her thumb against the touch pad, she read the text from Sarah: Are you home yet? No chat abbreviations from her sister-in-law, who taught English at her local comprehensive school and had vocal opinions on the subject of lazy spelling.

She curled up on the couch, wedging a cushion behind the small of her back, and dialled the number for Sarah and Niall's home in Camden.

"If it isn't the future Mrs. Troy." Sarah was obviously trying hard not to laugh, and failing dismally.

Lainie sighed. "I see the gossip columnists didn't waste any time."

"Oh, no. The photos started appearing an hour ago. *London Celebrity* is running two consecutive articles on the hot new romance, one in which they have you almost engaged, and the other which writes off the whole thing as a rebound fling. With some fairly sketchy allusions to Will and the timing. I wonder if they were written by the same person, if their staff ever bother to check what the next cubicle is writing, or if they just don't care."

"When in doubt, pick C." Lainie took another sip of tea. Her iPad was resting at the other end of the couch and she pushed it a little farther away with her big toe, in a symbolic gesture of rejection. "Sounds like business as usual, then."

"Can't say I think much of the lip-lock, though," Sarah said disapprovingly. Lainie could hear her mouse clicking. "I've seen steamier embraces during church services. He looks like he's performing CPR on someone he'd secretly rather have left at the bottom of the pool."

Lainie laughed, but she wasn't entirely amused. At all, in fact. "Accurate representation by *London Celebrity*. That's a first."

"The atmosphere backstage still a trifle chilly, is it?"

"It's social Antarctica. If it wasn't for Chloe, who's even nice to Richard and is totally oblivious to snubs and any underlying tension, performances would be about as much fun as drinks out with the Borgias."

"He can't be as bad as Wee Willy, though," Sarah said firmly, and Lainie almost snorted tea through her nose.

"Have I mentioned lately that I love you and Niall?" she asked, as she lunged for an old dusting rag to mop up the mess.

"Yeah, we're quite fond of you too. And don't avoid the question."

"I wasn't aware you'd asked one."

"It was implied in the statement. I refuse to believe that Troy can be as big a waste of testosterone as your genitally challenged ex. Bad temper aside—and having seen a bit of what you put up with in the media, I'm not sure I entirely blame him—"

"Blame him. There are people who deal with a lot more hassle from the media than Richard, and he perpetuates most of his bad press himself. If he kept his head down, he wouldn't be half as interesting. And it isn't only dodgy photographers who come under his fire. He's rude to almost everyone. Ask his dresser. Ask *my* dresser. Ask the girl who delivers the morning papers."

"Oh, I know the type, and I grant you they're hard to tolerate. There are at least two of them in my class every year, and it's depressing to know they might not grow out of it." Sarah was clicking her mouse again, and Lainie wondered what fresh delights she'd found in the news feed. "But he seems to at least trump Will in the romantic sense."

"Allow me to fall about laughing at the idea of Richard Troy being romantic."

"Well, I can't find any love rat rumours. He's never been involved in any sort of cheating scandal, has he?"

Lainie tried to remember what she knew about Richard's love life. As little as she'd been able to manage. He'd been linked with a few businesswomen and a high-powered barrister at one point. Never with an actress. Their fake relationship was probably a hard pill for him to swallow in a *multitude* of ways.

"No, his relationships never seem to last that long, but they at least take place one at a time. As far as I know. And he doesn't seem to hop from one bed to the next."

"Surprising, when you think about it."

"Not really." Lainie was dismissive. "You would have to have a skin like a rhino to put up with him. Or just no self-esteem at all and a faint aura of desperation."

"Ouch," Sarah said, sounding as if she was grinning. "I'm beginning to feel sorry for the man."

"Said no person who'd actually met him, ever."

"I wonder what he's like in bed," Sarah mused, and Lainie choked on her tea for the second time.

"Sarah! Married woman."

"I vowed to be faithful, not dead from the waist down. And whatever his faults, you can't deny your Richard is a bit of a dish."

"Please never refer to him as 'my' Richard again."

"Well, I admit the chemistry between you isn't exactly sparking off the screen," Sarah said—and *click*, *click*, *click* again. "Yeah. No. I'm not getting a 'let's split this joint and get naked' vibe. More of an 'I vaguely fear contamination' vibe."

"Funny you should say that." Lainie sighed. "Can we change the subject while I'm still able to sleep tonight?"

"Stirring lust?" Sarah asked with interest.

"Creeping horrors. How's my second-favourite niece doing?"

"Who's taken top billing this week?"

"Charlotte. She Photoshopped a collage for me involving Will and the T. rex from *Jurassic Park*. I've hung it on my fridge."

"Obviously Emily needs to up her game. She's fine. She's just being a bit…"

"A bit what?"

"A bit thirteen."

"Enough said."

"She's excited about the fête on Saturday, though."

"*Is* she? I wouldn't have thought cake stalls and sack races would be her thing."

"No, but Johnny Blake is very much her thing. She's highly impressed that you've managed to get somebody semi-cool to open a fête in Little Bottomsworth."

"Upper Bidford," Lainie corrected, and tried not to smile. "And Johnny Blake is a sweet kid, as far as these teenage YouTubers go. His mother is a leukemia survivor, so he wanted to support the cause."

"You know I'm all for the cause. I'm just not sure why we're fund-raising for the foundation in the remote Cotswolds."

"There are plenty of events planned in London over the next few months as well, but the villagers in Bidford wanted to help. They lost a seventeen-year-old to non-Hodgkin lymphoma this year."

"Oh." Sarah was quiet for a moment. "Dreadful."

"Yes."

"Well, we'll be there, and we're bringing cakes. I can't promise they'll meet the Women's Institute standards, but…"

"I really appreciate it, Sarah. Thanks."

"The whole family appreciates what you're doing with Shining Lights."

Lainie made a murmuring sound, dismissing not the sentiment but the need for it. Her gaze went inevitably to the framed family portrait above the heat pump, and zoomed in on one face.

Hannah had inherited her freckled cheeks and gap-toothed smile straight from their dad. She and Lainie were also the only ones who had copped his dark red hair. In appearance, their father was basically the lost Weasley. Hannah had stopped talking about dental surgery after Georgia May Jagger and Anna Paquin had made the tooth gap fashionable, but she had always moaned about the freckles.

At least until other problems had made them seem a comparatively petty complaint.

Lainie had thought then, and still thought now, that her little sister's face was adorable. Freckles and all.

Hannah had retorted that it was easy to say that when you looked more like Jessica Rabbit than Raggedy Ann.

A wave of grief hit her. She longed intensely for the sound of her sister's voice. Even at its most high-pitched whine. It almost toppled her where she stood, at least once a day, how much she missed the irascible little brat.

"We all miss her," Sarah said quietly into the receiver. "She would be really proud, you know."

"Not that she would admit it in a million years." Lainie bit her lip. "But, yeah. I know she would."

"And she would get a huge kick out of this thing with Richard Troy."

"Her opinion of my taste in men was always low."

"Well, after Wee Willy and Sir Stamps-A-Lot, we can only assume it's all uphill from here."

"We can but hope."

RICHARD COULD HEAR voices when he stepped into the foyer. One was female, high-pitched and came with a laugh that would have been invaluable as an air-raid signal during the Blitz. He followed the lingering scent of lavender floor cleaner to the kitchen. Mrs. Hunt had left the radio on for him again. She was convinced it was "friendlier" than coming home to an empty house. Apparently his housekeeper was confusing him with a dog with separation anxiety. Lovely woman. Absolutely no common sense.

He switched the radio off, silencing another paint-stripping peal of laughter. Then he began the arduous process of turning off almost every light on the ground floor. Mrs. Hunt also thought it was friendlier if he came home to a house lit up like a burlesque hall.

His thoughts became considerably more charitable

when he reached his study and found a tray on his desk, whisky decanter sitting ready. She'd also laid out a cigar from the box he kept for visitors, mostly uninvited former colleagues of his father. He didn't smoke, but suspected Mrs. Hunt had formed her conception of actors based on Victorian novels.

Pouring a couple of fingers of whisky, he dropped into the armchair by the window and looked absently out at the dimly lit street. Every few seconds, headlights flashed by and car tyres threw up a silvery splash. It was starting to rain heavily. He sighed, letting the tension drain from his muscles. The adrenaline buzz from the performance had worn off about ten minutes into the charity benefit. He had a perfectly competent assistant whose job it was to quietly disburse money into charitable donations and endowments. He had no problem parting with the cash. His objections lay in having to do it publicly, with second-rate champagne in his hand, for the edification of a bunch of social degenerates with cameras.

His iPad beeped with an incoming text message and Richard rolled his head to the side to look at it. He glanced at the clock on the mantel. It was bound to be from a woman. Men had the judgement to reserve this hour of the morning for sleeping, sex, or live-streaming American sports. Stretching out a lazy hand, he picked up the tablet. He trusted the message wasn't from the date he'd taken to the Ivy the other night. He'd realised that was a mistake the moment they'd been served with their entrée and she'd pulled out her phone to take a photo of it. She'd uploaded the image to a calorie-counting app, and then refused to eat it based on an arbitrary and almost certainly inaccurate analysis. He thought

Gearing's food was overpriced and barely worth eating too, but not because the man cooked with butter.

The text was from Lynette. A jubilant Lynette. She'd actually inserted a smiley face. The last time his agent had used an emoticon on him, he'd just walked out of a live interview. The symbol in question had involved a fist and several fingers, and was probably banned in the district schools.

She'd inserted a link to a trashy online rag that masqueraded as a news site. Against his better judgement, and partly under the warming influence of the whisky, he brought up the page and was greeted with the image of his own scowling face. He winced. Jesus. He looked like his great-aunt Harriet. It was something about the combination of the frown and the emerging beard.

His gaze moved to Lainie. She was standing at his side, her arms crossed over her breasts. With no compunction, he let his eyes linger there. He was willing to bet that dress had been designed on a flat-chested mannequin. His lips pursed in a silent whistle that would undoubtedly have earned him a smack around the ear had he been in feminine company. Lainie's own expression, as she stared directly into the camera, was heavily disapproving. She looked like she would happily garrotte someone with the chain of her handbag. No prizes for guessing whom. Richard's lips tilted unwillingly.

His eyebrow rose when he scrolled to the next set of images. They silently chronicled Lynette's arrival on the scene, Lainie reluctantly cuddling up to him, smelling sweetly and elusively of vanilla, and then the staged peck on her mouth. Her lips had been sticky with gloss and had tasted of synthetic strawberry. Like a throat lozenge. The tableau looked ridiculously fake. Back-

ground extras in a C-grade soap could pull off a more
convincing display of affection. There was obvious tension, but it was more of the angry than sexual variety.
It was bad acting, and it riled his professional ego. The
whole situation was bloody distasteful.

It came down to how badly he wanted the chair of
the RSPA. He was neither deaf nor self-absorbed to
the point of oblivion. He'd heard the murmurings. His
media reputation was becoming a millstone around his
neck. He was yet to be convinced, however, that the
way to redemption was on the arm—and presumably,
in public opinion, between the thighs—of an attractive
girlfriend. Even if she did moonlight as Mother Teresa
in her spare time. His apparent involvement with Lainie
seemed more likely to damage her reputation than polish his own.

Surprisingly, the thought irritated him. His eyes returned to the iPad screen. Scissoring his fingers, he
enlarged a headshot. His study of her features was less
dispassionate than it would have been only hours earlier. He must have been aware that she was a beautiful
woman, but symmetrical features, white teeth, glossy
hair and generous breasts were a dime a dozen. The
women—and men—he'd worked with over the past
fifteen-odd years blended into a composite Hollywood
ideal. If people couldn't offer anything beyond genetic
blessings and surgical enhancements, either by way of
wits or—to be frank—useful connections, their voices
didn't tend to rise above the clamour.

Lainie had been a mild revelation tonight. Jessica
Rabbit actually had a personality. And a fairly biting
tongue. He shook his head. She was wasted on the sim-
pering legs-and-lashes role they'd given her in *The Cav-*

alier's Tribute. She could probably have made a decent job of Helen. Chloe tended to oversimplify and oversex the calculating, sardonic character.

On the other hand, Chloe wasn't moronic enough to fall into bed with Will Farmer.

He moved one shoulder abruptly, trying to shake off the unusual feeling of restlessness. After the inane back-stage chatter at the theatre, his silent house was usually a refuge. Tonight, his thoughts seemed to echo into the corners of the large comfortable room, coming back to taunt him. For one insane moment he considered going into the kitchen and turning the radio back on.

He flicked over to his calendar and checked his schedule for the rest of the week. The space for Saturday morning was currently fantastically blank. He couldn't bring himself to insert the change of plan. A village fête. In October. It was like something out of Agatha Christie. Frozen dead bodies and all, probably, considering the weather forecast.

His chin lifted. He eyed the portrait of his father above the fireplace. The old man glared down at him. If Richard squinted, he could almost see the painted moustache quivering with rage.

The fête it was.

Silently, ironically, he saluted his father with the whisky glass and then drained its contents.

THREE

London Celebrity @LondonCelebrity. 3h
A rebound fling?
*Will Farmer's bitter rant as Graham and Troy heat up
the Metronome...tinyurl.com/puy26gy*

A NICE PERSON would have let him off the hook. There were no members of the Metronome goon squad lurking around Upper Bidford to bully them into obedience. Even the demands of her job weren't enough to entice Lynette Stern from the civilised city to a country village with no free Wi-Fi. Lainie *could* have offered to bluff an excuse while Richard stayed home to enjoy whatever he usually did on a Saturday morning. She assumed it involved excellent espresso and some heavy self-Googling.

Clearly, she was *not* a nice person. Because she had rarely enjoyed any sight more than that of Richard Troy at a village fête, wedged between two of the more terrifying representatives of the local Women's Institute. He looked as if he'd accidentally fallen through a portal into the third circle of hell.

A young woman with questionable maternal instincts shoved her defenceless infant into Richard's arms, ignoring his furious response while she unearthed her phone. While she took a series of images, musing aloud on the best one for Instagram, Lainie wandered over to appreciate the spectacle at close range. It was debatable who looked more wrathful: Richard, or the infant he was dangling at arm's length like a mud-splattered football.

"You do realise you're holding a baby, not a leaking bucket?" she asked conversationally, and he gave her a look that could splinter wood. "Against your chest, hand under his bottom. Honestly. You must have had a cuddle before."

"Yes, but women don't appreciate a hand under their bottom until I've at least bought them dinner," he retorted, and the WI president tittered into her jam scone.

Lainie pulled out her own phone and also took a picture. "Like I'm going to miss this opportunity," she said in response to his glare. "If the acting thing doesn't pan out, I can always hock this photo to the tabloids as evidence of your secret love child." She flipped the screen around to see how the image had turned out. Wow. Portrait of an Irate Actor.

The mother laughed as she retrieved her son. The baby was well wrapped and adorably squishy in his furry onesie. "My husband would probably come after him with a meat cleaver. That's him over there." She nodded toward the field where a rugby match was taking place against the neighbouring village. Lainie had no idea which player she was pointing at, but they were all equally well-endowed in the thigh department.

"Now there are *two* reasons to keep it." Lainie wiggled her phone at Richard, and he scowled at her.

"Delete it."

"Not a chance. I may make it my screensaver. I especially like the smear of drool on your shoulder."

He looked down at his coat and swore, swiping at the stain with his hand.

"Sorry," Lainie apologised pointedly to the group of women clustered about them. "His manners are a work in progress." She grabbed Richard's arm and dragged him away. "It's not the most promising beginning for your career in rubber-stamping and paper-pushing, is it? I think charming elderly women and chucking babies under the chin is part of the job description."

"I'm campaigning for the presidency of the RSPA, not running for mayor in the sticks." He cast a scornful look around the village green. The fête had opened an hour earlier, the ribbon cut by a bashful-looking Johnny Blake. Away from his vlogging camera, he was as awkward as the next teenage boy, but the young girls in the crowd had seemed to appreciate his stammered speech. And it was nice of him to make an obvious effort when he was out of his comfort zone.

Unlike some males twice his age.

Richard was poking at a chipped teapot on the table for the white elephant stall. "This is junk," he said, without even bothering to lower his voice.

"It's a white elephant stall. That's kind of the point. And who are you, the *Antiques Roadshow*?" Lainie cast a quick, embarrassed look around. She would estimate the ratio of people staring at Richard to be about ninety percent. It was too much to hope they were *all* hard of hearing. "If you could develop some sort of filter and a volume button in the next thirty seconds, it would really help me out."

"Exactly how long do we have to stay?" Richard stared in disbelief as a pig walked past with a blue prize ribbon around its neck.

"Until the last cup of tea is drunk and we've helped with the cleanup." Lainie was rapidly losing her sense of humour about the situation. "These people are kindly giving up their time, money and goodwill to help out a charity that means a lot to me. And sulking at a fundraiser for children with cancer is a total dick move. FYI."

Once again, Richard reddened slightly. A week ago, she wouldn't have thought him capable of changing colour without the aid of cosmetics. He thrust a hand through his tumbled black curls and looked away from her. All broody in an open-necked white shirt, and set against a pastoral background, he looked like a still from *Wuthering Heights*. She refused to be softened by the image. He could look as handsome as he wanted; it didn't make his behaviour any more attractive.

And he needed a shave. There was a fine line between designer stubble and scruffiness.

"Of course I'll support the cause," he muttered, and then added impatiently, "but I don't see why we can't just write a cheque." He repeated his derisive survey of the merrymaking. "You'll be lucky to break a thousand quid with this lot."

Lainie wasn't sure whether "this lot" referred to the fairground goods for sale or the villagers themselves. It was offensive either way.

"Because there are dozens of people here who care enough to want to contribute—" *and a good hundred more who've come along for the sole purpose of seeing your sour face, thanks to the social media grapevine* "—and they can't all afford to just 'write a cheque.'" She had the satisfaction of seeing his flush deepen. "And all of these events help raise the profile of the charity. We're trying to turn a spotlight on Shining Light. Not on the fact that Richard Troy has opened his fat wallet for something more philanthropic than a new sports car."

His face was unreadable. "You've made your point."

Not quite. "For the record, you're behaving exactly the way Will would."

Not that she would have got Will down here in a million years, PR stunt or no.

A nerve twitched above Richard's right eyebrow. "Is that blatant insult supposed to make me re-evaluate my life choices?"

She shrugged. "It would make *me* think twice."

He said nothing in response, but refrained from openly sneering when they went to greet the women running the cake stall. He even bought a bag of chocolate chip biscuits. He almost immediately handed them off to a thrilled middle-aged woman with a teenage daughter in tow, but it was the gesture that counted.

"I suppose," she muttered, choosing a plate of small sandwiches for herself from the savoury section, "it would be too much to ask you to judge the jams and chutneys."

"You suppose correctly." Richard took her elbow and steered her out of the way of the crowd. "Don't push your luck."

But his voice was surprisingly mild.

He even stood still for over twenty photographs with fans before impatience began to flicker at the edges of his smile and temper. Seeing the signs of an impending snap, Lainie excused them with a polite murmur. They each purchased a cup of hot cider—which was very good—and strolled toward a marquee that promised excessively large vegetables.

"Is that a joke?" Richard was reading a sign inscribed Largest Pumpkin Competition. We Hope You're Having a Gourd Day.

Lainie winced. "Well, it's a fairly cringe-worthy attempt at one."

"Not the god-awful pun. The competition itself. There's actually a contest for the largest pumpkin?"

"Oh, yes. Vegetable size is a cutthroat category, I gather. You know men. Always obsessed with the girth of their courgettes."

He ignored that and reached for her arm, foiling her attempt to take a sandwich from her plate. As ordered by Pat, he had picked her up outside her flat at an unearthly hour of the morning in order to beat the weekend traffic out of London, and she hadn't had time for breakfast. She was starving.

"Come on, then." He towed her toward the entrance of the marquee. Yet again, she was doing her best impression of a tugboat in the wake of the *S.S. Troy*.

"Arm," she said, looking wistfully at her sandwiches. "Attached to shoulder joint. And I'm trying to eat here."

"It's kind of a dick move to whine at a fund-raiser for cancer patients," he said without turning his head. "Just saying."

Touché.

"Jesus," he said inside the tent. "Look at the size of that thing."

Lainie looked from an admittedly sizable pumpkin to the gleam of reluctant fascination in Richard's blue eyes.

Escorting her to a party: no interest. One of her more

expensive dresses: totally unimpressed. Acting with her in a play: distinctly underwhelmed.

And then bowled over by a gigantic vegetable.

She chose to be amused.

"Do you think they use a special kind of fertiliser?" Richard went down on his haunches, looking at the pumpkin's bulbous backside.

Lainie unwrapped her sandwich plate and poked through the contents. "I expect they use hormone therapy. Like with chickens," she lied, and lifted a triangle of thinly sliced bread, hoping for cheese. Cucumber. Disappointing.

"Do they?"

She rolled her eyes. "I have no idea. Why don't you ask someone? Do you like cucumber?"

"What?" He glanced at her, distracted. "Oh. Yes. I suppose."

She handed him the sandwich and went back to her search for cheese. She would also settle for ham and chutney. Someone had got a little carried away on the jam front.

Richard ate the dainty triangle in one bite before he cornered one of the farmers. Presumably to enquire how he too could grow such a large gourd. The elderly man looked as taken aback as she felt.

One of the organisers of the fête stuck her head through the entrance flap of the marquee. Her brow cleared at the sight of them and she came over to update Lainie on their takings so far. Her name was Mary, and she was a nice woman. They had been corresponding by email for several weeks. It was her niece, a young local girl named Lexie, who had recently died. Lainie looked at a photo of a cheerful teenager with pretty brown hair and offered Mary her sincere sympathies. There was a lump in her throat. Lexie had been only a couple of years older than Hannah. So many kids. So much stolen potential.

After Mary had gone, Lainie studied her feet for several moments. She concentrated on her breathing exercises, which had proved a useful tool in more than pacing a monologue. She had regained her composure when an elbow nudged her, making her jump.

"Are you all right?" Richard's question was abrupt. When she looked up, he was frowning slightly and there was a trace of concern in his eyes. They had darkened to almost indigo.

He also had an air of impatience and wariness, and she felt the subtle shifting of his body as he moved his weight from one foot to the other. His body language screamed of reluctant, uncomfortable male. He obviously suspected her of imminent tears and was ready to dash up the nearest hill if they appeared. Or just order her, in his iciest tones, to stop being so *female*.

He would probably tell her she was habitually overplaying the sob scene. She almost laughed, and then wondered if she was becoming hysterical.

It must be the oddity of the setting. Standing in a marquee in the Cotswolds with a plate of depleted tea sandwiches, surrounded by pumpkins that would do Cinderella proud for transport, in the company of Richard Troy. Who was holding a plant pot in each hand.

Surreal enough for a Max Ernst painting.

"I'm fine," she said. In her confusion, the words sounded cold, and he stiffened at the apparent snub. "Thank you," she added, which seemed to make the sit-

the side of the tent like the Road Runner if she touched him again.

It seemed a fairly safe bet that he was not, as a rule, a hugger. He didn't even have to play that many love scenes onstage. Backtracking through his résumé, he had been frequently typecast as the villain in recent years.

It would be shabby and far too easy to comment on that.

"Where's Emily?" Lainie asked, interrupting Sarah's intrigued inspection of Richard's herb pots. "Were we abandoned for shopping on the high street?"

"No, she's over at the tea tent. Giggling with her best friend and pretending they're not spying on Johnny Blake. Whom I can't help noticing is a scrawny bean-pole in serious need of a shower, a comb, and a belt to hold up his trousers. I despair about the current state of teenage hormones."

"To be fair," Lainie said, "I believe you had a crush on George Michael when you were at school. He wasn't exactly a well-coifed bodybuilder, was he?"

"He was adorable." Sarah wrinkled her nose. "You eighties babies had no sense of style."

Niall was Lainie's second-oldest brother and Sarah was a decade her senior, but the age difference had never affected their friendship. They had clicked from the moment Niall had brought her home to meet his family as a university student.

"Says the woman who sat her A-levels in shoulder pads and a bouffant."

Richard was stirring restlessly. Their mutual ex-change of nonsense had provided enough cover for him to resurrect his usual shields. "Who *is* Johnny Blake?" he asked abruptly, and Lainie frowned at him.

"I introduced you to him when we arrived. He opened the fête."

"I may only just scrape in as an eighties baby," he said sarcastically, "but I haven't quite dwindled into senility yet. I recall the introduction. I'm still awaiting the explanation of his apparent teen idol status."

"He's a vlogger," Sarah explained. "He makes videos on YouTube."

"Oh. YouTube."

Henry the Eighth might have used the same tone on a visit to the London slums: "Oh. The common rabble."

And, well—yes. She supposed that if his experience of YouTube was limited to people posting iPhone footage of his public meltdowns, he was entitled to be jaded. She would have to introduce him to the life-altering joy that was funny cat videos.

They made their way back outside, and Lainie shivered. The sky was an ominous-looking grey now and it was amazing the rain had held off this long. There was a good reason why most village fêtes were held in summer. At least one could be *optimistic* about a hint of sunshine then.

She was suddenly surrounded by warm, masculine-scented wool. Her eyes, scrunched up against the wind, shot open and encountered Sarah's equally surprised expression. Richard, now *sans* his thousand-pound coat and probably freezing in his shirtsleeves, didn't look at either of them.

Too astonished to speak, Lainie touched a wondering hand to the thick, butter-soft cashmere. Richard's cheeks were going a bit ruddy in the cold air.

Or was he embarrassed? He looked definitely relieved when a stranger approached them and apologised
for interrupting.

Gratitude slid into gathering thunderclouds when
the man went on to ask, very apprehensively, if Richard was the owner of the Ferrari parked by the church.
Lainie didn't think he'd moved that quickly since their
first dress rehearsal, when Will had been let loose un-
supervised with his sword and had found it harder to
manoeuvre than anticipated.

She followed him at a less athletic pace, already
wincing. She hoped he hadn't been ticketed. That would
make for a fun journey home. It had been a very long
couple of hours in the car already this morning. Bob had
staged impromptu drinks with VIP guests after the previous night's show, and none of the cast had got home
before 2:00 a.m. Neither she nor Richard functioned
well on three hours of sleep and zero cups of coffee.

"My, my," Sarah said provocatively at her side.
"What was that I saw? Could it be? Was that possibly
a belated spark of chemistry?"

Lainie shot her a look. "There was a photographer
outside." She heard the defensive thread in her words,
and Sarah looked unimpressed.

"Not when I walked in, there wasn't. Just two smitten-
looking people snogging in a sea of pumpkins."

"We weren't snogging, and I'm not smitten." She
touched a fingertip to her borrowed coat again. Confused, yes. Smitten, no. "We're just doing our job."

"If you say so." Sarah pushed back a strand of limp
blond hair, side-eyed her and added wickedly, "Although I still think he's dishy."

"Then help yourself. I won't tell Niall that his wife is a shameless and mentally impaired hussy."

"Oh dear." Sarah came to a sudden stop, and her brown eyes opened wide. "I'm guessing Richard didn't inscribe his own car door as a fashion statement?"

"What?" Lainie asked blankly.

She followed the direction of Sarah's troubled gaze, and her heart sank. Richard and his hapless messenger stood in the midst of a murmuring crowd, all of whom were gathered in a circle around the Ferrari, gaping as if it were a murder scene. The unfortunate victim in the case was the driver's side door, which had been tagged. Fairly explicitly, and in deep gouges with a key.

"I'm also assuming that *Dick* is not meant as a chummy nickname."

"Probably not when it's wedged between an expletive and the word *head*, no."

Lainie regretted ever getting out of her warm bed and pyjamas. She didn't really want to look at Richard, but forced herself to do so. His lips were pressed together so tightly they had almost disappeared. The nerve ticking in his jaw was like a timer on a volatile bomb. She was surprised he hadn't already exploded. This was a positive show of restraint, and one she doubted would last.

Catching sight of the same photographer in the crowd of onlookers, happily snapping photos and probably planning a weekend break in Biarritz on the profits, she shook off the horrified inertia and went to Richard's side.

Up close, the damage to the prohibitively expensive car was even worse. And the message was offensive to the point of repulsion. Lainie grimaced. She might have called Richard at least one of those names in the privacy of her head—and possibly on the phone to a long-suffering relative—but this was just…foul. Insulting, abusive vandalism. Considering where they were, and why they were here, it was sick.

Mary from the Women's Institute obviously agreed. She looked appalled as she stammered an apology to Richard, making hesitant allusions to local tearaways.

"There's a youth centre in Brickford…"

An offer to reimburse him for the damages was made with obvious dread, an emotion silently echoed by Lainie. A sharp finger was poking at her own conscience on that score. It might not have been her idea that Richard tag along to her charity events, but it *was* still because of her that he was here.

God knew what it would cost to restore a carved-up Ferrari. Almost certainly more than she could afford if she wanted to continue feeding and clothing herself.

She heard a muffled giggle, hastily hushed. More than a few people, in fact, seemed to be finding amusement in the incident.

Proof in action of Richard's unfortunate public image.

For a woman who usually wanted to skewer Richard with a blunt pencil, she was strangely annoyed by the general air of "serves him right." When she looked at him standing to one side, alone, with the skin taut around his eyes and mouth, she felt almost…protective. He would give short shrift to any offer of sympathy, so she kept her mouth shut and settled for placing a tentative hand on his elbow. Even that she expected to be rejected with some force.

He barely seemed to notice her touch. His glaring attention was fixed on his poor sexy, wounded car. She could hear the low, harsh sound of his breathing and feel the muscles quivering in his arm. He looked and sounded so much like a bull about to charge that she experienced a fanciful pulse-jump when the wind whipped her long red ponytail in front of his face like a flag. Hastily retrieving her hair, she tucked it into the collar of her—his—coat. She felt additionally guilty about wearing it now. It might be easier to face public insult and property destruction if he wasn't freezing his balls off at the same time.

"I don't suppose," Richard at last spoke, very tightly, "that anyone saw it being done?"

Nobody had seen it done. Or if they had, they weren't prepared to admit it.

"You should file a police report," Sarah said, the voice of calm reason, and Mary immediately offered to summon the local constable.

Lainie, keeping a wary eye on the avidly interested paparazzo, said dubiously, "I doubt if there's much they can do, without witnesses…unless you have CCTV footage?"

They did have CCTV surveillance, but the camera was directed at the front of the church, not the rear side where Richard had parked.

"You still need to file a police report for your insurance company." Sarah nodded to the anxiously hovering Mary, who immediately went in search of Constable Porter, last spotted browsing the book stall.

Insurance! Of course he would have insurance. Stress was doing odd things to her intellect. Lainie could have twirled with relief. She hadn't fancied the prospect of eating baked beans and Marmite toast for dinner for the next six months.

Richard drew in a sharp breath through his nose and also glanced at the waiting photographer. The pap was looking a bit chagrined at such continued and unusual reticence from a man who had been known to blow his top over spilled tea.

"You do have insurance, don't you?" she asked quickly, trying to divert him. Her fingers pressed a warning into his arm.

He seemed to take in her presence for the first time, and he scowled at her. "Of course I have insurance," he snapped, pointedly picking her hand off and returning it to her. "That's hardly the point, is it?"

From the perspective of her wallet, it was very much the point. But she appreciated that his pride was more outraged than his finances. It was actually a relief that he had returned to grumping and glaring at her. It made it considerably more difficult to feel warming, sympathetic, dangerous things toward him. Richard was a less disturbing element when she could keep him tucked firmly in her mental box of grievances. Just pulling him out now and then to touch up the doodled fangs and devil's horns.

Mary returned with the police constable, and Richard continued to disappoint most of the crowd by not raising his voice or stamping his feet, either metaphorically or literally. He did mutter something about a clod-footed fool, but it was under his breath and not within PC Porter's hearing, so Lainie chalked that up to a win for public relations. She rubbed her finger over the car door to see how deep the gouges went, and he reacted like a fussy hen that didn't want people touching her eggs.

At some point in their association, her eyes were just

going to roll right out of her head and bounce along the floor like a cartoon.

Fortunately for his health, as she would have made creative use of the prizewinning pumpkin if he'd been rude, he was quite polite and gracious with her niece Emily, although clearly uncomfortable with—well, humans, really. His reserve with strangers was not limited to the youth. Emily seemed unimpressed by his efforts, but then Richard *was* over thirty. He also bathed regularly and covered his entire backside with his trousers, so he couldn't really be any less cool to a thirteen-year-old.

While Richard filled in his police report and Emily resumed her distant ogling of Johnny, Lainie and Sarah helped with packing up the tea tent and the baking stall. There were only a handful of items left unsold on the table. Unsurprisingly, the stuffed celery sticks had proved less popular than the chocolate brownies and toffee apples. There was a time and place to push the five-plus a day mantra and it was not at a charity carb fest.

Sarah was almost wriggling with her need to offer further commentary on the Richard situation, but was restricted by the presence of the WI. Lainie made a mental note to screen her calls for a day or two.

Once Johnny had left to catch his train back to London, Emily became impatient to return to her natural habitat. She tugged at her mother's sleeve with one hand, texted a friend with the other and whined. Teenage multitasking at its best.

Sarah allowed herself to be dragged away, still glancing mischievously from Lainie to where Richard stood, putting out stroppy vibes and making PC Porter visibly uncomfortable. Lainie emphatically waved her relatives off and went to thank Mary and the other women for their hard work. They promised to put through a transfer to the Shining Lights account as soon as the cash tally had been finalised.

They left just after one o'clock, with enough time to get to the theatre by four, barring a flat tyre, car accident or roadworks. Richard was a simmering, brooding presence behind the wheel, tapping the indicator impatiently whenever they were stalled in the flow of traffic. Lainie wished she was driving, so she would feel comfortable turning on the radio to break the silence. It always seemed rude to do it in someone else's car, like a tacit acknowledgment you weren't being entertained or would rather not speak to them.

True in both instances here. She *was* bored, and she also didn't want another squabble. They appeared to be incapable of having a conversation without it deteriorating into a spat. There was something about their personalities that rubbed and ground into sparks.

Perhaps best to avoid verbs like *rubbing* and *grinding*. They conjured certain images.

She watched the progress of the tic in his left eye. It was probably a good thing she couldn't read his mind. Her fragile ego might not be able to take the strain. "I'm sorry about what happened to your car," she ventured at last. Because she *was* sorry. And *she* had manners.

His fingers tightened around the steering wheel. "It's fine," he said, as if it hurt to open his jaw more than a centimetre.

"No, it's horrible, actually."

"I said it's fine."

Message and warning tone received.

With a sound that was meant to be a quiet sigh, but

which came out as a nose-blast of exasperation, Lainie stretched out her calf muscles and flexed her ankles. She still thought it was obscene that his car cost more than most people's mortgage, but she wasn't denying it scored well on leg room. The seat was comfortable too. She wiggled her bottom from side to side, enjoying the pliable cushion. A little bounce or two, to test the suspension. Not bad.

The silence suddenly became more pointed, and she looked up into Richard's aggravated, long-suffering stare.

"I see why you aren't supposed to transport the infantry without a car seat," he said, annoyed, and lightly grabbed hold of her knee when she bounced again. "Why can't you just sit still like a normal person? It's like being trapped in a small box with Tigger."

"Speaking of behaving like a sane person," Lainie retorted, her eyes fixed on his restraining hand, "congratulations on not going off like a Catherine wheel at the fête. Why so civil, *mon ami*? The little grey cells want to know."

The skin of her knee was prickling under his fingers. She delicately lifted them away digit by digit, and couldn't resist an admiring stroke of his fingernails. Hers were never that neat and smooth. Too many applications of polish over the years. His facial skin looked in better shape than hers too, which was a bit depressing when he had greasepaint slathered on it as often as she did and could give her at least six years.

"I don't know, Tig." He returned his hand to the wheel and his gaze out the windscreen. "It must be your soothing influence."

She didn't bother to respond to that.

They made it to work by ten to four, and already a few people were waiting outside the side doors of the theatre. Lainie stopped to pose for photos and sign a few tickets. It was still surreal every time someone stopped her in the street to ask for a signature, and she doubted if she would ever feel blasé about the compliment. Richard, on the other hand, cut a striding path through the hopeful group without looking at anyone and went straight inside. Apparently the limits of his civility had been reached. A small child started crying when the door banged shut behind him, most likely from fright at the sudden noise, but it seemed to underline Lainie's embarrassment. She felt she had to linger for an extra five minutes as some sort of poor compensation.

An elderly woman said to her loudly, "Personally, dear, I think you can do better than both of them."

She was quite chuffed about that as she made her way inside.

Backstage was crowded with cast and crew. Footsteps and voices echoed loudly from the catwalk above the stage, as lighting adjustments were made in the midst of strong disagreement. The acoustics in the Metronome were so good that the resulting profanities would be crystal clear in the cheapest seats.

A grip walked past, laden with equipment, just as Chloe decided to have a costume refitting outside the privacy of her dressing room. The crewman's concentration naturally faltered when his eyes almost bugged out of his head, and Lainie had to duck to avoid a head collision with the boom.

Ignoring the chaos she had caused with her corsets, Chloe looked up and waved at Lainie. "Hello!" she called, through a mouthful of sandwich. "I hear you've been larking about in the Cotswolds with Richard. That must have been fun."

From anyone but Chloe, that would unquestionably be sarcasm.

"That's one word for it." Lainie walked over and held a loose flap of silk for Chloe's dresser, Theresa, who looked as if she needed about three extra hands. Women had swaddled themselves in a *lot* of fabric in the olden days. Lainie quite enjoyed the palaver of walking and sitting in her own costume. She had literally got her bustle stuck in the greenroom door during opening week, and Will had had to get in there with his shoulder and wedge her out like a stuck cork. The corseting, she thought they could have dispensed with. Nobody needed a wasp waist.

Theresa hummed gratefully through a mouthful of pins, and Chloe put her hands on her hips, swishing her gown from one side to the other. It was not the most helpful behaviour when they were attempting to resize her clothing without turning her into a voodoo doll.

"I should take Benji for a day in the country," Chloe said. "The fresh air would do us both good."

Lainie had no idea if she was referring to her teenage son or her miniature dachshund, both of whom had been named after Chloe's grandfather. There was no polite way to ask. She settled for a vague, affirmative "Mmm."

"And it's nice about you and Richard," Chloe added, pausing in her fidgeting to smile at Lainie. "I hadn't really thought about you as a couple, but it seems to fit, doesn't it?"

Did it?

Theresa made another sound through her pins, apparently in agreement, and Lainie tried to look less appalled than she felt. Did people really see her as being temperamentally compatible with Richard?

Maybe they *both* needed to re-evaluate their life choices.

She left Chloe to her dreamy gyrations and cut through the wings, doing her best to ignore the sounds of the understudies' rehearsal taking place on the stage. It made her uncomfortable, listening to someone else reading her part. She started to nitpick her own performance, which was a bad idea a few hours before curtain.

On her way down the stairs to the principal dressing rooms, she almost walked into Will, who was coming up without looking, his eyes fixed on his phone. Probably sexting with the fangirl, she thought, examining her feelings on the subject. She was relieved to find she wasn't remotely jealous. She wasn't even angry anymore. There was merely a certain relief at having dodged a bullet, and an underlying shame that she'd ever entered into such a shallow relationship in the first place.

"Whoops," she said when she trod on his foot. "Sorry, Will. Excuse me." She went to move past him, and he glanced up sharply from his phone. His large hand shot out and wrapped around her upper arm, bringing her to a halt so swiftly that her feet skidded off the step. She swayed in his hold like a pendulum dangling from a clock and made a noise best transcribed as "Eek."

Will shoved his phone into his pocket and returned her to an upright position. She would have thanked him if he hadn't left his hands on her waist, and if he wasn't looking at her as if she'd just crawled out of a compost heap.

"What do you think you're playing at?"

She blinked. "I said sorry." She fumbled around and located her spine, adding pointedly, "I wasn't the one gawping down at my dirty text messages instead of looking where I was going."

A faint flush ruddied his cheeks. *Bingo*.

"That's what this is about, is it? How things ended between us?"

"Technically, things didn't 'end' between us. Not in the traditional sense of the word, where one person decides they want out of the relationship so they strap on a pair and man up about it. But minor detail." She raised an eyebrow, wondering if his nostrils had always flared so aggressively when he spoke. "To which 'this' do you refer?"

"Cut the crap, Lainie. You know what I'm talking about. You get your knickers in a twist about Crystalle and—what? Decide to revenge-bang Troy?"

"Her real name cannot possibly be Crystalle. Have you seen her driver's license? I bet you a fiver it's something like Joan."

"Richard-sodding-Troy."

"Or Mabel."

"Would you shut up about Crystalle!" Will blew out through his mouth and pushed a rough hand through his tumbled black hair.

It was funny, really. On paper, Will and Richard would sound almost interchangeable. Hair—black, eyes—blue, build…distracting. Surprisingly fit, both of them, for men who would rather be seen dead than sweating in public. In person, however, they didn't look remotely alike. Richard's hair was curly and his face was far more sculpted. He looked like a carved mask she'd seen in the British Museum. Will was pure Calvin

Klein pretty boy. He was aesthetically the more handsome, but Richard was sexier. Women would probably
want to tack Will's two-dimensional face to the wall of
their office, but they'd rather have a three-dimensional
Richard, mussed and sleepy, against their pillow.

Had she just admitted to finding Richard sexy?

She wondered when to expect the remaining signs
of the apocalypse.

By *comparison*, her mind hastily backtracked. Comparatively speaking, when the alternative was Wee
Willy and his revolving bedroom door, Richard was…
not unattractive.

She had to go. She clearly needed a power nap and
a strong coffee before the show.

"We are no longer personally involved, Will," she
said, narrowly avoiding a slip of the tongue and calling him 'Willy' to his face. She dodged around his restraining arm. "It's none of your business who I get
involved with."

"Oh, isn't it?" he retorted, following her to the bottom of the stairwell. They stood looking at each other
in the dim hallway. A door opened and then closed
again somewhere down the passage. Will's breathing
was quick and agitated, a loud rasp in an otherwise
quiet stillness.

After a moment, he relaxed the tension of his shoulders, apparently with an effort. "Sorry." He sounded
stiff, the apology dragged out of him. "You're right.
You can do whatever you want."

"Thank you," she said dryly. "Now, if you don't
mind…"

"I still think you can do better." Will's mouth twisted
into a grimace, and she was forced to remember why

she'd liked him in the first place. "Than both of us, I suppose."

"Will…"

"I mean, come on, Lainie. *Troy.* A city full of single blokes, and you pick the biggest wanker in the West End."

"It's a sorely contested title. And we've agreed this is none of your business. Now move, please. I need to be caffeinated, and you need to resume typing dodgy little comments in Mabel's ear."

Will raised his hands in surrender and stepped away, and she moved around him, reaching into her pocket for the key to her dressing room.

He started back up the stairs, pausing at the top to call down, "And it's Ethel. I saw her passport when we went to Paris for the day."

Ethel? The discarded trophy wife and wannabe glamour model, *Ethel.*

Quelle horreur.

PAT WAS ALMOST out the door when she suddenly came to a halt and retreated back into the dressing room.

Richard looked up from the script he'd been reading before her unwelcome interruption. He didn't bother to mark his place this time. From a promising first act, it had descended into melodramatic, historically improbable crap.

He smothered a yawn. God, he was tired. He'd had about three hours of sleep last night. The extra shot of espresso in his afternoon coffee was ineffective. He checked his watch. If Pat would kindly sod off, he could fit in a thirty-minute power nap. After her latest mandate, making herself scarce was the least she could do. He wondered if Lainie had received the news yet.

"Was there something else?" The question was pointed rather than polite.

Pat was smiling to herself. With one manicured finger, she smoothed back the immaculate blond hair above her temple. "That should put an extra cat among the pigeons." The observation was both clichéd and obscure. When he merely blinked slowly, uninterested, she added, with a nod toward the door, "Lainie and Will. A rather intense little tête-à-tête in the hallway." She looked thoughtful. "It might be about time for a statement from that corner. Perhaps I'll drop a few words in ears."

Richard had stopped listening to her. He was already on his feet. He wasn't going along with this farce so Lainie could pull a U-turn and dive back between Farmer's sheets. As Pat watched with great interest, he yanked open the door and strode out into the hallway. He was just in time to see Farmer's flat feet clumping up the stairs, probably on his way to the greenroom to sexually harass the catering assistants. It wasn't going to be necessary to speed him on his way.

It had been a trying day all round.

Lainie was walking toward him, headed for her dressing room farther down the corridor. She looked pleased with herself. A tiny smile tugged at her lips. Her red lipstick was almost the exact shade of her hair. She lifted her head and faltered when she encountered his narrowed gaze.

Richard debated speech, and then simply lifted her by the elbows and transferred her to his own dressing room. She didn't come quietly.

The stream of protest came to an abrupt halt when she caught sight of Pat. A vivid blush spread up from her neck. She was definitely a natural redhead. Completely unable to maintain a distance between her emotions and her complexion. Given their line of work, she ought to be thankful for the camouflaging qualities of greasepaint.

"Hello, Pat," she said stiffly, and then shot Richard a nasty look, as if he was responsible for the other woman's presence.

"Lainie." Pat smiled at her. "I hear things went well this morning."

"Oh." Lainie darted another glance at him. "Did you?" Her tone was sceptical.

"The *Digital Mail* is running a caption contest on the photograph of Richard fondling root vegetables. Last time I checked, they already had three hundred entries. Ninety-nine percent sexual innuendo, obviously."

Richard rolled his eyes but couldn't stop a faint smile when he saw Lainie's amusement.

"I'll have to remember to enter tonight." She lifted a delicately arched brow at him. "Was there a reason for that polite summons into your lair, by the way? Or did you just feel like showing off your biceps?"

"I thought you might have questions about Monday," he said blandly, and watched her expression change.

"Monday?" she asked suspiciously. She glanced from him to Pat. "Oh, God. Now what?"

"Your enthusiasm is noted," Pat said, heavy on the irony. "I've booked you both to appear on *Wake Me Up London* on Monday morning. You're on at half seven, so you'll have to be there at six. Get an early night tomorrow. Concealer can only do so much. We'd like to avoid the impression that we work our cast into walking corpses."

Lainie was obviously appalled, which perversely made Richard feel better. Bad temper put red flags under her cheekbones and caused her short, straight nose to wrinkle. It was all very ineffectual. She didn't have the face for intimidation. Her features were deceptively sweet. If she'd thrown tantrums as a child, her parents had probably smiled tolerantly and chucked her under the chin.

"You want us to do a TV interview? About...*this*?" Lainie asked, horrified.

"Could you not gesture directly at me when you say that?" Richard asked. He leaned back against the wall and crossed one ankle over the other. "It's bad for my self-esteem."

She ignored him and continued to address Pat. "I really don't think that's a good idea. Neither of us comes across that well in screen interviews anyway, and if we're supposed to be addressing our...relationship..." She managed to get the word out, but it rolled sourly around her tongue. She looked as if she'd taken a swallow of milk and realised it had gone off about six weeks ago.

"Speak for yourself, Tig," he said, and her sea-green eyes turned almost teal with irritation. Personally, he was starting to feel quite relaxed. There was something very soothing about letting Lainie fight their battles. She was so delightfully...flammable. "I always keep my head during interviews."

"That's why you've almost driven Lynette Stern into a nervous breakdown, is it? Allow me to send you a link to a clip reel on YouTube. It's a three-minute Not-

Safe-For-Work montage of your polite responses to interview questions. The censored version is one continuous bleep."

Richard's smile grew. "Have you been looking me up on the web?"

There was an audible click of teeth as Lainie pressed her lips together. She could probably make judicious use of Lynette's fuck-you emoticons.

"Ostensibly, the interview is to promote *The Cavalier's Tribute* and give an insight into what it's like to be a young—" Pat eyed them. "Youngish actor in the modern West End."

Lainie looked even more annoyed. "Well, I'm younger than Richard."

"You've always seemed practically infantile to me," he told her comfortingly, and her fingers closed around the ballpoint pen he'd left on his desk. He suspected he was about two minutes away from having it neatly inserted into his jugular.

"Obviously, Tara Whitlow is going to broach the relationship angle. I think it's best if you play for discretion. The less you say, the more the public will infer for themselves. Sadie Foster is likely to be voluble on the subject of her affair with Jack Trenton, so I'd prefer you to present a contrast. You've both had media training. I'm sure you'll behave sensibly."

It was admirable, the level of threat Pat could impart without altering the tone of her voice or intensity of her expression.

"Sadie?" Lainie flung his spare jacket off the desk stool, and he watched as fifteen hundred quid of full-grain leather sailed carelessly into one corner of the room. She sat down and fixed Pat with a furious stare. "Is Sadie Foster in the same interview slot?"

"And Jack." Pat casually removed a speck of fluff from her lapel. "It was originally their booking, to promote *Les Mis*. But the band scheduled to appear at eight had to pull out due to 'illness'—i.e. one of them has been carted off to rehab. So the producers have extended Sadie and Jack's slot, and decided to include you and Richard, as well. The Palladium has had enough free publicity recently. We need to keep our end up."

Lainie's response to that was short, explicit and unprintable.

Really, she was growing on him all the time.

FOUR

THERE WAS SOMETHING sadistic about installing harsh fluorescent lighting in a breakfast TV studio. Lainie took one horrified stare at her reflection and dove into a makeup chair. She didn't consider herself *that* vain, but *au naturel* was not working for her at ten past six in the morning. She was usually drooling into her pillow at this hour, halfway through a recurring sex dream about James Bond. Daniel Craig's body. Sean Connery's voice.

A smiling young woman appeared in the mirror behind her, holding a coffee cup in one hand and a bottle of foundation in the other, and Lainie tried not to actually weep at her feet.

"Hi, I'm Sharon," said the goddess, handing her the coffee. "Milk and two sugars, was it?"

"Perfect. Thank you." Lainie drank half of it in one go, while trying not to look directly at the sobering reality check in the mirror. In her head, her skin was not pasty to the point that it had actually acquired a green tinge. She did not have massive dark circles under her eyes. And she definitely didn't have two huge spots on her forehead.

Outside the open door, she heard the clatter of approaching high heels.

And faintly, in the back of her mind, the theme music for the Wicked Witch of the West.

Sadie Foster appeared in the doorway and posed, one hand propped on her hip as she looked around the room. Her sharp gaze fastened on Lainie, who had to suppress the impulse to lift her palm and cover the spots.

"Oh, right," Sadie said, with a snotty head-to-toe survey. "The Metronome." She frowned. "We've met, right?"

Said the woman who'd copied Lainie's answers in acting theory class for a year, and then attempted to maim her. Presumably, in Sadie's world, other people just blurred into one negligible composite of Not Me.

"A few times, yes." Lainie knocked back the rest of the coffee in one gulp, mentally swapping it out for a tequila shot.

Sadie swung her handbag onto a nearby table, where an intern was trying to set out a selection of accessories, and sort of...*flowed* into the chair next to Lainie's. She had the same ability as Richard to make her body go boneless and effortlessly elegant. She also had a similarly aristocratic, aquiline nose. The pretty-face fairy had been awfully generous where those two were concerned. And had obviously just whacked the good-manners fairy right out of her path.

"I want something like this." Sadie handed a torn-out magazine page to her own stylist, interrupting the other woman midway through her polite "Good morning." She nodded at Lainie's empty cup. "And a coffee. Black. No sugar."

Lainie, her eyes fixed on the mirror, saw the two stylists exchange glances over her head.

Sadie, oblivious to the undercurrents—and the fact that she was probably going to star in a Facebook rant later that morning—crossed her legs and yawned. "God," she said, flipping her gold wristwatch around. "Seriously, *who* would watch TV at this hour of the morning?"

"The studio gets some of its highest ratings between seven and eight in the morning," Sharon told her, beginning to dab primer onto Lainie's cheekbones. "A lot of people watch the show while they're getting ready for work. Hauling the kids out of bed."

Sadie shuddered. Lainie wasn't sure whether her nerves were upset by the idea of a nine-to-five, needy offspring, or both.

The bored brown eyes cut in her direction again. "So," Sadie drawled. "Anything lined up for the end of your run? Rumour has it that might be sooner than scheduled."

Lainie concentrated on the soothing motions of Sharon's hands. The cream she was using smelled like coconut. If she closed her eyes, she could pretend she was having a facial. On a desert island. Far, far away from the abrasive blonde presence beside her.

"And that would be just that," she said calmly. "An unsubstantiated rumour."

"*Not* what I heard." Sadie's voice was light and malicious. "I would have thought twice, if I were you, before I got into bed with Richard Troy."

Lainie's eyes opened, and she met Sadie's gaze in the mirror.

"Professionally speaking," the other woman said. She smiled. "Obviously."

"Obviously."

Sharon and her colleague widened their eyes at one another again, and Lainie grimaced. Snarky little scenes like this didn't help anyone's reputation.

"You could try the manager at Leather and Lace," Sadie suggested helpfully. "I've heard he's always looking for trained dancers." She raised her eyes to Lainie's forehead. "Or a Proactiv campaign," she muttered. Loudly.

On the other hand, it would probably give the studio a bit of free publicity if one of their guests mysteriously choked to death on a tube of lipstick.

Sharon coughed. "Tara's buzzing about the interview," she said tactfully. She picked up a damp sponge to blend in Lainie's foundation. "Mr. Troy doesn't give many mainstream interviews." She politely didn't add, "with good reason." "And she's been wanting to get Will Farmer on her couch for ages. In a manner of speaking." She grinned, wiggling her eyebrows suggestively, and then looked mortified as recollection obviously came back to her.

Lainie was too busy going into cardiac arrest to care about the social gaffe. "Sorry?" She pushed her hands down on the arms of the chair, half rising to turn and stare at the red-faced stylist. "What?" Her vocabulary had gone out the window, along with all sense of optimism about the morning.

"Well, *that's* embarrassing." Sharon bit down on a long purple fingernail. "Geez. Sorry."

"Will's *here*? Now?" Hundred shades of horror.

Sharon was visibly taken aback. Sadie looked as if she was mentally bouncing in her chair, clapping her hands with glee.

"Well—yeah. I think so." The stylist seemed eager to make amends. "I don't know for sure that he's arrived, but everyone had the same call time, so I assume he's down the hall with Casey. I can check?"

"*No*. No. Thank you. That's okay." Lainie breathed out through her mouth. She ignored Sadie, whose sharp little ears had pricked up like a fox terrier.

Pat.

Forget the prison guard gig. The woman should be directing presidential campaigns.

That was two for unfortunate death by lipstick. She reserved the right to adjust the number, depending on how the next couple of hours played out.

"You did *know* that the interview is with Richard *and* Will?" Sadie was all fluttery innocence. "Oh…dear." Laughter threaded her words. "*Awkward.*"

Lainie entirely agreed with her.

Sadie's stylist thankfully silenced her with coffee and the latest copy of *Vogue*, and Lainie let a subdued Sharon get back to work. She couldn't stop jiggling her crossed leg as the stylist finished her makeup and started on her hair.

Live TV. Will and Richard on one couch. Sadie stirring the pot. Jack—not the brightest bulb at the best of times, and probably hungover at this hour of the morning. She couldn't see any help coming from that corner.

No potential at all for career-trashing disaster.

Sharon had decided on a no-makeup makeup look, with natural waves in her hair, as opposed to Sadie's

full-on red-carpet glamour. It took gobs of product and
a depressingly long time to create the illusion that she'd
just woken up attractive.

Sadie was finished first, and was wrapped around a
barely conscious Jack when Lainie entered the greenroom. He was sprawled on a couch, head tilted back,
eyes at half-mast, seemingly unbothered by the tentacle-
like arms that entwined his shoulders. Will and Richard
were seated at opposite ends of the other couch, pretending that the other didn't exist. Will was playing games
on his phone. She could hear the tinny theme music.
He glanced up when she came in, scowled and then
went back to obliterating animated snack food. Richard was reading a newspaper. He didn't even bother to
raise his head.

And these hulking specimens of manhood constituted her past and currently imaginary sex life.

God, she hoped there were pastries on that refreshment table.

There were, so the morning wasn't a total loss. She
went with the one closest to her hand, to be polite. The
fact it was oozing the most jam and cream was merely
a bonus. She had no compunctions at all about eating
her feelings. She took a bite, cupping her hand underneath to catch the cream spillage, and said hello to Jack.
He detached his earlobe from Sadie's teeth and turned
to look at her.

"Oh, hey," he said, with a smile and wink. "How's
it going?"

"Great. Thanks."

Nope. No idea who she was.

The only free seats were on the four-seater between
Will and Richard. With a sigh, and as the lesser of the

evils, she sat down beside Richard. She would prefer an
indifferent silence to a sulky one. She also preferred his
aftershave. Although that was a bit of a misnomer when
he clearly hadn't picked up a razor this week. Chewing on a bite of pastry, she eyed him critically. They
hadn't even put much makeup on him. And he looked
fine. Good, even. Bastard.

"Is there something on my face?" he asked, without
much interest. The paper rustled as he turned the page.

"About ten days' worth of stubble, I imagine." Lainie
finished her breakfast and licked a glob of apricot jam
from her thumb. "I'm marinating in half a can of shine
spray here. You could have at least shaved."

Richard cut his eyes in her direction and then glanced
briefly at Will. "Like the Backstreet Boy over there?
Pass."

She was not going to smile.

"I'm not interested in stocks. Or farming." She
leaned forward to look over his raised arm. "I'll take
international news, please."

"There's a pile of magazines over there." Richard
turned the page again, interrupting her perusal of the
classifieds. "And nobody is reading them."

"Yes, but then I would have to get up."

"Great. You can bring me a cup of coffee."

Lainie propped her elbow on the back of the couch
and considered him thoughtfully. "Do we think that's
a good idea?"

He paused, his fingers tightening around the paper.
"Do we think *what's* a good idea?"

"More coffee. You do get a bit grouchy. It could be
caffeine sensitivity. Maybe you should just stick with

the one cup. I mean, live TV. They might not be that quick with the bleeper at the crack of dawn."

A muscle shifted in his jaw. "I haven't *had* any coffee yet."

"Oh." She looked at him sympathetically, wondered if a patronizing pat on the arm would be going too far. She risked it anyway. "Bad night's sleep?"

"No."

"Huh." Swinging her legs up beneath her, she rested her chin on her arm and frowned. "So—it's just *you*, then." She paused, counting to three in her head, and then asked helpfully, "Should we talk about that?"

"Take the bloody paper."

"Thank you."

A production assistant stuck her head through the door a few minutes later. "On in fifteen," she said, looking a bit flustered. "Someone will come to escort you to the set in ten minutes."

Lainie finished scanning the world news and flipped to the arts section. There was a new review of *The Cavalier's Tribute* in the theatre column. She wasn't mentioned. But—

"Do you think *The Cavalier's Tribute* is thematically comparable to *Chicago*?" she asked Richard, who was sitting with one ankle propped on the opposite knee again, frowning into space.

"I think Tom Reynolds should stick to reviewing at his intellectual level," he responded, still glowering. "Which would be open mic night at the local pub and the occasional panto."

Lainie lifted an eyebrow at his sour tone. "Cheer up. He called you 'gruff and overtly masculine.' That could be a compliment. And things could be way worse. I could be sucking on your ear in public."

They watched as Sadie touched her tongue to Jack's chin dimple, and simultaneously grimaced.

"Did you know, by the way?" Lainie asked suddenly. She lowered her voice, although she doubted if Will could hear her over the obnoxiously raised volume of his game. "About Will being here too?"

Richard's expression was difficult to interpret. His eyes moved from Will's lowered head and busy thumbs to Lainie's face. There was a sardonic twist to his mouth, so she expected a biting response.

"No," he said after a moment. "I wouldn't have sprung that on you if I'd known."

Huh. Sensitivity. That was new.

"Although it's probably to our benefit. If Farmer has to open his mouth without a script in his hand, everyone in his vicinity comes off well by comparison."

…And they returned to their regularly scheduled programming.

When another assistant arrived, clipboard in hand, Sadie retracted her tongue from Jack's face, Will reluctantly killed his game, and Richard touched his hand to the small of Lainie's back to guide her out into the hallway. She shivered and sped up.

The *Wake Me Up London* studio was decked out in tones of yellow and orange to look perky and refreshing. The lights were intensely bright, presumably to give the effect of sunshine, despite the dim sky outside. It was more like being in a sunbed.

Tara Whitlow, formerly of the BBC entertainment beat, was smiling into the cameras, rounding up a segment on student fashion designers. She tossed her curls over her shoulders and beamed as she teased the up-coming interview. The director cut to an ad break, and her smile faded. She rolled her shoulders, stretching out her neck, and stood up to greet them as they were herded onto the set. Her smile was perfunctory as she shook hands with them all, and Lainie didn't miss the shrewd stare that accompanied her own introduction. That couldn't bode well.

"Fantastic," Tara said. "If we could have Will, Lainie and Richard over here, and Sadie and Jack on the op-posite couch, please."

Lainie glanced at Richard as they reluctantly fol-lowed the directive. The moment her bottom hit the cushions and she saw the blinking red light of a cam-era, nerves struck. She really, really did not enjoy in-terviews. Richard's sarcastic comment about Will's inability to communicate off-script hit a little close to home.

Richard returned her a wry look, and then looked again, his blue eyes narrowing on her face.

She was physically trembling, literally vibrating with tension. This never happened onstage.

The surprise she'd felt at his earlier, almost friendly remark was nothing to her astonishment when he casu-ally reached out and took her hand in his. His fingers felt strong and rough as he linked them through hers, pulling her wrist over to rest against his thigh.

She let out a slow breath through her mouth.

"All right?" he asked evenly, and she nodded. She wrapped her thumb across his. Sitting up straighter, she ignored a poisonous look from Will. Her nerves had gone from a rolling boil to a slow simmer. For all his many and varied defects, there was something very reassuring about having Richard at her side, when he was *on* her side. He was unflappable in these situations.

Mostly because he didn't care, but still.

The director cued them in, the cameras moved into position, and Sadie went from zero to sixty: sulky diva to big eyes and innocent dimples.

"I'm delighted to have with me this morning five of the brightest young stars in the West End firmament," Tara said. "From the Metronome, Richard Troy, Elaine Graham and Will Farmer, and from the Palladium, Sadie Foster and Jack Trenton. Welcome, all! Thank you for being here today."

"Thank you for having us." Sadie offered the obligatory response.

"I'm doubly appreciative because I know free time is a scarcity when you're in the middle of a performance run. When we announced you would be stopping by the studio this morning, we had a lot of interest on Twitter about what it's like to work on the West End. Can you tell us a bit about that, what it's like behind-the-scenes? What does the average day look like for a principal player?"

Sadie and Will fielded that one, jumping in with a pack of PR-friendly lies that made the theatres sound like something out of an Enid Blyton book. All jolly midnight feasts and togetherness. As opposed to a hard, professional grind and a social atmosphere that could be like navigating a snake pit. If one of them came out with a smarmy "There's no 'I' in team," she was pulling a Richard and walking out.

The questions continued, with the PR puppets continuing to supply most of the answers. Sadie had a habit of inserting little side remarks even when Tara directly addressed someone else, so as to keep herself in the shot. Lainie kept a smile on her face and wished she were back at work. At the actual Metronome, not the sunshine-and-rainbows *My Little Pony* version Will was spinning.

For the first five minutes, Tara kept the interview focused on the performances. It was obviously polite opening filler, since anyone actually interested in the plots of the plays could look them up in five seconds on Wikipedia. Lainie waited, cynically and on edge, for the inevitable.

They came back from another ad break, and Tara's smile turned syrupy.

Here we go.

"I imagine things can become fairly intimate," Tara said, her eyes moving meaningfully between the two couches, "when you're working so closely together. And little birds have been Tweeting that there're a few love stories happening off-script, so to speak."

"Have they?" Sadie couldn't have looked more coy if she'd put a finger to pursed lips and gazed wordlessly into the distance. She reached out and placed a gentle hand on Jack's knee. "I try not to look at social media too much."

Richard raised his eyes to the ceiling, and Lainie bit back a smile. Stress was bubbling at the base of her throat, and it really wanted to emerge as a nervous giggle.

"You don't find it raises an issue, having relationships in what is, after all, your workplace?" Tara's voice was a little sharper behind the sugary gloss. Lainie would have been interested to know what she was like behind closed doors, or in the opinions of the studio interns.

"As you said, it's a workplace. We're professionals, and we don't bring our personal lives into the job." Sadie crossed her long legs and leaned back, smiling at Jack. He looked uncomfortable. Maybe he wasn't sure how to act when Sadie wasn't actually plastered to his face. "I think it's fairly natural that actors fall in love. You spend so many hours together, and you have something fundamental in common, which is always a strong beginning." She shrugged and smiled. Lainie was going to have to revise her opinion of Sadie's acting skills, because she was almost likable in this persona. "Add in a strong dose of chemistry, and, well…"

"And I suppose it doesn't hurt when you're acting out love scenes every night," Tara said, with a knowing smirk.

Sadie laughed. "It's only acting, of course, but—well, let's just say it can be more fun with certain people."

"But potentially risky, I would think, if you hit a bump in the road offstage and have to maintain a consistent performance?" Tara looked directly at Lainie and Will, but again it was Sadie who piped up.

"I imagine it could be a challenge, but I think anyone serious about their career would be able to put the job first. I can't speak from experience, though." She stroked a circle on Jack's leg with her fingertips. "This is new territory for me. Meeting Jack was an…extraordinary experience for me. I can't imagine making a *habit* of dating my costars." Demurely, she looked up between her lashes. Straight at Lainie.

Zing.

Lainie could imagine the *pings* as the #WMULondon Tweets picked up their momentum.

Tara's smile was more genuine now. She must have visions of high ratings dancing in her head. Pushing back her hair, she turned to the Metronome couch. "At the risk of being shockingly tactless," she said hopefully, "I understand things might have been a little... challenging at the Metronome recently, from a personal perspective."

"In what way?" Richard asked politely.

Tara's pause lasted only a fraction of a second, but she definitely hesitated. Straightening her back, she smiled again, narrowly. "Your recent breakup, Elaine and Will, was fairly well publicised. You've clearly managed to carry on in a professional capacity, but it can't have been easy. Especially when things have taken a...shall we say, unexpected new direction?" Her gaze went pointedly to Lainie's and Richard's entwined hands, and then returned to Lainie's face. "There's been a lot of speculation about your new relationship, Elaine, particularly when it's—well, fishing in the same pond, to put it bluntly. How are you dealing with that? And you, Will? It must be difficult for you."

Although the amazing Ethel and her magically disappearing knickers must soften the blow.

Will's fatuous expression was meant to be sensitive and long-suffering. She recognised it from his regular attempts at emotional blackmail when things hadn't been going his way. "Breakups are never easy," he said, lifting one broad shoulder. "But Lainie and I are still very good friends."

That trite cliché that covered up all manner of hurt feelings and homicidal impulses.

"No truth to the rumours of friction between you and Richard, then?" Tara pushed.

Richard shifted lazily at Lainie's side, and Will flushed. "As Sadie said," he replied after a moment, "we're all professionals."

Tara made a sympathetic little grimace at the camera, in lieu of just inserting the subtitle *Heartless Tart* under Lainie's close-up.

"It seems quite…fast, though," she said to Lainie, really picking up a stick and beating that dead horse into the ground. "When did you first realise that your feelings for Richard went beyond those of a colleague?"

(*A*) *When we spoke directly to one another for the first time, and I almost shanked him, and* (*B*) *Mind your own fucking business.*

Lainie could feel the heat in her own cheeks. She was not going to be made out to be the cheater here. Whatever she said in response would likely have been cross, blunt and definitely not Pat-sanctioned, but before she had a chance to land herself in hot water, Richard spoke up in a slow drawl.

"The last time I checked," Richard said, keeping his tone very light, "Lainie was a grown woman, capable of making her own decisions."

His eyes were fixed coolly on the vapid blonde host. Thwarted ambition, he suspected. She had Hollywood signs in her pupils and was obviously straining at the bit in this second-rate studio. If she had the slightest bit of self-awareness, she would realise that attempting to slut-shame another woman on live television was not going to win her any popularity points. He shrugged off the additional, more unfamiliar level of anger. If he did feel…protective toward Lainie, it was all part and parcel of the role they were playing. "I don't really think she needs to apologise for a private relationship between two unattached, consenting adults, do you?"

The host, whose name he'd temporarily forgotten, was taken by surprise. Perhaps she was unfamiliar with the reciprocal aspect of an interview, where her guests actually responded to her classless questions with more than Farmer's brand of arse-kissing.

"Do you have a partner?" he asked conversationally, and she blinked.

"Well, I—yes," she said, further startled and not recovering well.

"But naturally it's your first and only relationship. You haven't dated other people in the past. None." He maintained eye contact. "I'm giving you the benefit of the doubt. I wouldn't like to be irresponsible and just throw around implications of hypocrisy."

The suspiciously taut skin around the blonde's eyes quivered and attempted to crease. Lainie's warm fingers momentarily convulsed around his hand.

After a long pause, in which he heard a stifled giggle from someone in the crew, the host pressed her lips together and switched her line of attack. He could almost hear the cranking sounds as the catapult turned in his direction.

"As opposed to throwing plates?" she asked with pseudo-sweetness. She was scrambling to regain control. "Or public temper tantrums? The Metronome has been hitting the headline recently with rumours of internal conflict and diva behaviour. Would you care to address that?"

He lifted a brow. "Which aspect in particular? Or

should I begin with the plate-tossing and work my way forward?"

The blonde opened her mouth, but Lainie cut in. "Unfortunately," she said, "it's all true." She turned to look at him, and he watched the mischievous twinkle come into her eyes. His gaze moved briefly to her mouth, which was lifting into a cheeky smile. "I *am* a world-class diva. If I miss a cue or forget my lines, I just take it out on the props. Start chucking plates around the stage. Vases. Goblets. If I'm really frustrated, I'll drop-kick the silverware into the stalls." She winked at their visibly hostile host. "It's an extra ten points if you land a silver spoon in the royal box."

Trenton laughed suddenly, and Sadie directed a malevolent stare at the poor bastard.

With an audible intake of breath and a tighter smile, the host tried again. "You've gained something of a reputation lately, *Richard*, for being difficult to work with. There have been reports in the press as to breaches of contract, and details have emerged of a rather nasty email exchange between yourself and the Department for Culture, Media and Sport."

"Which is a shocking reflection on the state of journalistic ethics in this city. Hacking into government emails." Lainie shook her head with dismay. Letting go of Richard's hand, she crossed her legs and leaned forward, clasping her fingers around her raised knee. "What do *you* think about that?" she asked, with avid, wide-eyed interest. She seemed completely at ease now, after her initial bout of nerves, and ready to have a good natter over a cup of tea.

Even Farmer was starting to look reluctantly amused.

The harassed blonde looked like she needed a large glass of wine.

Richard leaned back and let Lainie have at it. He really had underestimated her.

The interview wound up with a rapidity that surprised no one. As they were ushered off the set, the forgettably named host eyed Lainie's rear. Probably weighing up the potential cost to her career against the satisfaction of soundly kicking it. Still grinning, Richard moved smoothly between the two women, just in case impulse won out over sanity.

An intern swept them back to the greenroom, where they'd left their belongings.

"Well...thanks," the teenager said, biting her pierced lip. "That was...great."

"By 'great'," Trenton said thoughtfully, when she'd departed in a hurry, "do you think she means 'total fucking disaster'?" He grinned and picked up Lainie's wool coat to help her shrug into it. The uncharacteristically chivalrous gesture annoyed everyone in the room except those immediately involved. Richard bit back a sarcastic comment when he saw Farmer and Sadie scowl. He had no desire to share even a fleeting sentiment with that company.

"For Tara Whitlow's ego, I mean," Trenton went on, happily oblivious to his simmering girlfriend. "I personally enjoyed the hell out of it."

"Well, I did *not*." Sadie grabbed Lainie's arm. "If you're that ignorant about how to behave in public," said the woman who'd caused widespread nausea by cleaning Trenton's eardrum with her tongue, "your management team shouldn't let you off the leash. It's our reputations that'll take the hit from your lack of control."

To the probable disappointment of all three men, Lainie failed to live up to the clichéd promise of her red hair and merely rolled her eyes in response.

"She's probably right, though," she admitted to him privately as they made their way down to the lobby, out of earshot of the others. "That may not be what Pat had in mind when she suggested we present a contrast to Jack and Sadie. I don't want to sound paranoid, but at times I got the feeling Ms. Whitlow didn't like us much."

Her phone trilled, and she dug through her bag. "Ten quid says it's Pat?"

"No bet." He held the door to the street open for her. "Watch the step, Tig."

The nickname slipped out again. He enjoyed the cranky looks it generated. He hadn't called anyone by a ridiculous nickname since his schooldays, when he'd shared a dormitory with One-Can Murphy and Mouse Philps. His own Eton nickname had been firmly consigned to the history books, never to be spoken again. Suffice to say that he'd paid dearly for the sports day folly of keeping his spare tennis balls in his pockets while wearing overly tight trousers. The entire upper school had thought he'd been a little too excited about winning the house cup. The recent coining of Byron by some moron on Facebook might otherwise have grated, but seemed trivial by comparison.

It was raining again, so they paused under the awning while she opened the text. Silently, she held it up for him to see.

To clear up any confusion on the issue, the point of this unholy alliance is to elevate Richard's reputation. Not for you to become mutually irritating.

Another beep. He could feel her breath warm against his ear as they read it together.

Fortunately, Tara Whitlow is a renowned twit. Behave like that at the Theatre Awards, and you're fired. Ditto Troy.

"She must be in a good mood," Lainie said, but she looked uneasy. She was an innate do-gooder. When the buzz wore off, she would end up mentally rehashing the interview countless times, probably wondering what on earth she'd been thinking.

Richard was slightly curious himself on that point. It had been a very long time since anyone had publicly leapt to his defence, and no one had ever done it with such an air of protectiveness.

Absently, he rubbed the heel of his hand against his chest. The troubled expression in her eyes was making him restless. "Talk about preferential treatment," he said, with a lightness that didn't reflect his mood. "The last time I did an interview, Pat texted me a link to a site on medieval torture methods. I should talk to the union."

He watched her. The air between them felt charged, as if he was attuned to her thoughts and reactions.

Oh, bullshit. He must be more tired than he'd thought.

Lainie smiled suddenly, and his heart actually thumped. He gritted his teeth and a muscle jumped in his jaw. He wanted to turn on his heel and walk away, like a fucking coward, and the impulse struck fiercely at his pride.

"As you called the union president an incompetent prick during your last interview, that might be counterintuitive."

A few years ago, he had participated in a black-and-white short film for the Royal Shakespeare Company. He'd had to communicate the passage of Lear's descent into madness solely through the alteration of his facial features. He had found that less difficult than it was to keep his expression bland now.

"The current president has a brain," he said shortly.

Unfazed by his sharp tone, Lainie gave him a distracted smile and began to text a reply to Pat. He was even more unsettled by the blasé response.

He checked his watch. They had to be at the theatre for a rehearsal at twelve. It was way too early to arrive yet. He didn't care. "I'll drive you to the theatre," he said abruptly, and Lainie also checked the time on her phone.

Casting him a slightly curious look, she hesitated, and then shrugged. "All right. I do need to talk to Olivia about my second costume change."

She followed him to where he'd parked the car and had just clicked in her seat belt when she swore under her breath. Her teeth sank into her very full lower lip. "I forgot. I have to swing by home first and feed Cat Richard. Just drop me at the Tube if you like. There's plenty of time."

He was beginning to feel as if he was doing surrealist improv.

Starting the car, he pulled smoothly into the traffic flow. At the first intersection, he turned in the direction of Bayswater.

"Cat Richard?" he asked, when they came to a halt behind a double-decker bus.

"My landlady's ginger tom." Lainie sounded too calm. He glanced at her. Yes, her eyes were full of laughter. "He's called Richard. I'm feeding him while she's away for a few days, and he has to have meals twice a day. Bowel issues."

This was actually his life.

It was raining more heavily when they pulled up outside the Victorian terrace where she lived. The street looked gloomy and run-down in the murky weather, and she'd better not have been walking here alone from the station at night.

"Do you ever drive?" he asked, as they made a dash for the front door. She pushed the key into the lock and glanced back at him. A raindrop caught on the end of her lashes, which were thick and spiky with mascara.

"No, I don't even have a license. I've never lived farther than a five-minute walk from a Tube station. Thank you for the lift."

She placed a certain amount of emphasis on that last part, and he said impatiently, "It wasn't a hint. How do you usually get home at night?"

"I beam myself into my living room like Spock. On the Tube. How do you think?"

"And then you walk home alone from the station?"

Lainie, apparently unaware that there was rain dripping down the back of his collar, turned on the doorstep to face him. People generally reserved that expression for very young and not particularly bright children. Her hand came up to cup his cheek for a moment, and if she felt him stiffen, she ignored it.

"This is Bayswater, your lordship. Not the red light

district of Bangkok. Chill. Your car might even still be
here when we get back." Her expression turned slightly
rueful. He suspected she was remembering what had
happened to his other car in the middle of a pictur-
esque country village. She had the tact not to resurrect that subject.

Pushing open the door, she led the way down a
creaking hallway and into the stereotypical living room
of an elderly woman. One hearty sneeze would knock
over several cramped pieces of furniture and at least
two dozen ceramic knickknacks. Lainie disappeared
into the kitchen, and he stood in the doorway, watching as she opened the fridge and emerged with an open
can of cat food.

Scooping the gelatinous sludge into a metal bowl on
the floor, she began to call for the cat. "Richard! Breakfast! Richard! Here, puss, puss, puss!"

Her voice had lowered coaxingly. It was husky and
persuasive, with an intriguing edge of command.

"Richard? Come here, baby!"

Jesus.

The cat, which was bloody enormous and did not
need to be fed twice a day, appeared at a leisurely stroll.
It sniffed the bowl disdainfully and then sat down to
lick its leg. Richard assumed they could now leave it
to eat in private. He didn't need visual proof as to what
constituted feline bowel issues.

Lainie picked up the cat for a cuddle, tucking its head
under her chin, and he saw it properly for the first time.

"What the fuck is wrong with its face?"

She looked offended on the cat's behalf, but seriously. A cross between Walter Matthau and a sundried
tomato.

Lifting the cat slightly away from her, Lainie looked from its grumpy face to Richard. And then back again. She walked over and held it up next to him. "Hmm."

"Don't say it."

"Hashtag twinsies."

Her laughter seemed to twine around him.

She bent to put the cat down, nudging it toward the food bowl, and turned to Richard. They were so close that he could count the tiny freckles on the bridge of her nose. Her smile faded. Her eyes, beautifully, intensely green, moved to his mouth, and he curled his fingers into fists.

"Richard." His name again, this time solely for him.

He closed his eyes for a minute, then, without moving a muscle, he deliberately distanced himself. "We've wasted enough time. Shall we go?" He could hear the chill in his own voice.

She looked away from him. "Right." There was a streak of pink under each high cheekbone. "Let's go."

When they walked back out into the rain, his bloody hands were shaking.

FIVE

London Celebrity @LondonCelebrity.now
*Love on the run: smitten Richard Troy front
and centre to support new love at
charity 5k...goo.gl/Ny5hFm*

IT WOULD HAVE helped if she'd got further than the couch
part of the couch-to-5k training plan she'd printed off
the internet. Lainie crossed the finishing line and immediately dropped her head toward the ground, leaning
her hands against her thighs and fiercely rejecting the
urge to vomit. She was embarrassingly unfit, but if the
chain-smoking, foulmouthed comedian two steps ahead
of her could finish with a smile on his face and no visible signs of nausea, then so could she. She straightened
with an effort, cringing as her back made an audible
cracking sound. Performing in a play was a physical
job, for God's sake. It required stamina. She didn't even
have the excuse of sitting behind a computer all day.

Camera lights flashed as more participants made
it over the line. They included several soap actors, a
controversial political commentator, a popular abstract
artist, and a DJ from Radio 1. The fund-raising committee had managed to put together a respectable hit
list of names for the Shining Lights UK 5k, considering
that Fun Runs were among the least popular of charitable events. She couldn't even say the term without an

ironic inflection on the first word. What kind of half-witted masochist actually enjoyed running on a drizzly October morning in London? On a weekday, no less, when there were plenty of people about with laptops and coffee cups, observing the mania with perplexity.

Lainie had tried to suggest an alternative—a bake-off, a rock concert—but the director of the foundation was a jogging enthusiast who refused to believe that other people might not share his predilection for spandex. She saw him now, standing by the refreshment table, doing some kind of yoga stretch and looking cool and unfazed. He didn't even have sweat stains in his armpits. Unnatural.

"Well done!" he called to her. "How was that?"

About thirty-five minutes of pure, wheezing hell, thank you for asking.

"Great," she said, desperately sucking air into her abused lungs. "Brilliant way to start the day." *If you enjoy unrelenting pain.*

"I beat my personal best time."

Which was true, in the sense that she had never run a 5k before and hopefully never would again.

Oh, well. It was all money for worthy coffers.

"Couldn't agree with you more," he enthused. "Nothing more invigorating than an early morning run."

The poor man had obviously never had early morning sex. Or a caramel latte.

He nodded toward the throng of spectators, shivering under their support banners. "Good to see the SOs out in force, as well."

"The SOs?" she asked blankly, trying to follow the direction of his gaze. Had she failed to swot up on necessary athletic jargon as well? Safety Officers? Sports Officials? Sulky Octopi? She had no idea.

"Significant others. Always helps to have a cheerleader on the sidelines, doesn't it?" He chuckled. "Yours looks a bit worn around the edges. Dragged him out of bed early, did you?"

Completely at sea, Lainie didn't respond. Then she finally saw what—or rather *whom*—he was looking at. Richard was leaning against a pop-up art installation. The enormous statue of a polar bear wore an identical frown and a similar amount of facial hair. The bear was evidently very worried about the status of global warming; a stroppy and still unshaven Richard appeared more concerned with his own warmth, or lack thereof. His hands were thrust in his pockets and he was doing the standing jig-dance of the cold and crabby, bobbing from one foot to the other.

Absently excusing herself from the grinning director, Lainie hurried over to him, blowing on her own ungloved hands. Now that she had stopped running, the chill was creeping in.

"What are you doing here?" she asked, amazed and irritable. This had not, as far as she knew, been on their agreed list of activities, and she couldn't imagine he was pining for her company. She felt justifiably annoyed with him for turning up when she was a redfaced, snot-nosed mess. Not that she had ever exactly bowled him over when she was a painstakingly curled, professionally made-up siren, either.

Although he hadn't seemed repelled during that one rain-saturated *moment* earlier in the week. Which she was never going to think about again. She'd been telling herself so all week.

He hadn't wanted to kiss her.

Had he?

Richard removed one hand from his pocket and held up his phone. "I had my instructions." It was hard to pull off a tone that snippy through chattering teeth, but he somehow managed. "A message from Pat. Payback for Monday. Either come to Hyde Park to bear witness to your feats of athleticism, or meet Will at the BBC for a joint debate on the impact of social media on the staging of live theatre—i.e. isn't it a pisser when someone gets a text message or live-Tweets during a performance?" He looked down at her, taking in the yoga pants and zipped fleece jacket. "This seemed like the lesser of two evils. Of course, that was before I knew it was going to be seven degrees outside and you were going to take about thirty-five years to complete the circuit."

"It was thirty-five *minutes*, thank you, and I was strictly middle of the pack. Loads of people aren't even back yet!" She glared at him, and someone took their photo. "Oh, for the love of…" *Deep breath.* She exhaled and said reluctantly, "I suppose you'd better give me a hug, then. Let them get their shot, so we can leave."

Richard eyed her with fastidious distaste. "You're sweaty."

Give me strength.

Or a blunt instrument.

When they'd left her house on Monday morning, she'd been mortified in the car. She'd actually *leaned into him.* In a kitchen that smelled like cat food. She'd been worried it would add a new level of awkward to their interactions, but fortunately he'd returned to being such a dick that it had been easy to quash any disturbing feelings.

"It's good for the skin," she snapped.

"And probably disastrous for cashmere."

Before she completely lost her temper, Richard leant down and swept her into his arms. To their onlookers, it must have appeared a supportive, affectionate embrace. It even included a cheeky bum-squeeze, which earned him a sharp pinch on the chest.

"Oy," he said, jumping. He spoke into her hair, his hands still holding tight to her waist. "I'm just following instructions here. Against my chest, hand under bottom, you said. Two easy steps for a successful cuddle." He anticipated the reflexive action of her right trainer and stepped back out of kicking range. "I'm not sure how you conned Pat into thinking you would be a good, even-tempered influence on me. I've clearly underestimated your acting abilities."

It struck Lainie that this was one of the few times she had seen him smile and mean it. The fact that he was a surly grouch aside, it was often difficult to tell with actors whether an emotion was genuine or an automatic playing to a role. They sometimes couldn't tell the difference themselves. She knew from experience that spending hours every day pretending to be someone else could become a habit difficult to break. She could go off duty, so to speak, and find herself performing the role of Lainie Graham, which could seem as artificial as any character she inhabited onstage.

Even in her relationship with Will, there had been an element of staginess, as if she'd been watching the love scene play out from afar and judging it with professional criticism. That embrace looked stiff; that comment seemed out of character; the chemistry was a bit lacking there; what would be her motivation for that particular action? No wonder so many marriages failed in the acting profession. Half the time they were unconscious stage productions, and every actor eventually tired of playing the same role.

And no wonder so many actors were in therapy. Fodder for the psychiatrist's couch, right there.

She shook off her clouded mood. There was *something* to be said for the dubious pleasure of Richard's company. It was ironic, given that their relationship was a complete hoax, but she never felt there was much pretence between them. Yes, they put up a show for the cameras, but he didn't whitewash his actual feelings toward her. And she had no doubt about her own toward him.

Or she hadn't. Until things had become a little… blurred. She at least recognised the frustration, annoyance, exasperation and reluctant amusement. It was a refreshing emotional catharsis, not having to hold back with him.

Richard Troy: human stress ball.

She ignored the tiny singsong voice that was making almost-kiss taunts.

Right.

Not holding back at all.

He seemed to be deriving some emotional benefits from being with her, as well. His expression was one of resigned tolerance when he reached over and caught her hand. "Come on, Tig. I'll shout you brunch."

She looked down at herself. "I can't go out to eat like this."

"You're fine. You hardly look like you put in any effort at all."

She was still trying to work out if that was an insult when they reached his car. The assaulted Ferrari had been swapped out for an equally lush Maserati this week—temporarily, she assumed, unless he just replaced a damaged supercar like it was a pair of ripped tights. His lifestyle was a wet dream for the average British male. He'd also managed to find a prime parking spot. She wondered if the force of Richard's personality was such that people just upped and left the moment he set his sights on their park.

Another photographer took their photo as they got into the car. Lainie resisted an insane urge to grin cheekily at her. She felt oddly light. Perhaps there was something to these exercise endorphins after all.

They ate at one of her favourite cafés in Bayswater, a few blocks from her flat. The décor was a bit naff and Ye Old Tea Shoppe, but it served incredible coffee and pancakes. Most of the restaurants in the area seemed to have gone over to the all-organic, all-healthy craze. It had been a personal mission to find one that didn't sneak greens into every dish, as if they were tricking toddlers into eating their vegetables. Lainie would rather have hips than drink pulverised spinach in her smoothies. She preferred her green food to contain the words *mint* and *chip*.

There was good people-watching in the summer, when it was borderline warm enough to sit at the tables outside, but they settled for a cosy table near the wood fire. Lainie looked at Richard thoughtfully as she cut into her pancakes, scooping up an escaping blueberry with her knife.

"What would you usually be doing at this hour of the morning, if you're not called in for rehearsal or scene changes?" It was half past ten, which in the world of evening theatre was most people's seven or eight. "Sleeping?"

Richard shrugged and swallowed a mouthful of poached egg. "Depends on what time I got home the night before, and whether I have another work commitment." He leaned back and picked up his coffee, giving her an unreadable look over the rim. "And obviously if I'm alone—or not."

She stabbed her fork into a strawberry and ate it with relish. She was fairly sure the berries had come out of a can, but they were still tasty. "A morning quickie sort of bloke, are you?" she asked, going there out of sheer nosiness. "Or is it wham-bam-get-out-my-bed-ma'am?"

He smiled against his will. "I'm sure you won't be surprised to learn that it's the latter. I prefer not to actually *sleep* next to someone if I can avoid it." He added smoothly, "Although I handle the situation as tactfully as possible, of course."

"Which, coming from you, probably means your poor girlfriends find themselves standing on the doorstep, wrapped in a bedsheet and clutching their knickers."

"Only in the summertime. If it's winter, I let them take a blanket, as well."

"How about that? A joke." Lainie was smiling, as well. She poured a bit more syrup on her remaining pancake. "What happened to the barrister? I remember thinking she looked nice."

"Which barrister?" Richard looked blank.

"Working your way through the profession, are you? That seems a bit risky in your case. With that short fuse, you don't want a stream of angry exes in the courtroom if you ever have to stand trial. The barrister you dated for like two months, you clod. *You*, at least, should remember her name. You took her to the Tony Awards. The blonde in the gorgeous Alice Temperley gown. The woman clutching your elbow all night." She forked up a piece of stewed apple. "You probably sat next to her in the venue. Most likely shared a car ride home. And…"

"Yes, I don't need the complete itinerary, thank you. You mean Barbara Greer. She's a judge, not a barrister."

"My apologies to her honour. Well? What happened?"

"Mind your own business." He drained his coffee cup.

"Spoilsport." She finished her plate with a contented sigh and picked up her own drink. Pancakes and hot chocolate were the building blocks of her happy place. "I wouldn't care if you asked me about my exes."

"How obliging of you." He idly twirled his fork between his fingers. "Unfortunately, I would rather insert this into my retina than hear the intimate details of Will Farmer's sex life."

"For that, you would have to read Crystalle Hollingswood's blog." She wrinkled her nose. "And then you really would want to stab yourself in the eye with a fork."

Richard was staring out the window and she thought he had stopped listening to her. She'd noticed that if he was bored with a conversation, he switched off and made no effort to disguise his lack of attention. After a few minutes, though, he asked casually, "Still heartbroken?"

"My heart didn't come into the equation." She was suddenly quite embarrassed and looked down at the tabletop, swirling heart patterns in the spilled sugar with her fingertip. "It was more about very shallow hormones in the beginning, and my pride later on. I wish it had never happened. It's a bit of a facer to realise I'm that susceptible to fairly empty good looks. Although he had his moments," she added out of fairness. "He's not a complete prick. Put it at ninety-five percent, with wiggle room if his conscience is playing up."

"It does seem to show an appalling lack of judgement on your part," Richard agreed coolly, and her mouth twitched.

She could always rely on him not to sugar the pill.

A group of tourists walked by the window, identifiable by their cameras, guidebooks and damp hair. If you spent much time in London, you learned to either carry an umbrella or look into the concept of hats. Or just run really fast to the nearest Tube station.

"They've been to the Tower." She nodded at the plastic gift bag one of the women was carrying. "I haven't done the tour there since I was about seven. I should make an effort to actually *do* more things when we have time off. If I get a morning to myself, I end up wasting it on a nap." Or watching four episodes of *Scandal* in a row on her laptop, but she could imagine his response to that without vocalising it.

"It's usually not worth the hassle." Richard raised his arms above his head and stretched. The joints popped in his shoulders, and his jumper rode up to reveal a slice of pale, tautly muscled belly. She shamelessly enjoyed the view while she finished her hot chocolate.

She was no longer necessarily *averse* to finding Richard attractive, she realised. It was just very surprising. And should remain at the sensible look-but-don't-touch stage. If she ever evolved into an outdoorsy person and went on safari, she might admire the dangerous beauty of the lions from a distance, but she for damn sure wouldn't get out of the car. Or some equally profound metaphor.

"There's always at least one idiot with a camera," the hottest old curmudgeon in town finished.

"I assume you're talking about journalists, not your well-meaning, misguided fans."

"Either-or." He frowned. "Both. It's all nonsense."

"Let me guess—you became an actor to *act*, not to become public property. The fame is an unfortunate downside to the craft. Et cetera."

"It is, to anyone with the gift and instinct for the stage, and not merely a need for constant, slavering attention." He looked at her scornfully. "Let me guess," he mimicked. "You share the good news on Facebook when you appear in the gossip columns, you can't get enough of people asking for your autograph in the street, and you simply adore being asked whom you're wearing by vapid journalism graduates who couldn't get a job reporting actual news."

"We're awfully snotty about the industry that pays our bills, aren't we?" Lainie refused to be provoked. She carefully set down her cup in its saucer and popped the free chocolate into her mouth. Moving it to the side of her cheek with her tongue, she added, "Although I forgot for a moment. You don't actually *need* vapid press to help you in finding work. It's easy to be high-and-mighty about the integrity of the craft when you could buy and sell the Metronome with your discretionary income, isn't it?"

A faint flush rose up Richard's neck, but she pushed past his obvious annoyance and continued, "And no, I don't particularly enjoy reading embellished facts and total lies about myself on the internet. But I can only be annoyed about it to a certain point before I become a hopeless hypocrite, since I read magazines and blogs myself." She ignored his snort. "Most people do. It's probably been going on since the beginning of time—people have always spied on their neighbours and they've always gossiped about public figures. Look at our play. Rumours running rife amongst the court. Your character would achieve fuck all without poking and prying into things that don't concern him. With the odd stagnant, boring exception," she finished, staring meaningfully, "to be human is to be nosy. I refuse to believe that even you wouldn't be secretly interested if you heard something shocking about, say, Jack Trenton."

"I cannot conceive of any possible circumstance where I would find myself enjoying a cosy gossip about Jack Trenton."

"No? What if I came to you and said that Jack got his role at the Palladium by sleeping with the director?"

"He did."

Lainie blinked. "What?"

Richard absently wiped up a coffee ring on the table with his napkin. "He was seeing Arnette Hall when he was cast, so I doubt if that was a coincidence." He sounded totally uninterested. "I don't think anyone believes Trenton is advancing in his career on the strength of his talent."

"But…what about Sadie? Weren't they going out then?"

Richard shrugged. "Since he hasn't been seen with six-inch nail gouges down his face, I assume not."

"How do you *know* this?" Lainie demanded. "And of all the cheek, criticising *other* people for gossiping."

"Nobody whispered the latest *on dit* into my ear over the watercooler. I saw them together at a hotel. If it was supposed to be a secret, they should have chosen somewhere less high-profile than the Goring." He leaned back and dug into his pocket to remove his wallet, ready to pay the bill. "That wasn't gossiping. *This*," he said, gesturing between them, "is gossiping. Which is why we're going to stop discussing it."

"So you didn't tell anyone?"

He looked disgusted. "What the fuck do I care about Trenton's personal life? If he has to shag his way through every casting office in the city to get a job, have at it. So long as he doesn't come within a foot of any production of mine."

He got up and went to pay for their food, and Lainie stared after him.

Well, *honestly.*

Outside on the street, she pulled up the hood of her fleece to protect her head against the drizzle, although she suspected her hair was a lost cause. She had now reached the post-exercise stage—admittedly a rare location in which to find herself—where the sweat had dried into a nice crusty sheen of salt on her skin and clothing. It was not pleasant.

"I need a shower." She grimaced and plucked at her top. She didn't think she actually smelled. Richard would never have kept quiet to spare her feelings. He would probably have made her sit on a towel and ride with the window open.

"Your pressing urge to traipse around the Tower will have to be put on hold, then." Richard unlocked the car door and held it open for her. "The British public *will* be disappointed."

"Well, I can obviously forget inviting you along when I go, since you seem to rank yourself on the Prince William and Clooney scale of paparazzi interest." She considered. "We could wear huge hats and sunglasses. Give you the chance to enjoy a day of anonymity. It must be a trial being in possession of such striking good looks and huge, pulsating…talent."

Richard slid behind the wheel and reached for his seat belt. "I think the idiots wearing sunglasses in pouring October rain would attract their fair share of attention."

He drove her the short distance to her flat, as it hadn't occurred to her that she could offer to walk home. Her body considered itself good for cardio for at least a fortnight. She automatically offered him a cup of tea—the English tradition: just finished drinking half a gallon of coffee and hot chocolate, therefore must be time for a cuppa—and was surprised when he accepted.

He followed her up the stairs to her flat, looking around the upper floors with avid interest and a growing frown. When she'd unlocked the door and he was standing in her tiny lounge, he asked rudely, "What pay grade are you on?"

Lainie went into the kitchen and topped up the kettle with water. "We can't all live in a mansion in Belgravia," she called back. "It would send the tax brackets haywire." Either the euphoria was still buzzing from her run or she was growing a thicker skin when it came to Richard. She didn't feel tempted to slip something more lethal than sugar into his tea. Progress.

She dropped tea bags into a couple of mugs and returned to the lounge while she was waiting for the kettle to boil. Dropping down on the couch, she smothered a yawn and pulled at her jacket again. She would strip it off and shower as soon as he left. There was no way she was getting naked while Richard was one flimsy wall away. "You'll just have to slum it for a few minutes. I'm sure you'll survive."

He sat down at her side, still frowning and obviously missing the subtle hint at his departure. He was subjecting her room and possessions to an intense scrutiny. A belated sense of guest etiquette seemed to return to him, as he offered an unconvincing, "No, it's…fine. Very…snug."

She eyed him. "I'm well aware that my entire flat could probably fit into your en suite. There's no need to strain something trying to be polite. I'm getting used to your particular brand of sledgehammer."

The kettle whistled before he was obliged to answer, and she went out to make the tea. She didn't think he would appreciate her pug mug, so she let him have her grandmother's Royal Doulton cup. After a pause, she added a handful of digestive biscuits to a plate. She might be finding him more tolerable, but she wasn't wasting the chocolate hobnobs.

He looked preoccupied when she handed him the pretty cup. The look he gave her when she sat down again was sharp and penetrating. "I didn't hurt your feelings, did I? About your flat just now?"

She came to a stop midbite of her biscuit. It grew soggy between her teeth and half of it crumbled into her lap. Coughing, she took a quick sip of tea. "Where did that come from?" she asked when her throat was clear. She brushed the crumbs from her knee into her cupped hand and deposited them into a tissue. Why did he continually make her feel like such a scruff?

"Did I?" he persisted. He had taken off his coat and pushed up the sleeves of his jumper. His forearms were ropy with muscle and dusted with a light covering of dark hair. It looked softer than the coarse hairs in his eyebrows, which were currently compressing wrinkles above the high bridge of his nose. He was being serious. He really wanted to know.

Lainie stroked her thumb around the rim of her mug. "No. You didn't hurt my feelings." She smiled faintly. "You make me hopping mad, though. And I wish you would have more consideration for other people's feelings in general."

In the interests of honesty, she added, "I'm not exactly soft-spoken myself, in case you haven't noticed. I can handle your acid remarks. I even—*very occasionally*—enjoy them. It's mostly when they're directed at other people that I balk. Especially when the balance of power is clearly on your side."

Richard was resting his arms on his knees, looking down into his own cup. The short black curls were tumbling against his forehead. His resemblance to the ideal of a romantic poet had never been more evident. "I'm aware," he said finally, in a low voice, "that I can be... difficult to get along with. And I don't always make allowances for individual circumstances. I expect people to just take anything I say and fire back." The corner of his mouth tilted. "As you do." He turned his head and fixed her with that intent blue stare. "I wouldn't want you to think I always intentionally aim to hurt."

Had there been a slight emphasis on the word *you*?

Lainie bit her lower lip thoughtfully. She wasn't quite sure how to answer. "I don't think you're a bad person, Richard. Perhaps a *little* more flawed than most," she teased, and he grimaced, "but I shall rise above that and keep a thick skin where you're concerned."

"Thank you," he said dryly.

"And if you really do hurt my feelings, I'll immediately and enthusiastically cry so you're aware of the fact."

He looked faintly appalled at even the joking suggestion—and generally uncomfortable with the way the conversation had turned. She could relate.

He leaned forward to put his cup on the coffee table and picked up the script that was lying there. The first page of the historical saga was scrawled and underlined with her notes. His initial movements were artificial—he was acting again, moving them out of an awkward impasse, and the script was the closest prop to hand. But his idle glance swiftly focused into intent interest. She conquered her first instinct, which was to snatch the papers out of his hand and sit on them, and settled for watching him warily from behind a sip of tea.

Richard flipped through a few pages of the miniseries pilot, skim-reading with a practised eye. "Are you doing this?" he asked, still reading. There was definite disapproval in his voice, and she bristled. This was currently her sore spot, and she was sensitive to the slightest jab at it. He glanced up when she didn't reply, giving her an ironic look. "Yet another talented stage actor decamps for the cheap thrills of television, I see."

She had stuck on the opening adjective. "Talented?" she repeated, astonished and totally ignoring the rest of his hoary old prejudices.

"That's what I said." He paused. "Well, within certain parameters."

"Which you may keep to yourself. I'd prefer my nice shiny compliment to remain untarnished, thank you."

Richard raised the script. "You should have a good chance of getting another West End role when *The Cavalier's Tribute's* run ends. Has the experience begun to pall?"

"No." Lainie tried not to sound defensive. "I love the theatre. But I don't see anything wrong in stretching myself. Trying other mediums." It was true. She just wished her confidence extended beyond the sentiment to her actual abilities. Her eyes narrowed. "I seem to remember the Great Troy lowering himself to do a few films back in the day. And I *know* you did at least one guest spot on TV." She had watched it on YouTube over breakfast the other morning. And Richard had been nominated for a BAFTA eight years ago for one of those films.

"Naturally. I would hardly air my criticisms of an industry without experiencing it firsthand, would I?"

"Just as a side note, you're the most infuriating person to have an argument with."

He looked surprised. "We're not having an argument. We're discussing your immediate future in your chosen occupation." He flipped through another couple of pages of the script and considered her shrewdly. "I suppose it's only fair that you get the screen bug out of your system. This doesn't seem like *complete* trash."

"I do not *have* the screen—"

"Have you been offered the role or are you still auditioning?"

She hesitated. "I had—have," she corrected hastily, "a callback for a third audition next week."

"Had or have?"

"Have. I *have* another audition next week."

She didn't like the way he was looking at her.

"You're faltering."

"I am not. I'm just…" Lainie realised she was chewing on her thumbnail again and removed her hand with an exasperated sound. She sighed. "I have…reservations."

"About the role? Don't do it, then. Listen to your instincts."

"Yes, well, my instincts are telling me it's a great role, and I would be rubbish in it."

His eyebrows went up. "You're nervous."

She set her chin mutinously.

"Get over it." Richard was uncompromising. His eyes didn't leave her face. "You wouldn't get a callback if they didn't think you had the right potential for the part. If you get it, and you want it, you do it well. And you *believe* you can do it well. There's no room in this industry for self-sabotage. There are plenty of people who will claw you down at the first opportunity. If you let them, you shouldn't be there. Time to look into teaching."

Lainie was silent.

"You're a competent actor. Grow a spine and act like it."

"I seem to have downgraded from 'talented.'" She looked at him. "You don't believe in coddling, do you?"

"Do you *need* to be coddled?"

Sometimes. Particularly at certain times of the month. But not, apparently, when it came to her career. Sarah's sympathy for her nerves, when they'd spoken about it on the phone, had made her feel even more uncertain. Richard's dictatorial straight talk made her sit a little taller.

She looked from the script to his cool expression. "Thanks."

"For the record, I still think you would be better off sticking to the stage." He carefully returned the script to the coffee table. "And I think you've misinterpreted the character's emotional response on the second page."

His eyes went to her phone, also lying on the table. "Is that a relative?" he asked idly, looking at Hannah's photo on her screen background.

Lainie's gaze also went to the freckled smile. "That's my little sister. Hannah."

"Cute."

"Yes, she was."

He stopped moving. "Was?" he asked after an extended pause.

Lainie picked up the phone, wrapping her fingers around it. It was a protective gesture, as if she could physically hold her sister's memory close, safeguarding it from any insensitive response.

"She died from cervical cancer." She never whitewashed the circumstances; she wasn't going to hedge about her sister's life and death to avoid a conversational gaffe. "About eighteen months ago, when she was sixteen. She was one of the youngest reported cases."

For at least thirty seconds, he said nothing at all. She knew; she was counting in her head. Stress tic. Eventually, and very, very gently, he reached over and took the phone from her resisting grip. He turned it over to look more closely at the photo.

"She looks like you," he said, and Lainie smiled faintly.

"I always thought so. She didn't."

"It's the eyes. Green as the sea and full of devils. She looks like a handful."

"Are you implying, by any chance, that it runs in the family?"

"Would I be so uncivil?"

Her smile grew. "She *was* a handful. She was a moody, stroppy little piece of work with too many piercings and at least one tattoo Mum didn't know about. She could get under my skin like no one else on earth." Her eyes turned ironical on him. "At the time." She added calmly, "And she was the relentless, pesky, foulmouthed light of my life."

"Hence the charity." Richard's face was unreadable. "You launched Shining Lights yourself?"

"Not exactly. I made a general nuisance of myself in some very influential buildings to get a few balls rolling, but it's a subject that unfortunately hits close to home for a lot of people. They came forward, a foundation was established and things have taken off from there. We have a great director. Albeit a slightly misguided one when it comes to organising a Fun Run during the coldest autumn in five years." She took back her phone, rubbing her thumb over the screen.

"It's admirable."

"It isn't, really." Lainie touched the corners of Hannah's smile. It had been so long since she'd seen that smile in the flesh. Far longer than eighteen months. "It was...self-preservation. I needed to do *something*. If I didn't do something constructive, I would have done something destructive. I was so mad. *So* angry, and I just...itched for action."

She bit down hard on her lip. "In drama, you know, and on the screen, it's all so...clean. The courageous patient, still smiling and joking on their deathbed. Going peacefully when the time comes. It's not always like that. Not that Hannah wasn't brave." She clenched her hand. "She was always brave, even when she was a toddler. She tried to climb the tree outside our house in Clapham when she was three because she wanted to see the bird's nest on the top branch. But she was angry. She was angry, and bitter, and *terrified* until the moment she died. And there was nothing to say. How can you possibly make it better? I knew what was going to happen, *she* knew what was going to happen and there was no way to stop it. And in the end, she'd be alone. I was holding her hand when it happened."

A different hand, a healthy, masculine hand, reached across and closed over hers.

Slowly, her palm rotated and she curled her fingers around his. "She still had to go alone."

Richard was stroking her knuckles in slow circles, trying to relax the tension there. She could hear him breathing in the minutes that followed her outburst. The combination of the sound and the touch, both steady and rhythmic, helped bring her back to herself.

She stirred, releasing his hand to self-consciously push back her hair. "Sorry. I didn't realise that was still bottled up." She managed a grim smile. "Apparently exercise has an unsettling effect on me. I knew there was a reason I avoid it."

"No. I'm sorry." He said it very simply, very matter-of-factly. "I *am* very sorry, Lainie."

She studied him. "Yes. I can see that you are." On impulse, and to their mutual surprise, she leaned over and kissed him on the cheek. Her lips nudged against his jaw, and the stubble there was rough and raspy.

Richard caught her upper arm as she started to pull back. He held her there, poised above him, his eyes—shockingly blue, full of questions—searching hers. She steadied herself with a hand on his belly and could feel a pulse thrumming under the soft fibre of his shirt. He seemed to make up his mind on a silently debated issue, and acted with his usual swiftness once he'd come to a decision. Her startled gasp was lost inside his mouth when he moved his hand up to her head, tangling his fingers in her hair and bringing her face to his in a rough, open kiss.

His other hand shaped the line of her shoulder and upper back, sliding down her rib cage to press firmly at the base of her spine. She gave under the pressure, her body coming down to rest half on top of his. Her leg jerked and she almost bumped her knee into an increasingly sensitive place, startling a muffled grunt from him. Without breaking contact with her mouth, he released her hair to grip her thigh, gently raising it and manoeuvring her leg across his lap. They both made tiny, urgent sounds of need at the new and intimate contact.

Lainie stroked the sides of Richard's neck, slid her fingers up to touch his earlobes. She cupped his jaw, feeling the muscles working beneath the warm skin, and attempted to angle the direction of his head. His kiss was both demanding and coaxing, playfully daring a response from her even as he took what he wanted.

Her lashes were fluttering as she kissed him back, and she was acutely aware of the barrage of sensation. The fierce, silky friction of his tongue against hers. The shivering stroke of nerves as his fingers burrowed under her fleece jacket, tickling her hip and tummy, sliding upward to brush the side of her breast.

A hint of sanity returned at that touch. Not because she was conflicted about a man touching her breasts. Her feelings were quite clear on the subject. Lovely in a sexual situation. Necessary evil during a medical exam. Sharp uppercut to the jaw in any other circumstances.

But she was usually wearing a lace bra in a sexual situation. Or, at the very least, separate cups of cotton. Not a clammy sports bra that gave her an epic case of mono-boob. Her generous assets were currently squished and flattened into a veritable shelf. It was not a sight she wanted to expose to Richard. And she still needed a shower.

And for God's sake, she was making out with Richard Troy. In the privacy of her flat. Where there was not the slightest excuse of a lurking photographer, unless the paparazzo had Spider-Man abilities to scale a three-storey building with no handy trees or drainpipes.

This would probably be a good time to remove her tongue from his mouth.

She pulled her head away and watched his eyes open. They otherwise stayed where they were, staring at one another and breathing heavily. His chest and belly pushed up into hers with each inhalation. It was extremely difficult to keep her fingers away from his shirt buttons.

When Richard spoke, his voice was a growly, sexy rumble. "Bad idea?"

He was still tracing slow, sliding circles on her bare stomach. She placed her hand over his to still the movement. "I'm only guessing," she said, "but I'd say disastrous." She looked regretfully at the impressive body sprawled under hers. "I think this situation is messy enough already, don't you?"

"Sadly, the situation seems to have been aborted before it had a chance to get messy, but I take your point." Richard lifted her off him completely, helping her to sit up. In the process, she made another accidental attempt to unman him with her kneecap. He dodged back out of harm's way, the momentum carrying him all the way to a standing position. "Christ! You should come with some kind of warning label."

"Sorry." She picked up her abandoned mug and took a fortifying gulp of lukewarm tea. Tea for shock: that was the idea, although she had always preferred wine after a stressful experience. She looked at the wall clock. Maybe not at half past eleven in the morning. Good Lord. She had almost seduced Richard on her couch, and it wasn't even noon. This was the day for all *kinds* of personal firsts.

"Could you stop knocking back cold tea like it's straight bourbon?" Richard asked her testily. "It's not the most flattering reaction to a kiss."

Was that what he considered a garden-variety *kiss*? Having a woman crawl all over him while he stuck his hands up her sweaty workout clothes? She didn't want to know the answer, so she kept her snarky internal response to herself.

Richard sighed and pushed a hand through his rumpled black curls. "Do we need to have the hackneyed 'so sorry—big mistake—won't happen again' conversation, or may we just take it as read?"

"No, I think that about covers it." Lainie summoned an unamused smile. "We did promise Pat we'd practise being nicer to each other. I think we can check that one off for today."

"Indeed."

She pulled at her top, suddenly impatient to be clean and dressed, and back in control. "I should have a shower."

"Since I assume I'm not being invited to either observe or participate, I'll accept my dismissal and push off." Richard bent to pick up his keys from the coffee table and hesitated, playing with them in his hand. Briefly, his gaze moved past her to focus on the bookshelf. His eyes flickered, darkening, before he visibly pulled himself together. "Do you want a lift to work today?"

"I can take the Tube."

"You have functional legs and there are coins jingling in your pockets, so I expect you can. However, you don't have to, as I'm offering a lift. Yes or no?"

She didn't want to be childish and silly about it. Lainie nodded. "Yes, okay. Thanks."

"Good. I'll be outside at twenty to four. Don't be late. Oh, and Tig?" Richard turned at the door. "Ten out of ten for effort, but the execution could do with some work."

She drew in a sharp breath, but before she could retort, he added innocently, "But then, you've never run a 5k before, have you?"

Left alone in her lounge, listening to the echo of his footsteps, she reluctantly smiled.

OUTSIDE IN THE STREET, Richard stood motionless, his eyes fixed sightlessly on the crumbling stone fence. The rain had dwindled to a light drizzle, but the air bit icily into his skin. He exhaled a long, slow breath.

Shit.

A couple of young women approached, pushing covered prams. One of them glanced at him with passing curiosity, and he grimaced, angling his body away from view with a discreet movement. He should probably count himself lucky it was almost winter. Right now, he was reaping the benefits of bulky, concealing clothing and nature's version of a cold shower.

He could still feel Lainie's soft skin under his fingers, the quivering of her stomach, the faint etching of stretch marks on the curve of her hip. Pale and perfect. Her breath had been warm against his neck, hitching when he touched her.

As a teenager, he'd been covered with acne, angry at life, and stuck at an all-boys boarding school. He was no stranger to sexual frustration.

It was more than that. He was… God, he was *bonding* with her.

Feelings—warm, strong, nauseating feelings— were springing up all over the place, unfurling in his chest, his gut, his groin. Sinking in deep with their little hooks.

Her obvious pain had reached out and grabbed him around the throat. He'd wanted her in his arms. Would have settled for holding her hand. Then she'd kissed him—on the *cheek*, for God's sake—and just about shocked his brain out of his skull. If he actually got her into bed, he might not survive the night. He looked up at the dull, overcast sky. Or late morning, as the slightly embarrassing case may be.

Bob's half-cocked plan was proving unexpectedly dangerous.

It had been a sour reality check, catching sight of Farmer's complacent grin over her shoulder. The digital photo frame on her bookshelf had been innocent enough until then, passing through a series of holiday snaps. Offering intriguing insights into Lainie's choice of swimwear. She did fairly spectacular things to a halter-neck.

They had looked good together. Smiling and pretty, healthy and happy. For a feckless little shit who dipped his wick all over London, Farmer had looked pretty far gone. He wasn't a good enough actor to fake it. Lainie's chin had rested on his shoulder, her eyes laughing into the camera.

He remembered, suddenly, interrupting a kiss in a back hallway on opening night. She had pulled free of Farmer, blushing. Richard had barely registered the scene, had felt nothing beyond fleeting contempt. Another of Farmer's brainless, easy conquests. That was all he'd seen.

He shook his head, a single, sharp movement, and left the narrow strip of lawn that functioned as a garden. Beeping the lock on the Maserati, he slid behind the wheel. He checked his watch. The panel beater was dropping off the Ferrari at one o'clock. His phone rang through the wireless system and he hit the answer button on the steering wheel.

"Troy."

There was a burst of static, then a voice that sounded like someone doing a bad impression of the Prince of Wales. "Is it Mr. Richard Troy, the renowned actor, I'm speaking to?"

No.

It's Helen of Troy, the mythical homewrecker. Richard curbed his impatience with difficulty. "It is, but it won't be for much longer if you use that description again."

"Noted." The speaker wasn't flustered. "This is Anthony Sutcliffe from the *London Arts Quarterly.* We're addressing the Grosvenor Initiative and its likely effects on cultural awareness, and I'd like to follow up on the views you expressed in your recent interview with Terry Gregson. Could we set up a time to meet? This week, for preference."

"I do have an assistant who handles my interview schedule." With Lainie's voice stuck maddeningly in his head, he tried to remain polite. "May I ask how you got my private number?"

"I did contact your assistant, Mr. Troy, but I understand you prefer to personally handle questions concerning Sir Franklin."

Richard had been reaching for his iPad to bring up his calendar, but now sat back. "I don't believe I discussed my father with Gregson."

"No." Sutcliffe sounded amused. "It was very circumspect of him, wasn't it? But I'm sure you'll agree that your father's legacy is relevant, to say the least. It's clearly going to have an impact on your own political path, which is one of the things I'd like to talk about."

Sutcliffe was correct. His father's…legacy, for lack of a better word, *was* relevant to the subject at hand, and it would certainly haunt his steps in any kind of political arena. Richard was prepared for that. He had to maintain a strong public presence, so simple avoidance wasn't feasible; however, the right application of insipid, meaningless diplomacy would disappoint anyone hoping for dirt. He'd encountered Sutcliffe's work in the past, and the man wasn't a threat. His self-confidence outstripped his actual ability.

He could—probably *should*—just agree to a meeting. The *Arts Quarterly* had a fairly minimal readership, but it was all useful networking. Unfortunately, the journalist had picked a bad time to make demands. He was in no mood to be cooperative.

"No."

"I beg your pardon?" The tinge of complacent malice had disappeared from Sutcliffe's voice. He was startled.

"No." Richard contemplated the terrace house again. The windows were shadowed, offering no glimpse of its inhabitants. "I don't particularly want to discuss my father, his political viewpoint, or anything else with you. If necessary, you can paraphrase the Radio 4 interview. I believe I made my position quite clear."

"May I ask why you're refusing?"

Journalists. They were like dogs at dinnertime—always hopeful of falling scraps.

He considered. "No. You may not. Enjoy the rest of your day."

It wasn't until he was stalled in busy Park Lane traffic that he let his mind release from its frozen trap. The hinges tended to slam shut at any drift into parental territory.

It was incredibly irritating that he was such a textbook cliché of dysfunctional wealth.

They were memories. Ephemeral. Powerless.

As he drove home, the scent of Lainie—perfume, sugar and temptation—seemed to linger in the air.

SIX

LAINIE ENTIRELY BLAMED the rain-splattered Fun Run. She never exercised, and she never got sick. Then she ran a 5k and had to take to her bed like an ailing spinster. Coincidence? She thought not.

It began innocently enough with a mild headache before the evening show. Fortunately, Meghan's handbag contained enough pills and potions to stock a small pharmacy, and Lainie was able to pinch a couple of ibuprofen tablets. The stash also included a jumbo-sized box of condoms. Meghan's usual workday must be a lot more exciting than her own.

Instead of improving after the medication, the nagging ache in her temples became a full marching band of drummers by the second act.

Will had picked a bad night to behave like a complete tosser.

Things seemed slightly off from the first line of the opening scene. Lainie was jumpy and fidgety, and for the first time ever, the adrenaline rush didn't wear off after the curtain had risen. She continued to be hyper-aware of her senses: the dust motes dancing in the beams of stage lighting, the swishing silk of her skirts, the smell of paint and turpentine from the backdrop touch-ups that afternoon.

Will was even worse. He was speaking too loudly, moving a little too deliberately, and he'd turned handsy. Every time they had a scene together, he was right up in her face and touching her as much as possible.

The unacknowledged catalyst for all of the upheaval was Richard. Richard, and herself, and the odd new vibe between them. To give him his due, he wasn't really doing anything to be provocative. His perfor-mance was a lot more consistent than hers or Will's. But the episode on the couch that morning seemed to have crashed through an invisible barrier. The tension between them was humming. It was as if there was an electric wire that connected her gaze to his, and when their eyes met—sparks.

Bob, in a hurried word at intermission, congratulated her on putting up a good show of chemistry. "But maybe tone it down a notch during performances. You're sup-posed to be passionately in love with Geoffrey at the moment, not eyeing up Bandero's codpiece."

Margaret was even more blunt: "You are aware that the entire audience is waiting for the plot twist where you boot Will off the stage and fall on Richard like a rampaging tiger?"

If the *theory* of Lainie and Richard as a couple had bothered Will, the visual evidence of their attraction was proving too much for him. He had never played his antagonism toward Richard's character with such con-vincing fervour. Richard, in his turn, was slowly being driven to react. There was a subtle edge to his voice as

he spoke his lines, and that small show of disquiet was
so unusual for him that Lainie was taken aback.

The crowning misfortune was that Richard's character was present onstage when she threw herself at
Will for their love scene. Her own character, Julietta,
was defiant and uncaring of an audience to her passion.
Lainie did not share her nonchalance. She had *always*
felt awkward kissing Will within five feet of Richard,
even when the latter had been a more distant thorn in
her side. The audience was at least separated from the
action by a certain amount of physical distance and the
metaphorical fourth wall. It gave an illusion of privacy
under the hot lights.

Richard was standing close enough to measure their
breathing patterns.

And Will didn't help matters by deciding to chuck
professional standards out the window and involve his
tongue in what should be a solely smoke-and-mirrors-
and-platonic-lips manoeuvre.

He was lucky she wasn't a violent person and that
she valued her career prospects, or he would have come
away from the encounter with a bloody chin. It took
considerable effort not to wipe her mouth with the back
of her hand. She glared daggers at him even as she
smiled and swayed into his hold, apparently besotted
and aroused.

There was a loud *crack* when Richard set down the
tankard of coloured water he was holding. His eyes
were glinting as he watched them. Usually, he played
his part in this scene with amused boredom: the malevolent aristocrat who viewed the lower-class Julietta
as a negligible speck on his horizon, a gullible bug to
be crushed beneath his boot. It was not, Lainie had al-

ways thought, much of a stretch for his acting abilities. She was fairly sure he had considered her a sort of
human prop in the past. An irritating prop that walked
and talked, had deplorable taste in men, and wouldn't
stay where it was put.

Richard, as Bandero, said something snide; Will
retaliated, and Richard suddenly grabbed him by the
throat. They were nose to nose, and the atmosphere had
nothing to do with pretence. Lainie thankfully seized
upon her cue and darted from the stage, crossing her
fingers and uttering a silent prayer that they made it
through to the curtain with no incidents. One thing to
be thankful for: Alexander Bennett wasn't in the house
tonight, so they wouldn't be hauled over the carpet tomorrow morning for unprofessional behaviour.

Her throat was scratchy, and she went to beg another
over-the-counter remedy from Meghan.

Her dresser frowned and touched a palm to her forehead. "You do look a bit flushed. How bad do you feel?"

"Bit achy." Lainie looked at the bottles of cough
syrup Meghan held in each hand and chose the children's version with the picture of the giraffe on the
box. Artificial cherry flavouring was one of her secret
vices. "I hope I'm not coming down with something."

"After what I've been hearing about you and Troy, I
suspect a brainstorm at the very least."

"Yes, well, there's a story there. I'll fill you in at
some point." Lainie swallowed a dose of medicine.
"Don't worry. I haven't lost my mind just yet."

Haven't you?

She ignored that traitorous little voice within and put
a hand to her temple. She couldn't wait to get home to

bed. She was starting to feel nauseous and the memory of the blueberry pancakes was coming back to haunt her.

"I'm not sure we can say the same for your menfolk," Meghan said. They could hear the raised voices from the stage as Will and Richard warmed up to their altercation. "I was actually kidding when I wished they would make more judicious use of their swords."

Lainie was plucking restlessly at the fastenings of her gown, and Meghan pushed her fingers away and loosened them for her. "Careful. You can't have them too loose or the show is going to go unexpectedly burlesque. You have too much up top to run around unsupported." She retied the ribbons. "And your feminine charms are obviously potent enough. Ten quid says one of them ends up a barbecue skewer yet."

The callboy signalled to Lainie before she could retort. With a muffled growl, she shimmied her skirts back into place and returned to the wings to await her cue. Only a couple more pages of dialogue to get through. Then she could take Chloe's dagger through the neck and drowse in her dressing room until the curtain call.

She was pallid and shaky by the time she performed her final scene. Her onstage death had never been more convincing. Richard caught her arm as she wobbled past him in the wings. He frowned down at her, the movement cutting a line through his heavy makeup. He was quite revolting in full costume. Dissipated wasn't the word for it. He looked as if he'd spent the past thirty years draining the contents of a distillery and neglecting to wash his hair.

"Are you all right?" he asked sharply. He put a large, cool hand to her forehead. She wished people would stop doing that. Her swipe at his fingers was feeble, and he looked even more concerned. "You look shocking."

"Look who's talking. You're probably single-handedly keeping the hair-oil industry solvent with this production."

"Go and lie down. Before you fall down."

Meghan was waiting to help her remove the blood-stained items of clothing before she had to reappear on the stage, and he spoke brusquely to her. "Get the medic to have a look at her."

"I don't need a doctor! I'm fine."

Her traitorous body succumbed to a coughing fit, and he raised his eyes to the heavens. "Medic," he repeated to Meghan. "Now."

The callboy gestured urgently for Richard's cue, and he returned to the stage with a reluctant glance back at her.

"You heard the man," Meghan said. "Get off your feet and I'll find someone to stick a thermometer in your ear."

Lainie glared at her. "Since when do you listen to the greasy dictator out there?" She stamped off toward her dressing room, aware she was being a total pill.

Her mood was not improved by the doctor, who had latent comedy ambitions and kept up a running stream of jokes about treating the walking dead. She, like the proverbial Queen Vic, was not amused. By the time Meghan half carried her back to the stage for the curtain call, she was drowsy and feeling strangely detached from her legs. She walked forward when nudged, and listened, as if from a distance, to the rolling thunder of applause. Will's hand was slippery with sweat, and she kept dropping his fingers.

"What's wrong with you?" he hissed close to her ear as they took the full cast bow. She wavered, and he made a grab for her. "Jesus! Stand up!"

Lainie turned a look of dignified reproach on him. "I'm fine," she said, very clearly.

And then she passed out on a West End stage in front of two thousand people.

SIGHT AND SOUND returned with considerable force and volume. She opened her eyes in the epicentre of a furious argument. Masculine voices snapped back and forth above her aching head, and she blearily tried to focus on who or what was responsible for the racket.

"I think I can manage to get her home without your assistance, thanks."

She knew that biting sarcasm. Blinking, she raised her eyes and looked up at the underside of Richard's stubbled chin. She was close enough to his skin that she could see the paint contouring on his jaw. She watched, fascinated, as her own finger came up and rubbed at the makeup, helping to blend in a smudgy line. That brought his face down to look at her, and his hand closed around her raised fingers, squeezing them.

His smile was grim—a thin, compressed slash in his bony face. She touched that too, feeling the smooth softness of his lips, testing their resilience. At her movements, the smile became a little more genuine and some of the tension eased from his shoulders. "You're hell on wheels for my blood pressure, Tig."

A muscle flexed under her shoulders. She became at least half-aware of her surroundings. Scenery flats towered above her, seeming far taller than usual, and there was a strong smell of paint. She was down on the floor backstage, on Richard's lap and in his arms.

"Tig?" repeated an incredulous voice, and she rolled her head against Richard's chest to look at Will.

He was looming above them, glowering down like an enraged genie. "She should be in bed," he said between clenched teeth. "The doc said she needs rest and fluids. Not a cuddle on a damp floor." He added snidely, "And being quite familiar with her bed, I'm happy to transport her there. I can also do it less conspicuously, in a car that doesn't look like the Batmobile."

Richard completely ignored him. He was still looking down at Lainie. With the pad of his thumb, he rubbed gently between her eyebrows, exactly where the worst of the pain was grumbling. "I know you were bowled over this morning, but this seems a bit extreme."

She closed her eyes on a wave of nausea and snuggled her nose into his neck. "Prick," she murmured.

"And on that sentimental note…" Richard rose to a standing position, still holding her. Even in her semi-comatose state, she was impressed that he accomplished the move with no visible staggering or hopping to keep his balance. It would have been a bit of an anticlimax with Will's critical glare fastened on them.

Meghan drifted in and out of sight with her belongings, and Lainie felt herself being lowered into a car. Camera flashes went off, voices clamoured, and Richard snarled something over his shoulder. He kept his body angled protectively in front of the open door, keeping her out of range for decent shots. The interior of the car was spongy and warm—her old friend, the Ferrari, again. Lainie stroked the leather seat and drifted off to sleep.

She was lying on her own bed the next time she woke, which was such a relief that she almost cried. Wonderful, familiar hands were helping her into her pyjamas. She blinked up at her mother. "Mum?"

"Bonus of having such a notorious daughter." Rachel Graham smoothed down Lainie's vest top. "When she takes a nosedive onstage, I read about it online five minutes later." She pushed back a lock of Lainie's sweat-tumbled red hair and smiled down at her. "You never did do things in a small way, did you, darling?"

"Oh." Lainie groaned and scrubbed her hands over her face. "I'm so not going to be happy about that when my head returns to normal size. Where's Richard?"

Her mum's eyebrows rose archly. "Your devoted swains are sitting in opposite chairs in the lounge, looking like thunder. I suspect words would be exchanged at some volume if it weren't for my inhibiting presence. As it is, they're quietly growling and snarling at one another like a couple of territorial bulldogs. You do lead an interesting life, poppet."

"Will's here too?" Lainie turned her cheek on the pillow, trying to find a cool spot. "Can you please get rid of him, Mum?"

"With great pleasure." Like Sarah, Rachel had borne the brunt of Lainie's initial reaction to the Crystalle situation. Without going so far as her husband's threats of castration, her opinion of Will was short and brutal. She pulled the covers up, resisting her daughter's attempts to kick them away. "In another five minutes, you'll be freezing. That temperature is raging." At the door, she paused. "And shall I also eject the other brooding presence?"

Lainie mumbled something into the pillow, and her

mother hid a smile. "I'll tell him he can come back for a few minutes in the morning, shall I?"

Will at his most belligerent was a puny opponent for her mother. Lainie heard the altercation, and he was ousted from the flat in less than sixty seconds. Richard was made of sterner stuff. It took her mum almost five minutes to get rid of him, and he insisted on having another look at Lainie before he left.

The bed dipped as he sat on the edge of it, his eyes fixed on her face. She stared miserably back, and he unexpectedly leaned down to kiss the spot on her forehead where the imprint of his thumb still teased. "I'll be back to check on you in the morning," he said. "Try not to succumb in the interim."

"Following your Pat orders?" Lainie asked drowsily, and he snorted.

"Completely flouting them." There was a tiny note of bewilderment beneath the sardonic words, as if he was surprised by his own behaviour. "I've been commanded to stay well out of the infection zone. They don't want to inflict more than one understudy at a time on a paying audience."

"Oh." Lainie's fevered brain struggled to cooperate. "Maybe you should stay away."

"I have no doubt whatsoever that I should stay away." He touched a light hand to her hair and stood up. "Nevertheless, I shall see you tomorrow."

IT WAS STILL dark outside when Richard followed Lainie's landlady back up the stairs to her flat the following morning. And he was still on edge.

He'd been trying to keep his focus away from Lainie when she'd taken a header into the stage floor and just about given him a fucking coronary. He'd been less immersed in his role than usual, partly due to Farmer's unprofessional stirring. He could cheerfully have thrown Lainie's ex-lover the length of the theatre. He had never liked Farmer. The antipathy was mutual, and now personal.

He wasn't used to worrying about someone. He'd pushed the speed limit to get her home from the theatre and away from the vulture press, thankful that he possessed a comfortable car for her. He hadn't realised her skin could go several shades whiter than her usual shade of pale. The spots of burning red on her cheeks and the purple smudges beneath her lashes had prevented her from looking like a black-and-white still.

He approved of her mother. Rachel Graham had calm eyes and a no-bullshit demeanour. And a way of handling Farmer that was almost artistic. He'd been less appreciative when she'd tried to evict him, as well.

He coolly returned Cat Richard's stare when he passed the lounging lump on the landing. The cat looked heavily disapproving, but could be feeling euphoric for all anyone would know. It was not a pretty face.

Twinsies. Jesus.

He knocked on the door, only just overcoming the instinct to walk straight through and into Lainie's bedroom.

Rachel answered the summons. She examined him thoughtfully, her eyes moving from his head to the soles of his boots. It was difficult to read anything into her expression. She would have made a very good Rosalind.

Her daughter was more of a Beatrice.

"How is she?" He moved forward, forcing her to take a step back and let him into the flat.

"Good morning." Rachel had an empty coffee cup in her hand, which she took into the kitchen. "Her temperature is still up. She's asleep."

Without waiting for further permission, he walked down the tiny hallway to the equally miniscule bedroom. Lainie was curled up in the middle of a double bed that left very little remaining floor space. The room smelled like her. Flowery. Sweet. With a slight undertone of sweat at the moment.

He sat gingerly on the edge of the bed, looking down at her, and touched his hand to her face. Her forehead and cheeks were burning hot against his fingertips. He smoothed his hand over her forehead, stroking back the damp, matted red hair.

She looked bloody awful, and he said as much to her mother.

Rachel's gaze moved to where he rubbed his thumb in a rectangular pattern on Lainie's collarbone. "It's a nasty bug. But she'll be fine."

Once more, the feeling that was attempting to crawl up his throat from his chest had nothing to do with a solely physical attraction, and he intensely disliked the sensation it left in its wake.

"Of course she will." She had the flu in the twenty-first century, not the bubonic plague in the seventeenth. He took her hand in his. With little awareness of his actions, he brushed her knuckles back and forth across his lips.

Rachel gathered a pile of dirty washing and quietly left the room. She looked thoughtful.

LAINIE'S EXISTENCE HAD narrowed to a series of brief, uncomfortable intervals between naps. Her mum stayed in her flat, sleeping on her couch—fortunately with no idea what other activities occasionally took place upon its cushions—and ferried her back and forth from the loo. They both balked at assisted showering, but Rachel did hover outside the bathroom door and insisted it be left open a crack so she could hear if Lainie faceplanted into the tiles.

"I'll shut my eyes and grab for a towel if I have to come in and save you. Although in case you've forgotten, fruit of my loins, I have seen your bare bottom before."

"There was less of it then," Lainie managed to retort through her congested misery.

Richard was quite often present during her periods of consciousness, and even Will made a number of determined appearances. She was amazed he even ventured past her bedroom door. He wasn't the type to mop a fevered brow and hold back hair to facilitate puking. It might be gratifying if he didn't spend ninety percent of his visits scowling at Richard.

She would usually be self-conscious about men sitting by her bedside when she hadn't had the strength to wash her hair. However, it was hard to care when she felt like something that had recently been dug out of a sarcophagus.

Her fever peaked on the third day, and she was almost delirious when Richard forced his way past her mother. The back of his hand pressed against her forehead and her cheeks.

"Shouldn't she be getting better by now? Does she need the hospital?" he asked through a fog. Her mum's voice was a low, soothing murmur. She smiled into her pillow. He was getting the "oh, these silly children" parental tone. Her dad never managed quite the same blend of reassurance and condescension.

Then she was drifting again in a pleasant, dozy sea, carried along on a boat of Paracetamol. Will swam by at one point, and she hastily rowed away. He tried to steal her hand, and she jerked it free of his grasp.

"Don't touch her." It was a captain's voice. Cool. Commanding.

Will, sneering, "Think you have exclusive rights, do you?"

"I think she doesn't even want your hands on her when she's unconscious. Wise woman."

Blessed quiet, and a sense of receding heat. Her eyes opened a crack. The room was dim and the strip of visible window between the curtains was black. Night. There was someone sitting on her bed. She could smell warmth and spice and man.

"Will?" she asked blearily, apprehensively.

A hand gently touched her cracked lips. "No. The better option."

She closed her eyes again and smiled against his fingers. "Richard."

The stroking touch moved to her cheek and played at the edge of her hairline.

"You smell nice," she said drowsily.

"Thank you. You smell like cherries and chemicals. I think it's the cough syrup."

"Sorry." The word was a sigh.

"It grows on you."

"What happened to Will?" she asked, a faint frown tugging at her brows. "Did he drown?"

There was a long pause. "Not unless he took a very

circuitous route home via the Thames." And, with an edge, "Do you want him?"

She moved her head fractionally on the pillow. It hurt too much to shake. He shifted, and she quickly moved her hand. Gripped a knee. "Don't go."

A feather-soft kiss on the tip of her nose, so lightly that it might have been part of the dream. "I'm not. Not yet."

"'S it late?"

"Almost midnight."

"Tired."

"Sleep, then." Another light touch on her cheek.

"No. You. Tired."

"I'm all right. I'm a hardy soul. Unlike those wee weaklings who go to pieces after one workout."

"It was *raining*."

She heard his muffled laugh.

"Play," she muttered. Worry was niggling at her, but she couldn't quite...

"Certainly, if you think you're up to it. I vote for strip poker."

Her body temperature was still at a level where humour didn't resonate. "No," she managed crossly. "*Play*."

"Is surviving without you, although only just. Your understudy is rubbish." He rubbed her fingers. "Don't worry about it yet. The theatre-going public are still getting their night out and their box of Smarties, and Farmer is leaving the stage in one piece on a regular basis."

"Don't hurt him," she said sleepily. She arched her back against the mattress, impatient with the persistent ache in her joints.

He slid a hand beneath her hips, gently kneading up her spine, and she made a soft sound of relief.

"Don't moan like that," he ordered with a husky half laugh. His face was close to hers; she could feel the tickle of his hair against her ear. "It gives me ideas, and the timing is inappropriate."

"Sicko." She smiled again without opening her eyes.

"Yes, you are. Hence my hesitation." His breath fanned her ear as he spoke. "You seem awfully concerned about Farmer there, Tig." He nudged her cheek with his nose. "You're obviously delirious in your weakened state. Repeat after me: I have no interest in Will Farmer."

"No interest," Lainie murmured obediently, and Richard carefully tucked a piece of hair behind her ear.

"He's an ugly bastard who doesn't have a quarter of Richard's talent."

"Richard…no talent…"

"We'll work on the deplorable ad-libbing when you're better."

Four days after her mortifying collapse, Lainie woke in the evening with a clear head. Her aches had dulled and her stomach had settled, and she felt almost like a rational human being again.

Her mother looked up from the armchair at the foot of the bed and smiled. "Feeling a bit better? You've lost that dazed look and your colour is better." She put down her iPad and studied her daughter approvingly. "Yes, definite improvement. You look mildly hungover, which is at least five steps up from yesterday's corpse."

Lainie ran her hand over her midriff, grimacing at the clammy feel of her top. "Always supportive, Mum, thanks." She looked around the bedroom. Despite the endless parade of sweating, tossing, turning and vomiting, it looked cleaner than usual. "Did you vacuum in here while I was out of it?"

"I also dusted, and I rearranged your wardrobe. Trousers at the left end, dresses at the right. This is a very small flat, Lainie."

"Meaning there was nothing else to do?"

"Meaning it wouldn't kill you to clean more often."

"I do clean. On Sundays." Not *every* Sunday, but most…well, some.

Rachel propped up the pillows behind Lainie's shoulders and helped her to sit up. "Do you think you can manage something to eat? I haven't been able to get more than a cup of instant soup down you the last few days. You won't have the energy to walk to the loo soon. What about some toast? A boiled egg?"

It had been a long time since her mother had brought her a sickbed tray. Lainie thought back to her school days. "Marmite toast?" she suggested, weighing the suggestion against any lingering nausea. It sounded quite tasty. She must be on the mend.

"Marmite toast it is. I'll bring you a cup of tea."

"You're a goddess among women."

She was shattered after eating the toast and standing up for a proper shower, but the joy of clean hair was worth the wobbly legs. Lainie lay back against a mound of pillows and carefully combed through the long, wet strands.

"What time is it?"

Her mum looked up from her book. "Almost ten o'clock." Correctly interpreting the reason for the question, she added, "The show will be over soon."

"I've missed three performances," she realised, dismayed, and her mother shrugged.

"It was hardly avoidable, darling. You couldn't even sit up without assistance. I'd say you're going to miss at least two more while we build your strength back up. You couldn't possibly make it through three hours onstage like this."

"They'll probably revert me to the understudy."

"Nonsense. Don't let the post-flu blues take over. You'll be back to work by the weekend. Put that phone down."

Lainie didn't look up from her dialling. "I'm just checking my voice mail." As she listened to the automated voice, she asked, trying to make the question casual and failing, "Has Richard really been here every day?"

The fake indifference didn't fool her mother. Rachel looked amused, and more than a little speculative. "He's not too good at taking no for an answer, is he? Yes, he's been here every day. Every morning without fail, usually before I was dressed, and each night after the show. I imagine we can expect his charming company shortly."

Lainie hit the button to listen to her messages and cast her mother a quick, concerned glance. "He hasn't been rude to you, has he?"

Rachel considered. "No. Not rude. Fairly abrupt, but I gather that's a personality quirk and not a cause for personal offence. And I think any curtness stemmed from concern about you. He's looked almost as bad as you have, my sweet. The stubble grows more alarming with each passing day. I assume he doesn't have to shave for his role."

"No, they actually add more hair," Lainie said, deleting a message from Bob. He was definitely not a priority call right now. She traced the pattern on the bedcovers. "*Has* he been worried?"

She could remember snatches of conversation. Gloriously strong hands. Whispers of kisses. Comfort.

"In his very stoic, sarcastic manner, darling," Rachel said lightly, "I'd say that was an understatement." She tilted her head. "Do you know, despite his unfortunate manner, I think you might have done all right there. He's a step up on Will, who unsurprisingly has been a bloody nuisance."

Lainie made a face and deleted another unimportant message. "He's only hovering again because of Richard. He can't stand him."

Rachel snorted. "The feeling is clearly mutual. I thought about baby-proofing the room when they were here together. No sharp or heavy objects in easy reach." Her narrowed eyes were mischievous. "I *had* thought you shared Will's dislike."

The flush that crept into Lainie's cheeks had nothing to do with fever. She avoided her mother's amused gaze. "I…it's complicated."

"You're not updating your relationship status on Facebook. I don't think it's at all complicated. Unless you go around kissing and cuddling *all* of your castmates, in which case we need to have a word about priorities. And I don't recall you muttering anyone else's name in your delirium."

"*Mum.*" Lainie's face was burning now. She started to reply, but broke off when she heard her agent's voice. "Message from Carey. Shit. I should have let her know I've been sick."

"Richard rang her."

Lainie's head shot up. "*Richard* rang her?"

"Eye on the ball, that one."

She wasn't sure how she felt about that, but Carey's three-day-old message wasn't going to pause to let her reflect. She listened, and her hand stilled on the blankets. When Carey's clipped, businesslike tones came to a halt and she had ended the call with a brief, "I hope you're feeling better soon," Lainie glanced at her watch and then tapped the screen to bring up her agent's number. She followed Carey on Twitter, so she knew she was regularly awake and still working at this time.

"Problem?" Rachel asked, watching her daughter's impatient fidgeting.

"It's that period drama I auditioned for," Lainie told her, putting her finger over the receiver hole in case Carey picked up while she was speaking. "The adaptation of Mollie Blair's *Somerset County*. The casting director bumped up the callbacks to this week. They wanted me to come in yesterday."

"Oh, dear. Can you reschedule?"

"I hope so. I—hi, Carey, it's Lainie... Yes, just starting to improve, thanks. Look, I just got your message about the *Somerset County* audition, and... Oh. Is there any chance of rescheduling? I think that... Yes. Yes, I know... I see... Yeah. It is unfortunate." Lainie scrunched up her face, and Rachel made a sympathetic grimace in response. "Okay... Yes, might as well have a look at it. You never know... Okay, thanks, Carey. Talk to you in a couple of days."

She ended the call and stared down at the phone. "Crap."

"No joy, obviously."

"No. Apparently the producer has a one-shot policy. Show up at your allotted time, or don't show up at all."

"I'm sorry, darling."

Lainie set her phone aside and leaned back against her pillows. She felt completely drained of both energy and enthusiasm. "Me too. I really wanted that role. Even after all my back-and-forth about it." She sighed. "I confessed my little confidence crisis to Richard."

"Oh? And what words of wisdom did he offer?"

"He told me to grow a spine and get over it."

That startled a laugh from Rachel. "He doesn't beat about the bush, does he?"

"He bulldozes right over the bush." Lainie hesitated. "I told him about Hannah too."

"Did you, darling?" Her mother's smile was a little wobbly. "Good. I'm glad you talk about her. I hope he was sensitive about it."

Lainie's eyes were unfocused as she thought about the past—both last year and far more recently. "Yeah. He actually was."

Rachel nodded, and Lainie put her hand over her mother's and held it for a moment. Hannah had been her parents' miraculous late-in-life baby, born ten years after their elder daughter, twenty years after their sons. At the funeral, their dad had called her an unexpected gift, a child they had been blessed to receive and to keep for as long as they had. It was one of the few fragments of speech she could remember from that day, which had passed in an unreal blur. Even when a death was inevitable, when there was theoretically time to mentally prepare, it still…stunned in its reality. She couldn't imagine what it was like trying to adjust in the case of an accident, when life changed—and vanished—in a split second of tragedy.

"She would be so chuffed about everything you've been doing." Rachel smiled at her. "Not just the charitable work, which, let's face it, would just bring on more groans about Saint Lainie—" Lainie rolled her eyes "—but all your career success. It would have made her year to read about her big sister in the tabloids. Endless mockery would have ensued."

"I know. I thought about that on the opening night of the show. That she wasn't there."

"Who knows? Maybe she was watching," Rachel said, and then paused. She made a face. "Or maybe not. Jacobean drama—not really her thing. She was more likely enjoying a free screening of the latest Channing Tatum film."

Lainie laughed. "She wouldn't have been all that psyched about a period drama either. She thought the only good thing about my going into drama was that I might eventually be able to introduce her to Zac Efron. Oh, well." She tapped her phone. "Maybe I would get a few more cool points for a romantic comedy. Carey is sending over a script for an independent film. Onwards and upwards."

Despite her blithe words, she was still disappointed over the missed audition, and couldn't hide her glum mood from Richard when he arrived from the theatre.

He stopped in her doorway when he saw her sitting up in bed—and not reaching for a bucket or visibly sweating, which made a nice change. A certain tension seemed to leave his shoulders as he surveyed her. "It moves. It's alive," he said drolly, in a very laconic Frankenstein impression.

"Confirmation that comedy isn't your forte." Lainie suddenly felt ridiculously shy. She yanked the bedcovers up past the neckline of her skimpy vest top, and he followed the defensive gesture with a quizzical brow. "How was the show?"

"Trying. I'm underpaid, and your stand-in is dire." He hitched his perfectly creased trousers and sat down on the end of her bed. "And your ex-lover is a blithering idiot." His sardonic eyes sharpened. "What's the matter with you?"

"I'm recently recovered from the plague. Pardon me for not looking my best."

"You look fine. Shampooed and combed is a good look for you. What's wrong?"

"Why would anything be wrong?" she hedged.

"I have no idea. That's why I'm asking," he said impatiently. "I can tell by your face. You must be an absolute liability in a poker game."

"It's nothing." Lainie pulled hard at a loose thread. "Just a job thing."

"Yes?"

"The audition for *Somerset County* was brought forward to yesterday, and obviously I missed it as I had my head in the loo at the time. Apparently the producer is not big on second chances."

"You spoke to Carey?"

"Yes. Nothing doing."

"Who's producing?"

She told him, and he nodded. "I've worked with him before. Fairly superhuman expectations of his cast and crew, and no patience with delays. He would have very little time for an actor who succumbed to illness anywhere near his set."

"Swell." Lainie reflected that they must have got on quite well together, being equally intolerant of normal human failings. She didn't say so aloud. Richard had actually been very—shockingly—patient with her during the past few days.

Typically dismissive of an unfortunate circumstance that couldn't be altered, Richard shrugged. "You can concentrate on your stage career."

"Yes," she said, deciding not to mention the possible rom-com yet. She could imagine his opinion of *that*, and it would be short, aggravating and mostly comprised of four-letter words.

He was studying her with a slight frown. "But you wanted it."

"Yes." She moved irritably. He was probably about two seconds from pulling out a sarcastic violin. A little mood music for her pity party. "Never mind. It is what it is."

"How philosophical of you." He looked preoccupied.

She tried to lighten the topic. "I suppose my new horizontal take on the traditional bow made a few headlines."

Richard seemed to make an effort to focus his attention on her. "I expect the charmer who filmed the whole thing on his camera phone can afford an upgrade to a better model this week. By the way, your dear friend Greta French whispered to her live audience about your mysterious long-standing disease. She fears your public collapse is a sign the end is nigh."

Lainie tried to be outraged, but her sense of humour got the better of her. She saw Richard's mouth twitch, and gave into a giggle.

He smothered a yawn, and she shook her head. "I

realise it would be beneath your dignity to confess that you're knackered, but you need to get to bed. You look like you haven't slept for a week."

"Feels like it too," he surprised her by admitting. He rolled his neck in a slow stretch and sighed. "Yeah. Bed. I'll get on that." One eye opened. "I assume I'm still not being invited to get on yours?"

"You are, as usual, correct." Lainie reached out and rubbed his stubbly jaw. "And, for God's sake, shave. My neighbours will think you're a drug dealer. My professional reputation has been embarrassed enough for one week."

Richard nudged aside her hand and stood up, groaning when a joint cracked in his knee. "Our fake relationship is prematurely aging me." He leaned over the bed, his face hovering inches from her nose.

"Can I help you?" she asked politely, and shivered when their breath mingled.

He eyed her mouth. "I'm considering whether it would be worth the risk of infection."

"I think that ship has sailed. You've been rubbing up against my germs for days."

"Well, in that case…"

His lips parted hers, warm and firm, his hand supporting the back of her head.

"Well?" she managed huskily when he pulled away a fraction. Her fingers were knotted in the collar of his shirt.

He looked down at her. "Results inconclusive, pending further investigation."

His mouth returned to hers, and she made a slight sound that might have meant anything. Protest. Need. Gratification. Doubt.

With her forehead leaning against his, she drew in a shaky breath. "Still just…rehearsal, yes?"

"Mmm." He nipped at the bow of her upper lip. His eyes were at lazy half-mast, a glittering glimpse of blue. "'Merely corroborative detail, intended to give artistic verisimilitude to an otherwise bald and unconvincing narrative,'" he murmured in agreement, à la *The Mikado*.

"I love it when you talk musical theatre to me."

SEVEN

London Celebrity @LondonCelebrity. now
*We're live-Tweeting tonight from the red carpet of
the National Theatre Awards.
Follow along for the best—and worst—dressed!*

"SMILE," WILL SAID warningly in her ear, as he followed his own advice. A trio of camera flashes went off, and a misguided young woman behind the crowd barrier proclaimed her love for him. He raised a lazy hand and waved to the cluster of predominantly female spectators. Silly screaming ensued. Will's star had risen recently after a series of guest appearances in a popular American drama. His hand tightened on Lainie's waist when she tried to step away. "People will think we aren't such *good friends* after all."

Lainie's fingers tightened around his, but her discreet tug didn't break his hold. There was only so much she could do in the full glare of the theatrical world, with a feverish tapping of thumbs feeding the intel straight into social media. She had too much dignity to get into a public scuffle with her ex-boyfriend.

But nor did she want to be photographed with his nose nestled in her hair. "The tragic news of your latest breakup was reported less than six hours ago," she hissed. He turned his head, and his lips ventured way too close to her face. She leaned sharply away. "What

I don't want is for people to think I had anything to do with Crystalle's Shock Heartbreak! I have no desire to ignite rumours about you and me again. Just stand for the bloody photo and then go elsewhere, please."

Will made a low sound of disgust. "Heartbreak. I'm sure she's sobbing her eyes out as we speak, curled up cosily back in her marital bed."

"Tell me you aren't expecting sympathy." Lainie saw Alexander Bennett getting out of a limo. "Bennett's here."

They amped up their smiles. Her cheeks were beginning to hurt. She still felt tired from the remnants of her flu bug. She'd only been back at work for one day, and everything still had a slight sheen of unreality outside the bubble of her bedroom. Another flash went off, and she resisted the urge to look down at her gown. Sarah and Meghan had joined forces to help her get ready, and they had taken numerous shots with a camera flash on, in both natural and artificial light. They had all been confident that her shimmery dress would *not* turn sheer in photographs, but a hint of paranoia lingered. She had worn her sexiest knickers as a morale boost, but she'd prefer that fact not to be made public.

At least not to *multiple* people. One person, maybe… *Don't go there.*

The cameramen at last turned their attention to the next newcomers, and Lainie hastened forward at some speed. She swore under her breath. It had been epically bad timing arriving at the same moment as Will. She had been unable to turn tail and run without creating an even bigger story, but appearing in the same photograph would be enough to have their relationship rekindled on gossip blogs. Add in Richard's conspicuous absence from the red carpet, thanks to a speaking engagement that had run late, and her sex life would end up resembling a Ping-Pong tournament. Bounced back and forth between the same two players.

Will seemed torn between tailing her and remaining behind to soak up his newfound sex symbol status. Unfortunately, persistence won out over vanity.

"No," he said from above her shoulder. Someone shoved against them, and he took the opportunity to put a gentlemanly arm around her. The subtle hip-squeeze was less chivalrous. "I'm not asking for sympathy."

Lainie glanced at him impatiently. At the moment, she was more concerned with getting inside the venue with her toes and pedicure intact. The street outside the Exhibition Centre was manic. A handful of names from the Hollywood A-list had dabbled in the West End this year, and had been nominated for a National Theatre Award tonight. Earls Court was chaos during rush hour at the best of times; the prospect of seeing a movie star in the flesh had provoked complete insanity. She was trying not to feel starstruck herself, whenever the pitch of screams peaked in volume and she saw another familiar face. This might be her first major awards ceremony, but she didn't have to act like it.

"I'm the one who ended it," Will went on, dropping his voice as they made it through the doors. It was still loud inside, excited voices laughing and chattering in every direction, but it was no longer deafening away from the added traffic noise and fan hysteria. "Although she didn't waste time grieving about it," he added sourly. His fingers spread on her stomach, pulling her to a stop. "Lainie. It wasn't working. It wasn't the same."

The press of stylish, heavily perfumed, glittering bodies formed a barrier that allowed her to push him away without being seen. "Will. I don't care. Your love life is no longer any of my business. Thank God."

"We had something really great."

"We did not. We had good sex, one shared interest and the inevitable result of propinquity. Would you like to add a suitably regretful 'I made a huge mistake,' just to complete the cliché?"

"Did you forget to eat before you came?" Will asked coldly. "You're always a bitch when you're hungry."

"Well, gee. Now I *really* want the makeup sex."

Will glanced around. A few interested eyes were turning their way, despite the competition of famous faces. "We'll talk about this later."

"We'll talk about this never. Enjoy your evening. Good luck in your category." Lainie turned away pointedly and latched on to the first acquaintance she saw.

In less dire circumstances, she would never have voluntarily entered into a conversation with the ghastly woman. Six seconds after her falsely cheerful "Hello! I haven't seen you for ages," she was being shown the other actress's Twitter feed, which included fashion commentary from the red carpet outside. It was a rookie mistake to read blogger opinions of your dress while you were still wearing it. Lainie forced a smile and tried to share the amusement. Personally, she thought her own critique was a little harsh. And she was fairly sure there was no *e* in the word *ho* unless it was being used in a gardening context.

She was pleased to discover that the awards were a sit-down-around-tables rather than a sit-in-neat-rows event, the important distinction between the two being

champagne—and lots of it. Lainie found her table and
saw Richard's name on the place setting beside her own.
She wasn't sure if someone had confirmed their atten-
dance as a couple, or if even the higher-ups in the acting
guilds bought into the gutter press's scandal-mongering.
Whatever—she was just relieved that Will hadn't been
put at their table to spice up the evening.

Her left-side neighbour was an icon of the theatre,
one of the Royal Shakespeare Company's living leg-
ends. The association with Richard had nudged her into
some exalted circles. The elderly actor was so charis-
matic and genuinely charming that he brushed aside her
intimidated shyness without drawing attention to it. He
immediately involved her in a fascinating discussion
about the current production at the Globe, and Lainie
was sipping Perrier-Jouët when the back of her neck
prickled. She sensed Richard's presence and caught a
whiff of his cologne before he slid into the empty seat
on her right.

He greeted her companion with a nod and a handshake—the posh gent's version of rappers raising their
chins and bumping fists, Lainie assumed—and then
raised an eyebrow at her. "You look very beautiful."

He looked like a press release for Armani. She did
love a good three-piece suit. Richard's eyes scanned
her clinging black gown, resting for an interested moment on the plunging neckline. She hoped he appreciated it. More double-sided tape had been employed in
that wrangling job than Santa's elves used at Christmas.

She met the glint in his blue eyes with a suspicious
narrowing of her own.

"Shoes on the right feet and everything," he added
in a congratulatory tone, checking under the table. He

opted for a sneaky grope of her knee while he was under there, and she jumped. "Sterling job at covering up the recent psychiatric episode."

"Translation, please?" Lainie asked, trying not to visibly squirm when playful fingers crept up the sensitive length of her inner thigh. She slapped them away with her clutch. It was gold-plated and apparently useful for more than housing her lipstick and emergency twenty quid.

Richard retrieved his hand and used it to pick up his champagne flute. His throat worked as he swallowed. "I gather that at some point between exiting your car and entering the building, you suffered a brainstorm and decided to rekindle the epic love story. Reports vary as to whether lips and partial nudity were involved, but I imagine the society page of the *Sun* will fill in the gaps tomorrow."

Was that sardonic humour in his face—or something else?

Lainie glared at him. "Always happy to provide cheap entertainment. Shall I ask Will to rub himself all over *you* in full public view, and see how funny you find it?"

The gleam in Richard's eyes took on a more dangerous aspect. "Define *rubbed*."

Her indignation beat a swift retreat at that look. It indicated he would shortly be happy to define *right hook* for Will. "It was just Will mucking about for the cameras, as usual." She didn't mention the Crystalle breakup or the belated show of remorse. There was an even chance that Will been knocking back whiskies in his limo and didn't mean a word of it. She would bet

her entire twenty pounds that he left the venue tonight
with another woman, regardless.

"How was your speech?" she asked, determinedly
changing the subject. "Were you audible? Eloquent?
Sober?" She grinned at him. "I envision a standing
ovation and at least one pair of knickers being thrown."

"That would have been disconcerting." Richard's
mouth twitched reluctantly. "Given that I was addressing the almost entirely male body of the Westminster
Operatic Guild. And there wasn't a woman there under
the age of sixty-five."

"I'm sure that's the prime age for knicker-tossing,"
Lainie said. "They would have practised their overarm
throw during the height of Beatlemania. You're almost
as cute as Ringo Starr."

Richard looked into his glass. "I think I need something stronger."

She pushed a bowl toward him. "Have a wasabi nut."

Without ever having *been* to a major awards show,
Lainie considered herself a veteran. She live-streamed
the Oscars, BAFTAs, Tonys, Emmys and Golden Globes
every year, and she didn't always mute the speeches or
take tea breaks. She had been not-so-secretly incredibly excited about tonight, despite the fact that she was
only nominated for an ensemble cast gong, which she
couldn't fool herself was anything but resting on the
laurels of Richard, Will and Chloe. It was still her first
nomination. Of many, she told herself, looking around
the glitzy, crowded room. She would take a note from
Richard's book of self-confidence and feel inspired and
ambitious instead of small and unworthy.

By the three-quarter mark of the ceremony, the ef-
fervescent buzz had dulled to a halfhearted fizz. It

turned out that sitting on an uncomfortable chair for three hours, intermittently clapping and having to listen in polite silence to the *long* acceptance speeches, was dull. A fast-forward button wouldn't go astray. And they lost the ensemble category, although the award went to a production that Lainie had enjoyed so much she couldn't be totally sorry.

As the winner for the best one-man show giggled self-consciously into the microphone, Lainie heard Richard let out a heavy, annoyed breath. She glanced over at him. He appeared to be playing both sides of an improvised chess match with the leftover wasabi nuts. She hid a smile, and he scowled at her when she ate one of his pawns.

"This is your category," she muttered when the host returned to the stage. "Sit up and quit fiddling with your nuts."

The elderly scion of the RSC snorted a laugh into his napkin. Richard looked unamused.

She hadn't been looking forward to the announcement of this particular award. Both Will and Richard had been nominated for a leading actor statue, Will for *The Cavalier's Tribute* and Richard for his most-recent-but-one role in a festival run of *Richard III* at the Old Vic. It seemed likely to prove an awkward few minutes no matter who won. She had weighed the other nominated performances and decided that none of them were of the same calibre. And unfortunately she had come to the conclusion that, in a fair judgement, there was only one possible winner this year.

The voting panel had agreed with her.

Richard's face was completely blank as Will went up to the stage to collect his trophy, but there was a telltale flicker in his jaw. First warning sign of an almighty male sulk.

The Cavalier's Tribute scooped another major award with Alexander Bennett taking the directorial honour. Lainie was thrilled on behalf of the production. She managed to muster some goodwill toward Bennett himself, although he made the task more difficult by giving the smuggest speech of the night. He could do with learning from Richard II's mistakes. It was wiser not to compare oneself to a deity.

When the host closed the prize-giving portion of the evening and directed everyone's attention toward the bar, there was a mass rising of bodies and an immediate outburst of chatter. Lainie turned toward Richard. "I'm sorry you didn't win."

He grunted, and she continued serenely, "Although you can't say it was unexpected."

That woke him out of his disgruntled apathy. His dark brows snapped thunderously together. "What?"

Lainie was unmoved. He might as well get the strop out of his system, so she didn't have to put up with it all night. "There's no question that you're the strongest actor in *The Cavalier's Tribute*," she said, shrugging. "You're well aware you're in a supporting role and stealing the spotlight from Will every night, with very little effort."

That produced a tiny smirk. She ignored it and went on, "But your nomination was for Richard III, not Bandero. It was an arts festival role that ran for three nights, and," she finished bluntly, "your performance was subpar."

"Oh, *was* it?" Richard asked dangerously.

She wasn't impressed by the intimidating tone. "Yes,

it was. And you know it. I saw that production on the opening night. It was the most mediocre, half-assed performance you've ever turned out. I bet you anything you like that you were more convincing during am-dram productions in your teens. I wouldn't have believed it was you behind the costume if your name hadn't been on the playbill." She held his wrathful gaze. Her own was calm and measuring. "You still deserved to be nominated. Your worst performance is better than most actors will achieve on their best night. But it would have been a biased travesty if you'd won. What happened?"

"What do you mean, what happened?" he asked rather nastily. "I lost. Deservedly, according to you."

"And you agree with me." Lainie spoke confidently. "I know how seriously you take the profession. You're a solid self-critic. And it must have gone against the grain to skate over a role like you did with that production. What happened?"

He was silent, glaring down at the table. She thought he wasn't going to answer, but finally he said coolly, "I was told about half an hour before curtain on opening night that a friend from university had committed suicide that morning."

"Oh God." Lainie reached out and closed her fingers around his fist.

He gently detached her hold. "It was irresponsible timing on behalf of the messenger, but it was my own failure that I let it affect my performance. The entire production was resting on my ability to convince in the leading role, and I let down every other person on, behind and in front of that stage." He raised one shoulder and let it fall. "Mea culpa."

"What did you say the other day about having superhuman expectations? Jesus, Richard. For all intents and purposes, your friend had died thirty minutes ago. I think you can cut yourself some slack. It was understandable you would be distracted."

"Perhaps. But not very professional." Richard hesitated. "It hit hard. Not just because of the loss of Derek, although that was a tragedy that should have and could have been avoided if his friends had realised in time. But his death recalled another…situation."

"Yes?" Lainie prompted quietly.

Looking at his set face, she was unsure if he would have gone on, even if Lynette Stern hadn't taken that moment to interrupt. The agent put a red-tipped hand on Richard's shoulder and he stiffened, his expression closing. Lainie felt the intimacy between them shut down as if an iron gate had been lowered.

"Richard," Lynette said briskly. "Good. Harlan Powell is looking for you. Hello, Lainie, how are you?"

"Fine, thanks." Lainie was still looking at Richard.

"He can't be looking very hard," he said to Lynette. "Since I haven't moved from my designated seat."

Lynette ignored the acerbic response. She tugged at Richard's arm, making him scowl. "He wants to discuss a potential role at the Globe. He's over at the bar."

"Of course he is." Richard looked irritated, but he rose to his feet. His eyes rested on Lainie. "I'll be back," he said briefly, and she nodded.

She was watching him walk away, and she jumped when Lynette touched her arm.

"Mind if I sit?" the agent asked, and then draped herself on Richard's vacated chair before Lainie had time to answer. It was a swooning movement that contrived to look impossibly elegant, but Lainie suspected Lynette's dress was so tight she couldn't bend at the middle.

"Help yourself," she said ironically.

The agent seemed to think the invitation also applied to Richard's champagne flute. "Thank God for the bubbly," she said, downing about a hundred pounds' worth of booze in one gulp. "I think I actually felt new wrinkles forming during Eliza Pimm's speech. These events make the Hundred Years' War seem like a momentary blip in time."

"You'll be sorry Richard didn't win," Lainie said neutrally.

"Mmm." The other woman eyed her shrewdly. "He was rubbish in that role. Some bloody moron blindsided him with the news of a school friend's death right before he went on. He pulled it together well enough, considering the circumstances. The average theatregoer might not have noticed a problem, especially if they weren't familiar with his usual work. Even some of the critics were fooled."

"Yes. I remember." Lainie remembered reading more than one glowing review with astonishment, wondering if they had been at the same play.

"But it was a definite low point on his résumé. Thankfully, it was only a three-night run." Lynette shot her a considering glance. "And how are things going with you two? I expected to be called to a late-night homicide scene by now."

Lainie smiled faintly. "And which of us would be sprawled inside the chalk outline?"

"Debatable. Richard has the worse temper, but he's also the more irritating."

"He would disagree." Her smile widened. "Possibly on both counts."

"No doubt." Lynette studied her. "Do you know, I think you're fond of him."

Lainie looked down at the tabletop. She traced a line through the ring left by her glass. "You're not, I take it."

"Frankly, I find him a walking, breathing migraine. One makes allowances, of course, for his upbringing," Lynette said, but she spoke without enthusiasm.

"His upbringing?" Lainie repeated, confused. "I gathered that *privileged* was putting it mildly."

"Oh, he's always been wealthy. Poor little rich boy to the core, and materially spoilt rotten. But it's the usual story: only child, parents absent for one reason or another, boarding school while still in nappies, succession of indifferent nannies in the holidays. His behaviour just screams it, really. Never been hugged in his life."

Lainie turned that over in her mind, weighing it against her own middle-class childhood with wonderful parents and more siblings than she knew what to do with. "I think there's a limit to which a person can excuse bad behaviour with a difficult-childhood card," she said at last.

"Oh, I expect most of his personality defects are his own," Lynette agreed, draining the rest of the champagne. "And he got shafted on the genetic front. Looks aside, obviously. His mother was an immoral bitch who'd go to bed with anything that bought her diamonds. And his father was a stiff-necked old sod. Sir Franklin Troy, you know, the MP. He died of a heart attack when Richard was at Eton."

Lainie actually remembered when Franklin Troy had died. She had been at primary school, and her usually mild-mannered father had gone off on a diatribe against the man. "Not wanting to speak ill of the dead, but…" Troy Senior had been rabidly right-wing and, in her dad's opinion, a bit unstable.

It was probably a good thing that she and Richard wouldn't need to have a fake family dinner with their parents to cement their fake relationship. She couldn't imagine it would have been cordial.

Lynette set down the empty flute and got to her feet. She was still rock-steady on her high heels despite the half quart of liquor she'd poured down her throat. "Well, must mingle, I suppose." She tapped Lainie on the back of her hand. "Pat and Bob will be pleased to hear that the little side performance is going well. Richard's reputation seems to be minutely improved. The redeeming influence of a good woman. It's a bit offensive, really. A month ago, the Operatic Guild would have been content to keep him at a safe distance, whispering behind their lorgnettes." Her lips lifted at the corner. "You maintain it *is* still an act, do you?"

"What do you think?" Lainie asked shortly.

Lynette looked thoughtful. "I think," she said before she disappeared into the crowd, "that I hope for Richard's sake you can't act as well as all that."

LAINIE SAT MEDITATIVELY in Richard's car, watching the lights of London out the side window. Traffic was still heavy around Earls Court; it had taken them twelve minutes so far to advance two blocks. The Ferrari came to a halt once again behind a hooting, hollering car full of teenagers. Tucking her wrap more tightly around her shoulders, she fingered the sequins sewn on the hem and turned her head to look at Richard. He, too, was quiet. He looked tired, his head tilted back and his eyes momentarily closed. His fingers drummed a lazy tune on the steering wheel.

"Long night," she said, for lack of anything else to say.

His eyes cracked open. They were glinting sleepily in the reflected lights from the street. "I've had more pleasurable evenings," he drawled. There was a pause. "Although the company could have been worse."

"I do believe that was a compliment." Lainie tucked a hand between her cheek and the headrest. "Feel free to elaborate. Don't spare my blushes."

"'The lady doth speak,'" Richard murmured, quoting one of Will's lines from the play. The rest was pure ad lib: "A little too much, methinks."

Lainie retaliated by borrowing words from Chloe's mouth: "'Thy pretty tongue, Bandero, leaves wounds.'"

"Well, that's an inapt choice if I've ever heard one," Richard remarked in his usual tones. He sat up straighter as the cars in front began to move. "I don't think I've ever personally been accused of speaking prettily before."

"You do all right," Lainie said. "Occasionally."

She sensed him cast another quick glance at her, but she had reverted her attention back to the window.

Another few minutes passed in silence, punctuated by jerky stops and starts in the flow of traffic. It was going to be dawn before they reached their respective homes at this rate. She was suddenly really hungry too. She tried to predict Richard's reaction if she asked him to take the Ferrari through a McDonald's drive-through. Her head turned farther to the side to hide her instinctive smile.

"Almost forgot." Richard took one hand off the wheel to reach into the pocket of his waistcoat. He had thrown the suit jacket into the backseat of the car, with shocking disregard for the artistry of its designer, and rolled up the sleeves of his shirt to reveal his taut forearms, lightly furred with black hair. She had been trying not to stare at him ever since. His hand came in front of her face with a piece of paper held between his first two fingers.

She took it automatically. "What's this?" she asked, opening it.

"The new call time for your audition for *Somerset County*," he said matter-of-factly, and she stared, first blankly at the piece of paper and then at him in growing astonishment. He intercepted the look and shrugged. "I pulled a few strings. They'll see you this week."

"But…" Lainie was aware that she was gaping and mouthing like a stranded fish. She pressed her lips together, and then tried again for a rational tone. "You can't just…" Rationality fled and her voice rose in pitch. "Richard! You can't *do* things like that."

"As you're holding a call time, evidently I can and I have."

"You can't just call people up and force them to give me a role!"

"I didn't," he said, with odious reasonableness. "I called and got them to reinstate the audition you had already earned on your own merit. I couldn't get you the role even if I wanted to. Mark Forster is a professional. He's not going to give a job to every woman who passes through my bedroom door just because I ask him to. Which I haven't."

"And which *I* haven't."

"No, you haven't. To my lasting disappointment."

She set her jaw. "I don't need favours and nepotism. I can succeed on my own."

Richard made an impatient noise. "Don't be naïve. Nobody succeeds on their own. And in this business, they grab hold of every connection they have and squeeze it dry."

There was an undertone to his exasperation that halted Lainie's next protest in her throat. His face was very set, and he was concentrating on his driving with far more intensity than earlier.

Had she actually hurt his feelings?

"Well," she said a bit feebly, after a pause. She added grudgingly, "Thank you."

His look was ironic. "You're welcome." He nodded at the paper. "Forster's private office line is on there, as well. He wants to talk to you about the charity."

"The charity?"

"Shining Lights. Regardless of the outcome of your audition, he's going to arrange for a portion of the profits from the production to be donated to the kids." Richard seemed to think that side note closed the subject. He returned his gaze out the windscreen, either ignoring or not noticing Lainie's stupefaction.

"You got him to agree to donate part of the profits to Shining Lights?" she said slowly, reconciling that fact with the picture she already had of Richard in her head. Trying to make the new pieces fit the existing puzzle.

"Yes." His shoulders shifted, just a little, and the uncharacteristic fidget brought home to her how uncomfortable and out of his depth he was.

A rush of intense, tender feeling almost drowned her. She actually made a slight sound, so taken aback was she by the sensation. She looked down at the paper in her hand again and made up her mind all at once.

Leaning forward, she pressed a sudden, warm kiss to the side of his neck, in the sensitive hollow below his ear.

He jerked, and the car swerved slightly. Swearing, he cast her a look that was an odd combination of warning and heat.

"The traffic is terrible," she said lightly.

"Cracking observation there, Sherlock," he said, taking refuge in irony.

"It would probably save time if you skipped the turnoff for Bayswater and just went straight on to your house."

He froze. She saw his hands tighten around the wheel.

After a single, comprehensive look into her eyes, he indicated to turn right toward Belgravia.

RICHARD'S HOME WAS one of those sparkling white mansion flats with black-and-white tiled steps leading up to the front door. She often passed similar houses on the various millionaires' rows, but never seemed to see anyone going in or out. They were like the residential versions of Willy Wonka's chocolate factory. She stood in a very plush lounge and tried not to think about the size of Richard's income. She failed, and blanched. Her own conception of financial independence had been shopping at Topshop more often than she did at Primark.

Richard handed her a cup of strong coffee. After that one betraying moment of stillness in the car, he had been behaving quite normally. She didn't know what she had expected—that he would flip a dimmer switch and activate mood music? Clearly she'd spent too much time with Will.

Sipping her coffee, she strolled awkwardly around the room. They were in Richard's study, and she was afraid to touch anything. It was like going into shops full of breakable knickknacks and feeling as if any wrong movement would bring a priceless ornament crashing to the floor. Not just when she was small and tagging along with her mother: she still tended to feel that way now.

She stopped in front of a large oil portrait set into the wall above the fireplace. Her eyes went from the intense painted features to the flesh-and-blood man sitting sprawled in a Regency chair. "You don't look much like your father," she ventured.

Richard swallowed a mouthful of coffee. "Not at all." He sounded completely unperturbed as he added, "Knowing my mother, it's possible there was no blood link. We can but hope." He frowned as he looked at the portrait. "It's inset into the wall and it appears that removing it would damage two-hundred-year-old fixtures around the mantel. Otherwise I'd have taken it down."

Lainie didn't know how to respond to that. She said, rather uncertainly, "Your father was…fairly conservative, I take it."

Richard snorted. "My father was about as far right as it was possible to move without falling completely off the grid. I'm not sure what policies his party actually supported. They were too busy opposing everything under the sun. Equitable rights, be they racial, sexual, or gender-oriented. Immigration. Public healthcare. Accessible education. The arts."

"The arts?"

"Hmm. A waste of time and public funds that ought to be directed into an aggressive overhaul of the military. The practise of licentious and unpatriotic tomfoolery by a bunch of Bohemian layabouts. Loose women and homosexual men." Richard swirled his coffee. "Franklin and his cohorts would have had ninety percent of the population exiled to Australia—still a jumped-up penal colony, by the way—if they could. Or just lined up against a wall and shot."

"Nice." Lainie sat down on the edge of the Queen Anne chaise. "I imagine he wasn't exactly thrilled to have a son who wanted to go to drama school."

"He died when I was still at school, and I hadn't made up my mind what I wanted to do at that stage." Richard grinned suddenly. "I think I was going through a very late-blooming astronaut phase, which would never have done. Rubbish at physics."

Lainie could suddenly imagine him as a teenager, and the image was more endearing than she would have expected.

"I did my first school play a couple of months before he died."

"Did he go?"

"No. He tried to have the drama teacher fired."

He wasn't joking. Lainie winced.

"At the time of his death, he was campaigning to eliminate almost all public arts funding. Government cultural grants were to be limited to a select few projects approved by the appropriate ministers, and art education was to be beaten out of the school curriculum with a barbed stick." Richard's voice was weary and disgusted. "Cultural resources were even more scarce then than they are now. The system needs a sharp boost, not to be dwindled into bleak totalitarianism."

Lainie was becoming clear on a number of things. "So first step, the RSPA," she said slowly. "To pick up the reins that your father dropped and turn the battle in the opposite direction."

"He would have approved the military allusion." Richard shrugged. "Perhaps not quite that dramatic, but yes. If he could have, my father would have done this country a monumental injustice in a number of areas. I intend to help correct at least one of them."

"It still must have been hard. When he had the heart attack."

There was a long silence, broken only by the sound of their breathing.

"He didn't have a heart attack," Richard said. "He was about to be found out in tampering with a parliamentary vote, and he shot himself in the head."

She drew in a sharp breath, and he continued, "My family had a PR team who make Pat look like a kindergarten teacher by comparison. They hushed up the truth about the suicide, the reason for it, the extent and range of my mother's affairs, and God knows what else." He met her eyes, and his smile was awful. "Pretty sort of background, isn't it?"

Lainie sensed instinctively that if she put a foot wrong now—and if she offered anything resembling pity—he would shove her so far out of his life, she would be left reeling on the street. "I hope," she said, in tones that were 5 percent compassion and 95 percent admonishment, "that you're not going to blame your tendency to behave like a complete prick on your parents. Because I would wager my entire salary for *The*

Cavalier's Tribute that you were a stubborn, bolshie little horror in your pram."

For a few tense moments, while her stomach twisted, Richard's face remained expressionless. Then he laughed, and it sounded genuine.

Taking her by surprise, he reached out, grabbed hold of her wrist and pulled strongly, tumbling her onto his lap.

"Bob Carson had no idea what he was setting in motion," he said, and he kissed her.

It took her a few stuttering breaths to catch up, but she had always taken direction well. She slid her hands along his jaw and into his hair, meeting the demanding thrust of his tongue with her own. He was stroking her own hair, sifting the silky strands through his fingers and humming his appreciation against her mouth. His lips trailed kisses along her cheek, her hairline and the curve of her earlobe. She jerked when he bit down. She could feel his hard thighs beneath her hip, and the subtle shifting adjustments of his body.

Lainie's fingers went to the buttons of his sexy waistcoat, tugging it open, and then to work on the fine lawn shirt beneath. She flattened a palm on his chest and gloried in the deep shudder that shook through his taut muscles.

Warm fingers traced the lines of bone in her shoulders and clavicle. His hand slid down her spine, igniting a shivering path of nerves as he lowered the zip of her dress, before he retraced his path back toward her neckline.

He came to a frustrating pause before the more interesting part of the proceedings.

Lainie's heavy eyelids parted and she inhaled sharply,

trying to catch her breath. "What's the matter?" she murmured huskily.

Richard tilted up her chin, forcing her to meet his gaze. His eyes were almost black with arousal. "Tell me you want this. Me."

It was enlightening that she could be this far gone with desire yet still capable of irritation. "Richard." She braced herself against his stomach. "I am prepared to stroke many things right now, but your ego is not one of them."

He didn't relax his grip. He was scanning her eyes, looking for—what? Reluctance? Sobriety? Temporary insanity?

"A few weeks ago, you couldn't stand me," he bit out, and she held his gaze without flinching.

"The feeling was mutual."

"No. I never hated you."

"No. You barely knew I existed." She added thoughtfully, "I think that's worse."

He moved an impatient shoulder. "I don't want to do this if it's not for the right reasons. If it's anything to do with what I told you tonight." Purposely crude, he said harshly, "I have no need or desire for a pity fu—"

Lainie's hand left his belly and covered his mouth. "If you want to retain the necessary equipment for this interlude, I suggest you don't finish that sentence." Her fingers moved, stroking his lips. "Richard. All I've had to do is *look* at you tonight and I want to curl up against you and purr like a cat."

His slow smile was equally feline. A black panther rather than a cosy house cat.

She put her hand over his and moved it down, sliding it over her jaw and down her neck to shape the heavy fall of her breast. Still he hesitated, until she ran a fingertip from the hollow of his throat to the top of his belt. His body arched sharply under her touch, and his thumb found a racing pulse under clinging silk. Her nails dug into his shoulders.

"A cat with claws," he murmured, and stood up with her in his arms. She breathed in the clean scent of his hair as he carried her up the stairs. Impressively, he managed to keep kissing her without walking them into any walls. His house was far too big for one person. It took so long to get to his bedroom that he was lucky he was sexy or the mood might have waned.

Her lashes fluttered open when his weight pressed her into a gorgeously plushy mattress. The silk dress was bunched around her hips. She could feel the coolness of the bedcover beneath her lower back and thighs. Richard leant on one arm, propping his body above hers. Slowly, he slid his free hand up her thigh, following the curves of her hip and waist. He looked down, his eyes intent as he watched the movement of his fingers. Catching hold of the folds of silk, he slid the dress up, bunching it in his hand. Her breath quickening, she arched her back, and he pulled it carefully over her head. She heard the crack of static from her hair as it tugged at the loosened strands.

His face was so close that she could only focus on one distinct feature at a time. Eyes, the black lashes lowered. The sharp aquiline plane of his nose. His lips, parted and a little thin. Very gently, still focused on the touch of their skin, he laid his palm on her midriff, spreading his fingers wide. He lowered his head and kissed her tummy, right in the hollow between her ribs.

She was slightly self-conscious about her stomach.

She didn't have the DNA or the will power for visible abs. Generally, she preferred men to pick a direction—up or down—and not linger in the middle region. It was so obvious from Richard's expression that he found her completely and unconditionally attractive that she let out a slow breath and relaxed in his arms.

He tugged her legs upward, bending her knees, and kissed the inside of her thigh. His mouth came down to blow warm breath against her expensive knickers—and she gave herself a mental high-five for leaving the Spanx at home again. She didn't need any Bridget Jones-esque comedy for their first time together.

Raising her hips, she wiggled the underwear down her legs and sent it flying with a careless flick of her foot. Their hands met on his belt buckle. She grinned up at him, her eyes sparkling and happy, and he touched the pad of his thumb to her lower lip.

When his body came down on hers again, both of them shivering at the slide of bare skin, she wrapped her arms around his back in a tight hug.

He lifted his head to look at her. "Okay?" His voice was rough and raspy.

In answer, she slid her toes up the back of his thigh, lifted her hips and pointedly arched an eyebrow.

His grin flashed as he adjusted his weight, and his head lowered to her neck.

Where she had expected a rush of blurred sensations, she received lingering clarity, as if the world had come into focused high-definition. She felt every moment of the hours that followed: the brush of his hair against intimate flesh, the warm suction of his mouth on her neck and her breasts, his soft kiss on the sensitive inner flesh of her upper arm when she reached back to the headboard, his hands—everywhere, it seemed.

There was one moment when they tried to roll to a different position and he kind of got trapped between her breasts, which was super awkward, but, she informed him kindly, *could* have been sexy if she'd been flat-chested and he'd been flexible.

It was worth it for the novelty of seeing him dissolved into laughter.

She had imagined Richard as a selfish lover, and she was wrong. He demanded, but he gave. He seemed fascinated, enthralled by her, which in turn made her feel intensely desirable. He made her feel far more beautiful than any couture gown or luxury cosmetic could ever do. It was a *real* beauty—messy, sweaty, intense. And it left her reeling.

MUCH LATER, THEY took a bath. Or rather, Lainie took a bath. Richard hijacked it, and didn't even have the decency to sit behind her so she could prop herself against his chest.

"How come you get my cosy self for a cushion, and I have to lean against cold marble?" She threaded playful fingers through his chest hair.

"My bath," he said, wrapping her legs across his lean belly so he could tickle her feet, "my cushion."

He stretched against her like a slick, satisfied seal, rubbing his wet hair into the curve of her neck. Lainie closed her eyes and dropped her head back. The water lapped at the drooping ends of her intricate hairstyle, most of which had been thoroughly mussed by Richard.

"What did Harlan Powell want?" she asked.

Richard traced interlocking circles on the inside of

her knee, drawing patterns with soap bubbles. "Mostly to talk about himself. He did mention a possible role in *Macbeth* next year."

"Oh," she said sleepily. "Good. As Macbeth?"

"I don't see myself as the Macduff type, do you?" His hand reached back to cup her cheek, providing a handy pillow against the hard surface of the bath. "I also ran into Eric Westfield, the RSPA vice president."

Lainie's eyes opened. "And?"

"Looks hopeful. He wants to have us over for dinner a week from Sunday. Smart casual dress." Richard sounded amused. "He obviously thinks you're a stabilizing influence on me, Tig."

"Interesting." She kissed his ear and smiled against his damp neck. "I would never have guessed he was so insightful."

EIGHT

London Celebrity@LondonCelebrity.3h
Are things getting serious?
Sources say "totally infatuated" Elaine Graham and
Richard Troy are spending "almost every night to-
gether."

LAINIE'S NUMEROUS OLDER brothers were all thick-necked, wide-shouldered, brown-haired and green-eyed. Richard took her word for it that it wasn't a mirrored reflection of the same large man. To a one, they obviously hated his guts. Compared to the Upper Bidford Women's Institute, however, they were about as intimidating as Cabbage Patch Kids.

The children were a different story.

"Bear," said one of the smaller girls. She showed him a dilapidated toy. Most of the fur had been sucked off one ear.

"Bear," she said again, more insistently.

He wasn't sure what she was looking for by way of a response. To start with, it wasn't a bear. It was a cat. Possibly a mouse. Less likely, a squirrel. Definitely not a bear. The kid was related to Lainie, so he suspected she wouldn't appreciate being corrected on that point.

Gingerly, he took the mystery animal from her. "Cute."

The lie seemed to satisfy her. To his relief, one of

Lainie's sisters-in-law appeared with a carton of ice cream and a box of waffle cones, and the little girl took off running. He turned the slightly sticky toy over in his hands, wondering where to put it. Through the hot cycle of the washing machine would be his first instinct.

"Can I get you a cup of coffee, Richard?" another woman asked, and he glanced up. She was tall, forty-odd and sharp-featured. Victoria, who was married to Lainie's eldest brother, Ryan. The one who'd attempted to break Richard's thumb during their handshake.

"Victoria is a university professor," Lainie had said in the car, on the way to her parents' house in Fulham. "She claims to be political, but she's mostly just stroppy."

"Black, thank you," he said. "No sugar."

A healthy shot of whisky wouldn't have gone astray either. He couldn't remember if he'd been nervous the first time he'd stepped onto a West End stage, but he couldn't have been as uncomfortable then as he felt now, at a one-year-old's birthday party. As was becoming his new state of normal, his eyes sought out Lainie. She was standing talking to Sarah, who'd been refreshingly pleased to see him. The baby propped on Lainie's hip was wearing a pink headband, so presumably was not the guest of honour, as the name on the birthday cake had been Cooper. She was bouncing up and down again, but her niece seemed to appreciate the rocking motion more than he had when she'd done it to the springs of his Ferrari.

He'd read an abysmal script a few months ago in which the protagonist had been struck dumb by the apparently sensual sight of his love interest clutching an infant. Watching Lainie sway with the baby, Richard's

main thought was for the welfare of her clothing. These
kids had consumed enough food to feed a barracks. It
seemed like tempting fate to jiggle one up and down.

She did look beautiful, holding the baby. She had
managed to look beautiful holding a sick bucket. She
was beautiful, in a way that had nothing to do with a
perfect smile, or large breasts, or gorgeous hair, and
had everything to do with *her*.

Although the boobs and hair were a nice perk.

She looked over at him, smiled that perfect smile,
and for a moment he couldn't fucking breathe.

He'd played this, onstage and on film, countless
times before age had sharpened his features and his
reputation had tarnished his character, and he'd been
more frequently cast as the villain than the lover.

He'd had no idea.

Lainie's gaze shifted down to his hands, where he
still held the revolting stuffed animal. Her smile grew.
She said something to Sarah, who also looked at him
with amusement, and handed her the baby.

He could smell her perfume as she came toward him.
Her hair brushed silkily against his cheek as she sat
down on the couch at his side and rested her chin on
his shoulder for a moment.

"I see you've been left in charge of Mister Ed. You
should feel privileged. He's Libby's favourite."

"Mister Ed?" Lazily, he rubbed his nose against her
cheek.

"Ryan used to watch reruns when he was a kid. He
told her it would be a good name for a horse."

"A *horse*?" His attention returned to the toy, and he
turned it over in his hands. "It's a cat. I'll accept a fox
at a push."

"It's clearly a horse." She took it away from him and set it down on the coffee table, next to a naked Barbie doll with a shorn head, one leg and an understandably fed-up expression.

Victoria came back with a cup in each hand. "Black coffee, no sugar," she said, handing him one. "Tea with milk and two sugars." She passed the other to Lainie.

"Thanks, Vicky." Lainie took it and sipped, with a grateful sigh. She flicked a glance at him through her lashes. "You're surviving, then."

He swallowed a mouthful of coffee. "Just." He raised the cup. "Although if one of your brothers helped make this, I should probably check it for traces of strychnine."

"Yeah. Sorry about that. They don't usually behave like the Corleone family. Will set kind of a bad precedent."

"Story of his life."

She grinned. He watched her narrowly, but there were no shadows in her eyes. Not a hint of lingering anger or regret. From her demeanour, Farmer might have been only a passing acquaintance. The corner of his mouth curved upward.

Another of the children, a small-to-medium-sized boy, came toddling over with a melting ice cream cone and laid a sticky miniature hand on Richard's knee. He sighed and looked around for a suitable toy. Mister Ed was obviously private property, and he didn't want to sacrifice the Barbie. The little boy looked like a holy terror, and her life had obviously been hard enough.

Lainie came to the rescue with a neon-green foam sword. Her ungrateful nephew whacked her around the ribs with it before charging off to decapitate his siblings.

Lainie looked at Richard ruefully. "Most of them will be taken off for a nap soon."

He wouldn't mind one himself. He had an entirely new respect for people with kids. They were exhausting. He also questioned the sanity of teachers, nannies and anyone who voluntarily wrangled the little beasts en masse. Naturally high spirits seemed to go into warp speed under the influence of pack mentality. He watched a card game disintegrate into something more like a reenactment of the Battle of Waterloo.

He'd occasionally wondered if he'd missed something, being an only child. Grievous bodily harm, by the looks of it.

"Thank you for coming." Lainie spoke in his ear. He turned to look at her. Her green eyes were level and serious on his. "I do appreciate it. I know this is so not your scene."

It wasn't. He hadn't met a woman's family since his university days. And his girlfriend at the time had also been an only child. But this was obviously the centre of Lainie's world, and he…cared about Lainie.

He shrugged. "We said we were going to spend the day together."

When they'd made plans for their day off, she'd forgotten about the family gathering, but needs must. The rest of the week was going to be packed with performances, meetings and duty appearances, so there wasn't going to be another chance to spend time with her away from the prying eyes of the public.

There were no paparazzi here. No pretence.

Just the vaguely threatening stares of her five hundred brothers.

One of them dropped into a seat opposite, a half-empty coffee cup in his hand, and Richard sat calmly under his scrutiny. It was the youngest. Cal, the only one with a beard.

He looked fairly unhappy about the proximity of Richard's hand to his sister's thigh.

Too bad.

"So," Cal said, with suspicious civility. "Richard."

"Cal," Lainie returned warningly.

"Rumour has it you're a bit of a prick."

"*Cal!*"

Her brother's face remained politely enquiring.

Richard's lips twitched. "That does seem to be the general consensus."

Cal leaned back, frowningly inspecting his jumper, which bore traces of his children's lunch. "And are you?"

"I believe your sister has said so more than once." He smiled slowly, looking down into Lainie's indignant face. "And I respect her opinion."

She shook her head at him. Reluctant amusement lightened her eyes to a gleaming shade of mint.

Cal watched them in silence. "Good enough." He stood up, drained the last of his coffee, and clapped Richard on the shoulder as he passed by. "Welcome to the family. See you in two weeks at the next birthday party."

"I'm adopted," Lainie said. "I share no genes with these people."

Richard glanced pointedly through the archway into the other lounge, where her freckle-faced, still partially red-haired father was playing Playstation with the teenagers. He tugged gently on a lock of her own hair.

Lainie put her hand up to rescue her scalp, her fingers closing over his. "Coincidence."

Without thinking, he nodded at the framed photograph on the mantel. "Your sister is indicating otherwise." He belatedly recalled that she'd almost cried the last time they'd talked about Hannah. It was still a novel experience, keeping a watch over someone else's feelings.

Fortunately, her eyes remained clear. Her expression softened as she looked at her sister's image.

"That's Auntie Hannah," said yet another childish treble, and he looked down at a young girl with a brown ponytail. He was relieved to see that this one had clean hands and looked old enough to entertain herself.

"She could curl her tongue like me." She demonstrated. "Can you do that?"

"Yes, Richard," Lainie said provocatively. She widened her eyes at him. "What can *you* do with your tongue?"

"Are you being gross?" her niece demanded, and Richard snorted. Lainie's cheeks reddened.

Taking pity on her, he stuck his tongue out and curled it, to the resounding approval of his younger audience.

"She could do cartwheels too." She looked at him expectantly.

"No," he said firmly.

"Yeah, Auntie Lainie can't do them either." The little girl looked disparagingly at her aunt. "Mum says it's because she has a heavy top."

Richard bit back a grin. His gaze moved to the…top in question, and Lainie pinched him.

"She can do *some* stuff, though," the precocious child

grudgingly allowed. "She can sit on the ground and put her foot right up behind her head."

"Can she?" He eyed Lainie with new interest. "That sounds…useful."

"I did it once and almost broke my hip," she replied deflatingly. "Don't get your hopes up."

"He can curl his tongue like Auntie Hannah, Gran," the little girl said to Rachel, who had come into the room to gather up dirty plates.

"Is that right?" Lainie's mother glanced at Richard, and then smiled at her granddaughter. "You can take these plates to the kitchen for me, please, madam."

He got to his feet, still holding his empty coffee cup. "Let me," he began, but Lainie took the cup from his hand and a stack of plates from her mother.

"It's okay," she said, nudging him with her elbow. It was a very casual, gentle, affectionate action, which somehow rendered him motionless. "I can do it."

Her niece trailed in her wake, holding a single plate and looking martyred.

Rachel stood looking at the photo of Hannah. Slipping his hands into his pockets, he remained silent.

"She was a good person." Rachel turned her head to look directly at him. "So is her sister."

He didn't so much as blink under her steady regard. "I'm aware of that."

"Good," she said, unsmiling. She continued to watch him for several seconds, then nodded and returned to the kitchen.

He walked over to take a closer look at the family photographs. He was standing near the open door to the hallway, well within hearing range when his name came up in conversation.

"So, what do you think of Richard Troy, up close and personal?" He didn't recognise the female voice, but instantly identified Victoria when she responded.

"He seems to have a few more brain cells than the last walking ego she had in tow. But once again, Lainie takes up with an up-himself actor."

"He doesn't seem *that* bad." The unknown woman sighed. "Do you reckon it'll last?"

"No."

"They do seem pretty into each other."

"She seemed to be pretty into the manwhore too."

"Vicky…"

"Besides, do rebound relationships *ever* last? None of mine did."

The voices trailed away and he heard footsteps going up the stairs. He was still standing by the doorway when a trio of kids came tripping through. They were all clutching plastic swords.

Apparently Lainie's brothers had dispatched an execution squad.

One of the two boys looked him up and down. "Are you a pirate?"

Richard dropped the murderous scowl and resisted a self-conscious urge to touch a hand to his unshaven chin. "No." His response was curt. "Sorry."

The boy persisted. "But you *could* be a pirate?"

Technically, he *had* been a pirate, although he suspected the kids were after a more interestingly bloodthirsty performance than was required by Gilbert and Sullivan. He eyed the plastic sword that the other boy offered, and shrugged. He'd worked with less convincing props, and he was in the mood for wielding a weapon. And thanks to the past weeks of work on *The Cavalier's Tribute*, his swordplay wasn't too rusty.

The children grinned from ear to ear when he threateningly brandished the sword. The female pirate, who looked a lot like Lainie, growled and took a violent stab at him with her own weapon. It was lucky the room was childproof, with no breakables on display.

"You're the baddie," the first boy informed him bossily.

"Again, that seems to be the general consensus."

The swordfight continued amidst rising giggles, and did a surprising amount toward working off his bad temper. He fielded off an enthusiastic slice and creased his face into another angry scowl, much to his opponents' delight. Eventually—naturally—the Lainie-lookalike declared herself the victor, for no other reason than that she wanted to be.

Amused, Richard lowered his sword in surrender. He heard a deep chuckle. Turning, he was slightly embarrassed to see Lainie's father watching the game.

"Fence at Oxford, did you?" Simon Graham asked, grinning.

"No, but I've had good motivation to practise recently. Attempting to skewer Will Farmer."

Simon's amusement visibly increased. He studied Richard. "So, you're Franklin Troy's son. You're not much like him, are you?"

Richard's half smile faded. He rubbed the back of his wrist over his sweaty forehead. Looking down at the sword in his hand, he flipped it around, extending the handle for the kids to take. "I hope not."

LAINIE STOOD IN THE doorway to the kitchen, biting down on the edge of her thumbnail. Richard nodded and responded to something that her dad said. He was still flushed and ruffled after his impromptu playacting with the kids. She'd almost dropped a plate when he'd started channelling Captain Hook. At least three members of her family had obviously given him the thumbs-up. She couldn't help remembering the last time Will had been with her family. Like Richard, he'd looked as if he'd wandered into the monkey cage at the zoo, but he'd been even more hopeless at hiding his discomfort. And he definitely hadn't bothered to muck about with her nieces and nephews. He'd spent most of the time on his phone. Probably texting Crystalle, in hindsight.

"I so knew it." Sarah's voice was smug in her ear.

Lainie removed her thumbnail from her mouth long enough to respond. "Did you? I didn't."

She still wasn't sure quite how this had happened. How, in a matter of weeks, she had ended up…

"Totally smitten," Sarah said. "Both of you."

"I am," Lainie admitted. She reached down and clasped her sister-in-law's arm, holding it for support. "I don't know about him."

He was still snarky, sarky, snobby Richard Troy. But sometimes—

"Lainie. Last month, the man would barely have recognised you if he fell over you, outside the theatre. Today, he came to your parents' house for a baby's birthday party, put up with your brothers acting like something out of a Tarantino movie, and let a bunch of lunatic children attack him with plastic swords. He's a goner."

She affectionately pulled Lainie's hair, much as Richard had done earlier, and went to corral her offspring.

Lainie felt strangely tongue-tied and shy of Richard

as they put on their coats, ready to leave. His knuckles
brushed her nape when he automatically reached out to
pull her hair free of her collar. She looked at him and
then quickly away.

"Tig?" His fingers closed loosely around her wrist.
"What's the matter?"

"Nothing," she said, still not looking at him.

"Lainie—"

"Bye, Lainie. See you later, Mr. Troy." Phil, her oldest nephew, gave her a one-armed hug as he passed. She
belatedly lifted a hand to squeeze his shoulder. She had
to stretch up to do it. He was almost as tall as Ryan now.
"Oh, happy birthday to you too, by the way," Phil said,
and Lainie's head snapped up in time to catch Richard's faint grimace.

"Birthday app," Phil explained, raising his phone. He
pushed open the front door with his elbow, making a
face at the drizzling rain outside "Your name came up
on the celebrity list when I was uploading some photos
of Coop. Meant to say something before, but I forgot.
Hope the rest of the day is a good one."

He departed with another casual wave, and Lainie
stared at Richard. He looked annoyed.

"It isn't your birthday, is it?" she asked apprehensively.

His frown deepened. "Well—" he said reluctantly,
and she released a sharp breath.

"Why didn't you say something? We could have done
something to celebrate."

"You've just answered your own question."

"You're exasperating."

In the car, she kept one eye on the passing streets
while she checked her email and Facebook. She'd been

linked to a new gossip article. They'd been papped leaving Richard's house.

"Why is it," she demanded, scrolling through the photos, "that you look good in every single photo, and I look borderline okay in one out of ten?" They stopped at an intersection, and she held the iPad for him to see. "Look at that. It's like James Bond and something out of Fraggle Rock."

He didn't bother to turn his head. "Don't be ridiculous."

"You could have told me my hair was doing that." She glanced up. "Wait! Stop at Sainsbury's, please."

Richard shot her a look. "Why?"

"Because I need to buy stuff."

"What stuff?"

Fortunately, there was one single advantage to having grown up surrounded by large and irritating men. She knew how to effectively end a line of questioning. Employ the dreaded tampon. "Oh, you know. Women's stuff."

He flicked the indicator without another word. He waited in the car while she sped into the supermarket, hugging her coat across her chest and ducking her head against the rain. When she finally emerged, staggering under the weight of her bags, he looked bored and irritable. She dove thankfully back into the passenger seat and ran her fingers through her damp hair, trying to smooth down the frizz. Her clothing smelled strongly of wet wool.

Richard turned around and stretched to look into the backseat. "So, by 'women's stuff,' you actually meant your entire weekly shop."

She flipped down the overhead mirror to check that

her mascara was still attached to her eyelashes. "Well, I figured since we were here…"

The comment he muttered under his breath was un-complimentary and mildly offensive to her sex in general, but she'd taken ages to make up her mind in the bakery section and he'd been waiting in the car for over half an hour, so she kindly let it go.

Neither of them could cook much more than tea and toast, so they also stopped to pick up takeaway for dinner. She wanted pizza. He wanted Thai. They compromised with Moroccan.

They were going back to her flat for the night, since her landlady was away for the weekend and Lainie was on cat-feeding duty again. Richard carried the bulk of the shopping bags up the stairs for her and then seemed confused about what to do with them. Obviously, his housekeeper usually did the supermarket run. When he frowned down at a packet of dishwasher cubes and tried to put them on the biscuit shelf in the pantry, she firmly removed it from his hand.

"You could do me a favour and go down and feed Cat Richard," she suggested tactfully. She wanted him out of the way for a few minutes anyway. "The food is in Mrs. Talbot's fridge. You can give him the rest of the can. And make sure his water bowl is topped up." She assumed a helpful expression. "The water is in the tap. You just hold the bowl underneath and turn it to…"

He nipped her earlobe with his teeth in retribution.

When she heard his footsteps going down the stairs, she quickly put away the frozen food and then went hunting through the rest of the bags for what she needed. She left the boring things to put away later. Clearing room on her limited bench space, she set out the peach-and-apricot pie she'd bought. A dessert from a boutique bakery would probably be nicer, but she'd never have got away with that side trip. Besides, she highly doubted that Richard had ever eaten a supermarket dessert, and everyone should have a new experience on their birthday.

She was pushing candles into the top crust when he reappeared.

"I swear to God, that cat was smirking at me. What are you doing?" He halted in the doorway, staring at her handiwork.

"Putting in your candles. I'm going with three on one side and five on the other, because I think the crust will collapse if I try to stuff in all thirty-five. You shouldn't be so old."

There was a long silence. She looked sideways at him. His face was completely blank.

"It's a pie," he said at last.

She stood back to admire it. "You don't like cake." He'd turned down the Victoria sponge someone had brought into the theatre for Theresa's birthday last week.

"No. I don't." Slowly, Richard walked over to stand at her shoulder. He looked down at the birthday pie. "What's with the M&M's?"

"I needed something to spell out 'Happy Birthday'."

"Does chocolate go with fruit pie?"

"Chocolate goes with everything." She bit her lip as she looked up at him. She was a little more apprehensive than she was prepared to let on. "What do you think?"

"I think you're slightly insane." He suddenly pulled her close to him and pressed a rough kiss to her temple. "Thanks."

She wrapped both arms around his lean waist and rested her forehead against his chest. "Happy birthday."

The pie was actually fairly tasty. They ate it with forks straight from the serving plate, sitting on the floor of her small lounge. It didn't really go with the chicken tagine, but she'd eaten far stranger combinations during her student days. Her stomach lining had been trained the hard way with months of pot noodles and post-clubbing kebabs.

Not for the first time, she wished she had an open fire. The heat pump kept the room warm, but it wasn't as conducive to doing sexy things on the rug. Richard was sprawled on his back, one arm tucked beneath his head, his shirt riding up. The pastry calories probably wouldn't venture anywhere near his flat belly. Genetics played a mean game of favourites. She was lying on her stomach. She was well aware that he could see directly down her top, and her cleavage tended to look better from this angle than when she lay on her back and her boobs slid toward her armpits. Problems of the naturally top-heavy, as her sister-in-law had rudely put it.

She contemplated just rolling on top of him and seeing how things progressed, but decided in favour of the pie, for the present. She'd been too on edge about exposing Richard to her family, and vice versa, to eat much at the party. Propping her chin on one hand, she reached with the other to skewer a mushy piece of apricot. As she chewed, she eyed him thoughtfully. "So, how horrifying was today, on a scale of one to ten?"

"I had a better time than you're likely to have next Sunday, at Westfield's house." Richard folded back his other arm, and his biceps flexed invitingly. She determinedly ate another mouthful of stewed fruit.

"Your family is very…you." He smiled faintly. "Open. Friendly. Talkative."

"Loud, demanding and bossy?" She extracted a red M&M from the remnants of the pie and put it in her mouth. Richard lazily opened one blue eye and followed the sweet's progress.

He contemplated her lips. "Your family obviously love you a lot. I'm glad you have people who watch out for you."

And who watched out for him? She hesitated. "Richard…"

"Mmm?" His eyes were closed again.

"How did your mother die?"

There had been no details on Wikipedia, only the bare fact that Anna Troy had passed away two years after her husband. There were a lot of photos of her taken just prior to her death, when she'd been linked to an Italian racing car driver. The images had firmly established the origin of Richard's dark, sculpted looks. It was the similar jaded look in her eyes that had affected Lainie most. Anna had been in the arms of a smiling, super-hot man, surrounded by dozens of laughing people, and she'd looked lonely. She'd probably died lonely.

Hannah had died alone, despite the fact that her hands had been held tightly, but she hadn't died *lonely*.

Lainie didn't want Richard to *live* lonely.

He was quiet long enough that she regretted asking, but he did eventually answer. "Ironically, *she* did die of a heart attack. The postmortem revealed an arterial blockage."

"Did it happen in England?"

"In Italy. She'd been seeing an Italian. I think he genuinely grieved for her, to give him credit." He sat up suddenly and shoved a restless hand through his black curls. "They weren't exclusive, though, and could go days without seeing one another. The coroner thought she'd been lying there for about eighty hours before her body was found."

"That's awful." She reached out to him. Very lightly and gently, she spread her fingers on his abdomen, and he put his hand over hers. "I'm sorry."

"So was I. Sorry *for* her, mostly. I really hardly knew her. She wasn't a particularly good mother. I'm sorry she died like that, and that she never seemed to get much happiness out of her relationships."

Lainie scooted closer and curled up next to him, sliding her hand across his chest in a hug and touching her nose to his cheek. He bent his arm to hook loosely around her neck.

There was a heavy weight to the silence, in contrast to the lighthearted sensual thrum of a few moments ago.

Geez.

Way to rain on his birthday.

Unable to just sit there while he had that look on his face, she carefully released him and got to her feet. Walking across to the table, she opened her bag and rifled through it to find the DVDs.

"I got us a movie," she explained, holding up the first of the cases.

"Is it a romantic comedy?" he asked suspiciously, and she tried to imagine his reaction to *Pretty Woman* or *While You Were Sleeping*. He would probably disapprove of the idealization of prostitution in the former. The latter might be good for her conscience. She and Richard had originally faked their relationship, but it had been with reluctant mutual consent. At least one of them hadn't been in a coma at the time.

"I do have high expectations for the comedy, yes."

"What is it?" He sounded even more suspicious.

"You'll probably guess from the theme music." She turned on the TV and started the DVD player.

She looked at him between lowered lashes when the disc began to play. It was a makeshift copy, so there were no menu options. Alas. She would have paid a great deal for behind-the-scenes special features.

It took less than five seconds for his entire body to stiffen. "What the f—" He snatched up the plastic case, turning it over to see if there was anything printed on the front. His eyes—intensely blue, incredulous and wrathful—snapped to hers. "Where the *hell* did you get this?"

"Shh!" she said, grinning. "You're on. Oh, my. Sexy pompadour, Troy." Richard lunged for the remote, and she held it out of his reach. "No way. Student Richard Troy, strutting his stuff with the T Birds? I've been looking forward to this all day."

Richard's expression was beyond price. "*Where*," he repeated, dangerously, "did you get it?"

"Victoria knows a lot of people at Oxford. I caught her in a good mood, and she called in a favour. Someone scavenged in the drama archives. And struck gold, I have to say. Did they have to sew you into those jeans?"

"Off. Right now."

"And miss you doing the finger-pointing to 'Greased Lightnin'? Not a chance in hell." Still grinning, she held up the other DVD. "If it softens the blow, I had Mum burn this to a disc. Behold my sixteen-year-old debut as Ado Annie in *Oklahoma!* I didn't even edit out the part where my sash catches on a wagon wheel and I fall into a wooden trough. Fair's fair. And I promise I won't leak yours to the tabloids next time you piss me off."

Richard's younger self pulled out a comb and ran it through his slick bouffant of hair in slow motion, and she tried really, really hard not to laugh. The current incarnation had lost his implacable cool. His cheeks were burning bright with colour.

A bit of summer lovin' commenced on the screen, and he winced. "Oh, for fuck's sake." He took the other disc from her hand and held it up menacingly. "This had better be embarrassing. I mean complete and total humiliation."

"I'm singing 'I Cain't Say No,' I have hair extensions and braces, and it was a single-sex school so my love interest was played by a fifteen-year-old girl, who was just about concussed by my left boob during the finale. It ain't good."

"Fine. Let me know when it's on, and you won't mind if I answer a few business emails in the meantime. You can sit on my lap and block the TV."

"Check us out. Compromising and everything."

He staunchly ignored the rest of his adolescent performance, but looked reluctantly amused as he typed into the iPad with one hand. His other hand played with the ends of her hair. And she had the pure joy of hearing him laugh heartlessly when her own teenage self flounced and pouted her way across the stage.

In bed that night, she lay on her side, watching the rhythmic rise and fall of his bare chest as he slept. A light scattering of black hairs trailed down his chest, circling his flat nipples, and she followed them with a fingertip. Lowering her head, her hair slipping down to pool on his skin, she touched her lips to his in a whisper of a kiss. He murmured her name, but didn't wake. When she rolled over, sliding her arm under the pillow and closing her eyes, she could still feel his body, warm against her back.

She fell hard into sleep and would happily have stayed there if Richard's phone hadn't rung at dawn. Not even dawn. The bedroom was still dark when she cracked her eyes open at the insistence of his frigging annoying ringtone.

"Richard." His leg hair was tickling her foot. She pressed her big toe against his calf and gave it a shove. "Phone."

He didn't even alter his breathing.

The phone kept ringing.

"Phone."

He clearly had no intention of getting up.

Swearing under her breath, Lainie sat up, rubbing her forehead. She leaned over him, brushed the tumbled hair from his eyes, and put her lips against his ear. "*Phone.*"

He made a grumpy noise, but still didn't move.

"I don't know what you're grunting at *me* for. It's *your* phone."

His response was to put his head under his pillow. He pressed it against the ear closest to her mouth.

"Fine. I'm answering it. But you're going to regret it if it's some other poor woman you conned into bed." Leaning heavily on his back, she reached over his recumbent body and snagged the phone from the bedside table. "Never mind. It's Lynette. If you shagged her, I'm too intimidated to compare notes."

She swallowed a squawk when Richard retracted the

long leg he was dangling outside the covers and tucked his cold toes into the curve behind her knee. Sliding her thumb against the touch pad, she reluctantly answered the call. Any communication from Lynette or Pat was liable to spell trouble. "Hello?"

There was a brief silence. Lynette managed to convey her amusement before speaking a word. "Good morning, Lainie. It's a little early for you to be answering Richard's phone, isn't it?"

Lainie wasn't sure if she meant time of day or brevity of relationship. Bit of a cheek if it was the latter, considering that Lynette was partly responsible for tying them together in the first place. "We've taken up hot yoga," she said blandly. "You have to get up very early to do hot yoga." Didn't you? "It's part of Richard's new healthy-living image. We're considering naked meditation in Hyde Park next."

"I'll start drafting the press release now. Is Richard there, or will eagle pose end in catastrophe if he takes the phone?"

"He's here." She ruthlessly pulled the pillow away from Richard's head and one blue eye stared narrowly up at her. "Lynette wants a word."

With a sigh, he heaved himself up to a sitting position and took the phone. He looked even more of a grouch than usual first thing in the morning. And the stubble situation was acute. He was verging on a full lumberjack beard now. No wonder she had patches of irritated red skin in interesting places.

"Is the theatre on fire?" His voice had a throaty edge. "Are *you* on fire?"

Lainie couldn't help smiling. He was just so…cute. All rumpled and sexy and cranky. The covers were bunched around his hips. She leaned forward and kissed his chest. Evading the grab he made for her, she scooted out of bed and snatched up her fleecy dressing gown. She didn't fancy freezing to death in the loo. It would make embarrassing copy for the gossip blogs.

When she returned to the bedroom, Richard was off the phone and typing something into his iPad. He tapped the screen a few times, then tossed it aside. Eyeing her dressing gown, he came up on his knees and caught her around the waist. He, apparently, had no issues with subarctic nudity.

"Nice," he said, running his hands up her arms. "Take it off."

"It's warm." She captured his sneaking fingers and entwined them with her own. Leaning forward, she rested her forehead against his. She lightly kissed the bridge of his nose. "Morning."

"It's six thirty. It's dark. That's night. Bedtime." With deft movements, he pulled his hands free and yanked open the belt of her dressing gown. It was slipped from her shoulders and thrown haphazardly behind her. Ignoring her laughing protest, he pulled her hard against him and pushed her down on top of it.

She wriggled beneath his heavy body, getting into a more comfortable position, and he gently kissed her cheek. She could feel the heat and hardness of his sleep-warmed skin along the full length of her torso. His mouth drifted to hers. He nudged her thighs with his knee, and she agreeably parted her legs, lifting them to hug his hips. He hooked an arm under her bent knee, lifting her teasingly against him.

"Warm enough?" he asked wickedly, as he bent his head to her neck. She closed her eyes, her breath quickening. His touch was leisurely, almost lazy. It was a slow drift of pleasure, rather than the intense, driven heat of their previous intimacy. She could stay in the moment, keep tabs on her own body. Focus on his.

The heat pump in the lounge was on a low heat overnight, not nearly enough to counteract the predawn chill of autumnal London. The bedroom was cold. Richard was not.

A warm hand slid firmly up her ribs and lifted the weight of her right breast. His thumb moved to flick and circle. Her back arched. Sinking her fingers into his messy curls, she tugged his face toward hers.

"I assume the Metronome is *not* on fire?" she murmured.

He moved his hand down her hip, sliding it beneath her, seeming to enjoy the feeling of her skin. His lips returned to her neck, moved up to her jaw and cheek. "No." He nudged her cheek with his nose. It was an affectionate gesture, and she relaxed her grip on his hair, shaping his head with her palm.

When he would have kissed her mouth again, she held him away, staring up at him, content to just…look, for a moment.

His cheeks were already flushed. Men, in her experience, tended to pull the same facial expression during sex that they made just prior to a final touchdown in a televised rugby match. Utter concentration. Leashed anticipation. Perspiring forehead. Ready to celebrate the successful try with a triumphant shout, a pat on the back and a beer-fuelled nap.

Bad time to get an urge to giggle.

He smoothed her hair back from her own damp forehead, rubbing his thumb against her temple. "Tig." His voice was deep and rough, and effectively banished any ill-timed amusement.

She watched her fingertips as she traced the edge of his ear, stroked the side of his neck, tested the strength of his shoulder. The muscles there were flexing as he kept his weight propped on one arm.

Her gaze returned to his. His eyes were almost black. No trace of sleepiness now.

"What did Lynette want?" she asked quietly. The room felt hushed. She touched his chin. Ran her thumb across his lower lip.

He caught it, briefly, between his teeth. "To spread the misery of insomnia." He shifted against her, and they both drew in a hitching breath. "She's had an email from…" He exhaled sharply when her hand crept sneakily down between them. "Ministerial bigwig. Requesting that I speak on cultural funding at a parliamentary conference next month."

"What?" Lainie's lashes had drooped to a languid half-mast, but she looked up at that. She withdrew her prowling hand to grip his biceps. "That's awesome. It's exactly the sort of opportunity you want, isn't it?"

Richard retrieved her fingers and firmly returned them to their previous site of exploration. "It's a very good start."

She had questions about the conference—very bright, astute questions—but he'd never know how perceptive she was, thanks to his bossy, demanding lips.

God, he tasted good.

"You're not bad at this sex thing," she gasped a few minutes later, her arm inadvertently tightening in a chokehold around his neck.

He reached up and loosened her grip, pulling her

hand around his torso so she could grip his back. Taut muscles moved under the smooth, warm skin there.

"Although, you know, regular rehearsals. Important for any performance."

The tip of his tongue teased hers. "You're adorable," he said. "Stop talking."

She let the man hone his craft.

NINE

THERE WERE A NUMBER of things that Lainie liked to do
on Sunday afternoons, and they all involved pyjamas.
They did not include choosing a suitable outfit to wear
to dinner with a man who licked the hands of brand-
new acquaintances, but needs must. With a cup of tea
in one hand, held at a safe distance from her outfit,
she examined her reflection in the mirror. Midi-length
pencil skirt and knockoff Chanel jacket from Topshop.
Decorous heels. Sleek waves of hair.

She looked like a bustier, ginger Jackie O. Pity she
didn't have a pillbox hat. When dressing for a part—
today's role being a sort of political consort, which
seemed more hilarious every time she thought about
it—might as well go all out.

The front door buzzed, and she checked her watch in
surprise. Richard wasn't supposed to be picking her up
for an hour. They had been so busy with performances
and appearances that she'd barely spoken to him the past
couple of days, except for brief stolen moments alone
in their dressing rooms. She would have liked time to
eat her chocolate biscuit and put on her lipstick before

he arrived, but she was looking forward to seeing him properly, in private.

She was smiling when she pulled the door open, but her expression quickly sobered. "Will."

He lowered the hand that was raised to buzz again—always impatient—and shoved it into the pocket of his crisp trousers. His black hair was combed in a smooth wave above his ear, and he was freshly shaved. The *GQ* effect was not as appealing as lazy stubble and tangled curls.

"I want to talk to you," he said with no preliminaries, already pushing his way past her into the lounge. "I've been trying to get you alone all week, but you're either dashing off to interviews or slobbering over Troy in the wings."

Untrue. She had decided opinions about public displays of affection in the workplace, and Will knew it.

Closing the front door, she hoped that Richard didn't break the habit of a lifetime and turn up early after all. She strongly suspected that these confrontations between former and current lovers were less titillating than they were presented in fiction. In fact, she would put her money on them being a bloody nightmare.

Will stood by her coffee table, watching her through narrowed eyes. His arms were folded. Chin up, pecs out, lips set. Great. She had the haughty Jacobite Geoffrey in her flat.

"You didn't congratulate me at the Awards last week."

"Congratulations."

"I expect you were devoting your considerable talents to consoling the loser," he said nastily, and she clenched her hands.

"Mind your own business," was all she said, but it was a struggle to keep her reply mild.

"I looked for you later, but Jack Trenton said he saw you leaving early with Troy."

From what she recalled, it hadn't been that early. The public part of the night had seemed interminably long. The private part, she wouldn't have minded extending. And repeating more times than they'd managed in the days since.

She shrugged, and Will looked at her intently. "Trenton and Sadie Foster have called it quits."

Unsurprising, if Jack was shagging his director and didn't fancy the idea of castration.

"He had a few too many after the ceremony. You know the way his mouth runs off. Admitted they were only in it for the publicity. He can't stand her."

A warning bell sounded in the recesses of Lainie's mind. She continued to say nothing.

"Which got me thinking," Will went on, still watching her fixedly, waiting for any change of expression. "Bob Carson and Pat Bligh seem *very* interested in your private life at the moment. And you took up with Troy pretty fucking quickly. One day you're not even on his radar—" Lainie couldn't help wincing at that "—and the next you're in his bed. I reckoned it was a rebound fling," he said with odious complacency, "but is it even that much?"

Lainie gave one short, hard tug on the hem of her jacket to straighten it. "Dropping the unconvincing impression of a Yard 'tec, are you implying that I'm faking an affair with Richard Troy to get my name in the tabloids?"

"No," Will said, surprising her, but he added, "I don't

think you would lie for publicity. You've never wanted cheap fame, and you've always had a high standing in the press. Particularly after what I did to you." That last was stated candidly. "But Troy's name has been mud this year. Suddenly, he's looking a bit more like the blue-eyed boy, with his sweet, philanthropic girl-friend. If she'll give him the time of day, he can't be all that bad. Such an earnest little do-gooder as she is." His scrutiny was now positively unsettling. "I've been thinking about it all week, and I realised there is one reason why you might agree to back up a harmless lie."

Lainie had never deluded herself that Will was unin-telligent, whatever his more carnal failings. Nor was he above using said intelligence in a morally questionable way if he thought it would benefit himself.

In other words, he would run squealing to the press at the drop of a hat.

She told him what was, in essence, the truth: "I don't want to be hurtful, Will—" and she really didn't, no matter how badly he'd knocked her own pride "—but there's nothing fake about my feelings for Richard—" there wasn't, not any longer "—and we are sleeping to-gether." Not that it was any of his business.

Will's jaw worked. "What could you possibly see in him? He's a self-serving, bad-tempered bastard who wouldn't lift a finger to help you. Unless it was to push you onto his mattress."

She damped down on the growing anger. "What I feel for Richard, and why I feel it, is my own business."

And Richard's business. The fact that they hadn't had that particular conversation yet made this one even more inappropriate.

"You're delusional."

Some of the fury escaped. "Will, you gave up the right to even come here. How I choose to move on is nothing to do with you. Would you just *go*?"

He caught at her words like a mousetrap snapping down on an agitated, waving tail. "So it *is* because of what happened between us? Lainie, I've told you that I'm sorry—"

"You haven't, actually, but it's irrelevant. *I'm* sorry, but you're not even a factor. You're part of my past. A memory that reminds me how much better I have it now." Brutal, but true, and she was too cross to continue shielding his ego.

"So you'd rather lower yourself to his level. A complete dickhead, who's incapable of caring about anyone but himself."

"Says the man who broke up with me by way of a gossip column and another woman's bed. His level is so far above yours in so many ways, this whole argument is obsolete. Leave."

"Is that right? You want to take a poll? See who agrees with you? There are reasons everybody hates him. How many people have gone home from the theatre feeling like shit because of Troy?"

She bit her lip, unable to refute that fact, and he pressed his advantage.

"He's a user. A poor little rich boy," Will said bitterly, unconsciously borrowing Lynette's words, "who stood on old family money to get where he is, and who wouldn't get out of bed in the morning if it wasn't to his advantage. He's using you, and you're buying it."

"Charming. While you, of course, were always the height of sincerity."

"My feelings for you were genuine. I admit I made a mistake—"

"Yes, you did. And you made another one in coming here today and talking a load of bollocks." She opened the front door again and pointedly held it ajar.

A flush crept into Will's cheeks. "I'm worried about you. Whether you choose to believe that or not. He's not right for you. He's not right for anyone."

"Oh, bullshit."

"He's a prick, Lainie. A spoilt, entitled brat."

Oddly, that made her smile. "I know," she agreed readily, almost fondly.

Her amusement seemed to further enrage him. "And look at his family. A mother who whored around Europe. Father a demented old bigot. Whose death, by the way, was supposedly brought on by Troy Junior."

"Richard did not cause his father's suicide!"

It was probably the stupidest, most careless thing she had ever done. The words just flew out of her mouth, propelled by sheer outrage and the instinct to defend. To protect.

And didn't she make a right arse-up of that?

Will frowned. "Suicide? Didn't he have a heart attack?"

Her heart was a thumping beat in her throat. Lainie drew on every ounce of acting experience she'd ever earned and kept her face blank.

Will jerked his head dismissively to one side. "Whatever. Just…think twice. That's all I'm saying. As your friend."

Feeling shaky, and not entirely convinced the danger could have passed that easily, Lainie nodded impatiently. She just wanted to be rid of him. "Fine. Whatever. Goodbye, Will."

"*Think about it.*" Will reached out and gripped her arm.

"Think about what?" The voice came from the top of the stairwell. Lainie almost jumped out of her demure two-inch heels.

How much had he heard?

Richard was leaning against the wall, one hand tucked into the pocket of his tailored trousers, his leather jacket hanging open over a cashmere jumper. The query had been cool and uninterested, but he was anything but relaxed. His eyes were fixed on the spot where Will's fingers bit into her arm.

She could almost see the tip of the panther's tail twitching, ready to spring.

Will responded by turning pink and inflating his chest, and Lainie groaned audibly.

Testosterone. It was massively overrated.

And please, God, let him have just arrived.

"Nothing." Lainie yanked away from Will's restraining hold. "Will was just leaving."

"You seem undecided, Farmer," Richard said softly. He pushed away from the wall and advanced toward them. "Do you need a helping hand down the stairs?"

Will's face was uncharacteristically ugly. "Try it."

"Oh, for God's sake." Lainie turned on Richard and put her hand on his chest. It was an instinctive movement, as if she was simultaneously laying a claim, declaring her allegiance and foolishly trying to hold him back from any rash action.

He looked down at her fingers, spread against the fine wool jumper, and then into her face. A more genuine smile tipped the corners of his lips. "Saving me from myself again, Tig?"

"Wallowing in the dirt *with* you, more like," Will muttered, and Richard's whole body tensed.

Lainie gripped his upper arm with her free hand. "Don't even think about it. I will never let you use me as an excuse to behave atrociously. Just let it go. He doesn't know what he's talking about."

After a dangerous pause, Richard touched his thumb to her eyebrow, smoothing the curve. "What have I let myself in for?" he murmured.

"You've never been so lucky in your life," Lainie retorted.

"No, he hasn't," Will agreed jerkily, and Richard's hand stilled against her face.

Will abruptly turned his back on them and left, his footsteps muffled on the worn carpeting of the stairs.

Richard watched him go and then looked at Lainie. "You look upset. What did he say to you?"

It was more what Lainie had said to *him*. How could she have blurted out Richard's most private business like that, and to *Will*, of all people? She briefly debated confessing the disastrous slip, but what was the point? It hadn't seemed to interest Will much. If Richard confronted him about it, it would only underline the fact that it was a card to be played against him.

The cowardly justification did not sit well with her conscience.

"Just the usual." She let her hand slip down his chest and drop away. "His ego playing up. He made a mistake; I'm making a bigger one. So on and so forth. Although I got a comment that could almost be interpreted as an apology for the Crystalle debacle, if you squint hard and replay it in slow motion, so that's new."

"And a bloody long time in coming. Idiot. Does he often visit you at home?" Richard's eyes were still uncomfortably shrewd, and Lainie shook her head.

"No. Not even very often when we were together. I gathered he had the same objection to perfectly decent Bayswater terraces as you do. He said he'd been trying to talk to me at the theatre, but I was too busy canoodling with you in your dressing room."

"Canoodling?" he repeated, some of his preoccupation sliding into a wicked gleam. His arm slid around her waist to tug her into his body. "What does that involve, exactly?"

His lips found the curve of her neck, and Lainie moved involuntarily into the nuzzling kiss. "I believe you've answered your own question," she said on a breathless laugh. Her hand came over his marauding one as it explored the length of her spine and ventured farther south. "And any further practical demonstrations will have to wait until later, because we're about to be late for your very important date."

"Sod it," Richard said, and he kissed her hard. "You're right. I'm not the political type. Let's have a lie-down instead."

"You're an actor." Lainie slipped her hand between their lips. "Act like you're the political type."

SOCIAL GRACES. HE DID them well when he wanted to, Lainie thought later. Over the flickering candlelight on a Knightsbridge dining table, she watched Richard being effortlessly charming to the very objectionable vice president of the RSPA. Not so long ago, that fake pandering had been supremely irritating, but now it at least seemed to be in pursuit of a worthy cause. Every so often, their eyes met, and Lainie had to hide a smile at the expression she read in his.

He hated every moment of this.

She had attended more congenial dinner parties herself. Eric Westfield, who was staying on as VP after the new incumbent took over the presidency, and who obviously had more money than the average merchant bank, had not impressed her at their first brief meeting. On closer acquaintance, she thought he was loathsome. The other guests at the table had ostensibly been invited to chat with Richard, but behaved as if they were paid actors whose only task for the evening was to laugh at Westfield's jokes. Richard, she noticed, confined himself to a brief smile, and only if the pun was halfway successful.

Westfield's wife was also present, but she was so quiet Lainie kept forgetting she was there, and the poor woman seemed to be an afterthought for her husband, as well. Karen Westfield was about Lainie's age and well dressed, but she was either half-asleep, texting under the table or highly medicated. She might have been pretty. It was hard to tell when all that was visible was a forehead and hairline. Lainie tried more than once to engage her in conversation, but received no response. It was a little weird. Westfield might as well have put a ring on a life-size doll, introduced her as his wife and propped her up at the table.

Of course, if the alternative to spacing out was socializing with Westfield, she understood Karen's defence mechanism. The arts patron stroked her knee under the table for the third time in the past hour and she jerked back in her seat. The impulse to kick was almost ungovernable. At her sudden movement, Richard looked at her and frowned questioningly. She forced a smile and shook her head. He had uncharacteristically put himself out to secure a major funds boost for her charity. She could sit down to dinner with an unsubtle lech for him.

Although if Westfield's hand crept any higher than her knee, she reserved the right to take sharp action.

Richard was still looking suspiciously from her to Westfield. "Where do you stand on the Grosvenor Initiative, Eric?" he asked, and Westfield's attention was thankfully diverted from her legs.

Lainie turned gratefully to answer a query from the society matron opposite about her usual schedule at the Metronome. "*So* interesting to meet someone in the *theatre*," with an inflection that suggested "the theatre" was a euphemism for something a bit more risqué. *That* type of unwanted attention she could handle.

After the dessert plates had been cleared by a hovering maid, Westfield looked at his wife for the first time all night. "*Karen!*"

She jumped and her head rose—pulled by the puppeteer's strings, Lainie thought despairingly. Karen stood, and it appeared the women were to be dismissed to coffee in a separate room. Because apparently this was *Downton Abbey*. She widened her eyes at Richard as she passed him and saw his lips twitch.

She'd hoped Karen would regain her personality and become magically talkative away from her husband's depressing influence, but no such luck. The woman sat down on an armchair in a very stately drawing room, crossed her legs and pulled out her phone. She *had* been texting under the table, then. That was a relief. Lainie had been imagining some sort of brainwashed Stepford scenario. She rather meanly hoped that Karen had a lover. A young fit one with table manners.

When she could no longer bear the social banter of the other two wives, she excused herself to find a bathroom. There were four to choose from on the second floor. She had dried her hands, reapplied her lipstick and was just closing the door when a masculine hand slipped around her waist and squeezed. She froze, her heartbeat picking up. The blunt-tipped fingers didn't belong to Richard.

Oh, God. How perfectly, hideously undignified and cliché.

HE FELT AS IF he were in the second act of a Sheridan play. Removal of the feminine element, followed by whiskies, cigars and subtle digs in the billiards room. Richard pushed away from the wall where he'd been observing the halfhearted game of snooker in progress. He checked his watch. Another hour, and they could leave without causing unnecessary offence.

And he could find a mutually satisfying way to make this up to Lainie.

The beginnings of a headache were thrumming in his temples. Abruptly, he moved his head, trying to relax the tension in his neck. He put a hand to his shoulder and massaged the ridges of bone.

After sitting at that dinner table, he was finding it difficult to remember why he wanted to keep on side with Westfield. And if he was right in his suspicions about what had been going on *under* the table, cordial relations were going to break down fast. He had been prepared to sacrifice a certain amount of personal dignity for the RSPA chair, but he drew a line well before exposing Lainie to sexual assault.

His eyes suddenly narrowed. Two minutes ago, Westfield had been standing at the bar, pouring another round of drinks. The liquor was now proceeding down the gullets of a couple of middle-aged stockbrokers, and their host had vanished.

Without bothering to excuse himself, Richard turned his back on the third stockbroker, who'd been trying to bore him into unconsciousness for the past quarter of an hour. He strode out into the hall, closing the door behind him. The women had gone upstairs. His head cocked, he stood tensely, listening.

At the sound of her muffled cry, he wasted no more time. Swinging nimbly around the bannister, he took the stairs two at a time.

When he found them, his frustration with the evening exploded into sheer fury.

PUTTING HER HAND over Westfield's wrist, Lainie pulled it away and turned around to face him, inwardly groaning. She had seen this scene played out on a hundred different sets, from melodrama to slapstick comedy, and it usually ended in torn clothing and at least one fat lip.

How to remove herself from this situation without completely scuppering Richard's chances at the RSPA chair?

She tried simple avoidance first. "Excuse me," she said evenly, going to step around him. She threw in a bit of marital guilt: "Your wife will be wondering where I've got to."

Westfield obviously had no conception of how to

follow a cue. He snorted and latched on to her again. "Karen never wonders anything. Except when I'm next going away on business and what present she'll get when I return."

Lainie seriously doubted that Karen waited impatiently for his return, even if he did come bearing duty gifts. "Yes, well, I should still—*mph!*"

The rest of her sentence was swallowed up in his mouth as he pushed her against the wall and kissed her. *Kiss* was too romantic a term for it. *Assaulted her*, to give things their proper name.

She tried to twist her face away, making a sound of disgust in her throat. Her hands pushed ineffectually at his barrel-like chest. The moment she got out of this, she was investing in a set of hand weights. Westfield's horrible clutching fingers started pulling at the hem of her skirt, which was thankfully too tight to rise above her knee. Then he yanked, and there was a distinct ripping sound.

Oh, I don't think so.

Her outrage was becoming tinged with genuine fright now. She kicked him and he grunted, but apparently a bit of violence just spurred him on. His mouth sought hers again, and she exclaimed in fury, shoving against him.

Finally—*and about bloody time*, she thought with unreasonable, panting anger—there was a loud, bitten-out curse from somewhere behind them and a swift movement. Westfield skittered away on his heels like a spooked crab, Richard's right hand fisted in the back of his jacket.

The older man went to speak, his face a dark unhealthy red, and Richard took a vicious step forward, angling his body in front of Lainie. She had a bizarre moment of déjà vu from the play. She was almost waiting for the clink of swords, and for Richard to burst out with a good old "you godforsaken knave!" or "blackguardly cur!"

"What the *fuck* do you think you're doing?" Richard's voice was low and deep. He looked at Lainie. She almost took a step back under the impact, and his anger wasn't even directed at her. "Are you all right?" he asked her tightly, and she nodded.

"Yes." Her hand—shaking, she realised—went unconsciously to the torn hem of her skirt, and Richard followed the movement. The muscle in his jaw jumped.

Westfield, who apparently had no instincts for self-preservation at all, continued to play to stereotype. "Just a bit of fun, my boy," he said, in an attempt at just-one-of-the-lads jocularity. "She didn't mind."

"Yes, I could see how much Lainie was enjoying herself. Pinned against the wall and screaming."

"She's been asking for it all night," said the stupidest man in London.

Richard calmly pulled back his fist and punched the other man on the bridge of his nose.

Lainie winced at the sound. Their dubious host let out a vaguely animalistic grunt. Blood dripped between his raised fingers as he glared daggers at Richard, but a muffled, distant laugh seemed to return him to some sense of his surroundings, and he didn't retaliate with his fists.

He jerked his chin toward Lainie, still clutching at his nose. "Don't be a fool, man. Throwing away a good opportunity for a woman like her?"

"And what kind of woman is that, exactly?" Lainie

asked, irritation breaking her out of a shocked trance. "One who can't be bribed with presents to let you touch her?"

Westfield's lips twisted. With blood settling into the grooves between his teeth, he was the stuff of nightmares. With his free hand, he reached into his pocket and pulled out a torn piece of newsprint, shaking it open. Lainie looked down at it and felt her skin creep. It was a page from one of the more disreputable tabloids, and the centre image was of a close-up of her from the Theatre Awards red carpet, looking very décolleté. He was actually carrying around boob shots of her in his pocket? Gross.

"Doesn't look too choosy and virtuous to me," Westfield said nastily, and their collective attention focused on the second photograph.

It was one of the ones taken with Will, and the paparazzo had caught them at an unfortunate gold mine of an angle. It appeared that Will had his hand in a place where most women would have qualms about being touched in public. Lainie's face was turned toward him—most likely to hiss at him to keep his distance—and anyone could be forgiven for thinking that they were kissing.

Richard gave the image one hard look. After a brief pause, he said, "Talk to her like that again and you'll seriously regret it." His voice hardened into lethal quietness. "And if you so much as shake her hand in future, I'll hear about it."

"Is that so?" Westfield was completely ignoring Lainie now, which seemed to put a final cap on his insulting treatment of her. He raised a scornful eyebrow.

"Well, you won't be hearing about an appointment to the presidency. Now or ever."

Richard's expression didn't so much as flicker. "I find the prospect of continuing to share a city with you sufficiently revolting. I have no desire to sit next to you in a boardroom." He held the other man's gaze with a cool stare. "Get her coat."

It was a blatant challenge. Showdown of the alpha males.

Men.

To her astonishment, Westfield drew in a sharp breath—and fetched her coat. He held it out to her with disdain, and Richard intercepted it. Gently turning her, he helped her slide it on. His hands rested on her shoulders, a reassuring, warm weight.

They left without a word to the other guests. Lainie doubted that Karen would notice their rude departure. She probably hadn't noticed their arrival.

Outside on the street, Richard exhaled sharply and his breath fogged in the crisp night air. He ran a hand through his hair, scrubbing the short curls as if he was dislodging dust and grime.

He looked at her, but before he could speak, she said, "I'm sorry."

Shock and regret were catching up with her, and she could very easily cry in front of him.

"For what?" he asked, and she couldn't read his tone.

"If you hadn't brought me tonight, you wouldn't have lost your chance at the presidency."

"The bastard invited you. And then assaulted you in his own home. *Christ.*" Richard's fingers closed into a fist against his scalp. "*I'm* sorry I let you in for that." Some of his control seemed to snap. His hands came

out and caught hers, pulling them up roughly to link
their fingers. "Do you think I want any favours from
a man who thinks he can put his hands all over my..."

Lainie stilled. "Your—what?"

Richard's jaw worked as he looked down at her.
"My..." Suddenly, he released her hands and cupped
her face, bringing her up on her tiptoes and her mouth
to his. His kiss was forceful and demanding—sheer
outraged male. Both Will and Westfield in one evening,
Lainie thought hazily as she kissed him back. She supposed it was pushing the point a bit far.

"Mine," he said. "Just mine."

Pulling back to take a much-needed breath, Lainie
rested her hands on his chest. "There's a distinct scent
of eau de caveman around here."

His only answer was to kiss her again. Then he
wrapped his arms around her waist and gave her a
simple hug, burying his face in her hair. "Are you sure
you're all right?" he asked, sounding more in control
of himself, and she relaxed a little.

"Yes. But I'm still sorry that it happened, Richard."

Richard touched the back of his finger to her cheek.
He lifted one shoulder dismissively. "It's a setback, no
more. Westfield has a lot of clout in the Society, but
he's not as indispensable as he thinks. He operates at a
purely financial level, and wealthy philistines are two
a penny in the City."

"Do you think that—"

Richard's phone vibrated in his pocket, cutting her
off, and he gave the screen an impatient glance. "Lynette." He checked his watch and frowned. "Who is
usually driving back from her parents' place in Man-
chester at this time. Hold that thought, Tig."

Lainie wrapped her coat more tightly across her chest as he answered with a brief, "Troy." Scuffing the toe of her shoe against the pavement, she was only half listening to his side of the conversation, her mind still replaying the horrors of what had gone on inside the house, when Richard seemed to freeze at her side.

It wasn't just that his body stilled. It was as if his entire personality iced over into a remote automaton.

She raised her eyes to his face and discovered him watching her. She didn't like the look.

"How much do they have?" Richard asked. The question was completely toneless. His gaze didn't budge from Lainie. She frowned back, trying to ask through her expression.

Pulling his key from his pocket, he beeped the lock on the Ferrari, jerked open the rear door and lifted his iPad from the backseat. He was still studying her with disconcerting impersonality while he brought up a web browser and started a news search.

"Yes," he said into the phone, and switched his gaze to the screen. A betraying nerve convulsed beside his eye. "Yes, I will." He ended the call without saying goodbye, and silently turned the iPad around to show Lainie.

It was a breaking news item in *London Celebrity*. Richard Troy's Secret Family Tragedy Revealed! blasted the headline, and then in smaller type below: *Late MP Sir Franklin Troy's 1994 "heart attack" shockingly outed as a suicide.*

Richard flipped the iPad over and continued to read the article. Lainie was unable to speak.

"Coincidence?" he said at last, almost casually. He closed the iPad with a decisive snap, and it might as well have been a sound effect for his fracturing temper. "Because I don't remember telling anyone else my private family business recently."

"I'm sorry." Lainie barely recognised her own voice. She wasn't even aware that she was going to speak until she heard the words. "I'm so sorry, Richard. It just… slipped out. There's no excuse."

"It just 'slipped out'?" Richard repeated with awful sarcasm. He was very pale. "You just 'accidentally' contacted the tabloids and mentioned that, by the way, that insane bastard Sir Franklin Troy shot himself."

"Does it say he shot himself?" Lainie was bewildered as well as absolutely horrified. How much digging had Will had time to do before he'd sent off his tattling email? And where would he have the resources? He was hardly MI5.

"No, it doesn't. I see you had enough circumspection to at least skimp on the details." He shook his head once, as if he'd sustained a blow. "*Why*?" he bit out. "It doesn't even make sense. It's completely out of character."

"I didn't tell the press." Lainie closed her eyes. "I would never do that."

"Then…what? My house is bugged? *London Celebrity* is hiring long-range telepaths now?"

"I told Will."

Richard went still again, and his fiery eyes went oddly blank. "You told Will."

"Yes." It was a strangled rasp. Lainie put out a hand to his arm, but wasn't surprised when he deliberately removed it. "He made me furious with something he said about you, and it just…slipped out. I'm sorry."

After a moment, Richard said, still without expression, "I'll take you home."

"Richard…"

He opened the door for her. With a last helpless glance at his impenetrable face, Lainie slowly got into the car.

It was the worst drive of her life. As they neared the familiar sights and lights of Bayswater, he asked without looking at her, "Did you tell him why?"

"*No*, I did *not*." Lainie jerked around in her seat. "Of course I didn't!"

"It'll probably come out anyway," Richard said, as if he was making a casual remark over the breakfast table as to the cunning inevitability of the British media. "It isn't the best foundation on which to campaign against Westfield's influence. Bad enough to have a father who was a known fascist about the arts. Not a good look when he's a vote-fiddler, as well."

Lainie put her hand to her forehead and said nothing.

When the car pulled up on her street, Richard walked her to the door. He was silently, remotely polite for the first time in their relationship. And she hated it.

Before he left, he looked down at her. A flash of intense emotion faded into indifference. "I suppose we got a bit carried away by the pretence."

She still didn't reply.

"It's easy to lose sight of reality when you're immersed in a role," he went on, echoing her once-upon-a-time sentiments. He paused and the muscle in his jaw jumped again. "However, I think that particular run is over."

It was a good exit line, delivered with so little emphasis that it avoided going too soap opera.

She didn't watch him drive away.

TEN

THIS WAS, NO DOUBT, the place in the script where Lainie was supposed to take to her bed, sobbing out her broken heart into a carton of ice cream. She had taken that option when Will had fractured her pride.

She wasn't letting go of Richard so easily.

After a terrible night's sleep, she got up on Monday morning and put on one of her favourite outfits. As a little confidence boost to start the day, a flattering jumper ranked dismally below a naked, sleepy cuddle with Richard.

Her bed smelled like his cologne. He'd left a shoot-'em-up spy novel on her coffee table. Her chocolate biscuit supply was suspiciously depleted. His presence was all over her flat.

Stuck fast in her heart.

She had left Bob's office, a hundred years ago, in a complete strop because she was going to have to put up with Richard Troy out of work hours. And he had changed her life—in every way—for the better.

She had to fix this.

God. She hoped she could fix this. Because if not—

She squeezed her eyes shut. She couldn't think about that.

She rang Sarah before her sister-in-law left for work. "You're a subcommittee member for the Literary Society," she said, without any preliminaries, and Sarah yawned. Lainie heard the sound of clinking china and cereal falling into a bowl.

"Good morning to you too. Was that a question or an accusation? Yes, I am, for my sins. Why? Do you need a book rec? I've heard good things about the new Booker Prize winner."

"And the Literary Society occasionally attends the same events as the Royal Society of the Performing Arts, yes?"

"Again, yes. Unfortunately, I do associate from time to time with the RSPA and the giant stick up their collective derrieres. I repeat: why?"

"I need contact details for the current president of the RSPA. I've already tried online. It's like looking for info on the Secret Service."

There was a pause and a crunch while Sarah ate a mouthful of her breakfast. "I imagine I can find out for you. Do I want to know what you're up to?"

"I just…" Lainie stared into her untouched cup of tea. She couldn't break. She wouldn't. This was too important. This was the rest of her life. "I need to put something right."

"I see." Sarah hesitated. "Didn't you say Richard was angling for the next chair of the RSPA?"

"Yes. He was. Is." Lainie sighed and shoved back a loose strand of hair. "Long, ugly story. I'll fill you in when I know how it's going to turn out."

Well.

Let it turn out well.

"I'll hold you to that. Hang on a tick. I'll make a few calls and get back to you."

Armed with an address from an amused Sarah, who said it was all jolly fun, really, like a spy film, Lainie splurged and took a taxi to Mayfair. She still had a few hours before she had to be at the theatre for a rehearsal with the other three principals.

Which at this stage was shaping up to be a right barrel of laughs. Will had left two messages on her phone. He'd sounded drunk in the first one and sulkily defensive in the second. She'd deleted them both, cutting him off halfway through an inadequate apology. She'd tried to call Richard, but his phone was off. The landline at his house had rung eight times before a breathless woman had picked up, sounding as if she'd either run up the stairs or been interrupted midorgasm. Fortunately for all of them, she had identified herself as Richard's housekeeper, thus saving her boss from castration.

No, Mrs. Hunt was sorry, but Richard wouldn't be available all morning. He was meeting with his agent and a PR team.

Ominous.

Lainie stared bleakly out the car window. As usual, it was raining. The weather was so wet and foggy that she couldn't even tell where they were for most of the journey. She tried to pick out familiar shops and landmarks, keeping her mind directly in the present, refusing to let it wander down dangerous alleyways that made her stomach feel hollow with anxiety.

Jeremy Steinman, the current president of the RSPA, was a retired barrister who lived in a block of mansion flats. Fortunately, he was at home. She had very little patience for anything else going wrong today. A tall, handsome man in his late sixties, he eyed her with twinkling curiosity as they shook hands. "Not that I'm not gratified to receive a visit from a reigning princess of the London stage," he said, smiling, "but to what do I owe the unexpected honour?"

Lainie hadn't really thought this through. She had just needed to do…*something*. Losing Will had led to an embarrassing, wallowing period of self-pity. Losing Richard was unacceptable. Ditto to treading all over his life goal.

This, at least, she could try to put right.

Her intention had been to assess the situation when she arrived and could see for herself what type of man Steinman was. If he was another Westfield, the mission was futile.

He was not another Westfield. Steinman's brown eyes were clear and kind. There was a gentlemanly dignity in the way that he regarded her. She put the chances of his groping her knee across the coffee table at zero.

She had come prepared to leave her own dignity at the door, to schmooze and network and be horribly fake if she had to. After a few minutes of conversation with Steinman, she decided to just be honest. Accepting his invitation, she sat down on a comfortable chair and she told him about their abbreviated dinner party with Westfield the night before. The way the other man had acted toward her, his parting sally to Richard, and the apparent ruination of Richard's chances at succeeding Steinman.

"I'm aware it's not very pretty behaviour on my part either," she said bluntly, nervously crossing her feet

at the ankles. "Coming here to tell tales. But it's unfair if this is the reason Richard loses his nomination.
I don't know if he's the lead contender." She paused,
but Steinman's face remained imperturbable. "But he
should have his chance. He's ambitious and...well, atrociously rude at times, but he gets things done and he
has integrity."

She didn't think it necessary to add the unspoken:
"Unlike some people."

Her decision to accost Steinman felt disastrously im-
pulsive as he regarded her in silence. At last, he smiled
ruefully and said, "Troy's a lucky man." He sobered.
"First of all, I sincerely apologise to you, Miss Graham,
on behalf of the Society, for last night's disgraceful behaviour. It will not be swept under the rug. And I'm not
at liberty to comment on the pending decision regard-
ing my successor, but I assure you that Troy will not
be blackballed through the prejudice of one member.
Regardless of the position that person currently occu-
pies on the committee."

She got the impression that Steinman wasn't the biggest fan of his veep either. Perhaps that was why he was
stepping down.

Lainie didn't particularly want a cup of coffee, but
she accepted Steinman's pleasant offer and stayed for
almost an hour, chatting about a number of current plays
and art exhibitions. It seemed less melodramatic than
marching into his house, pointing an accusing finger
and storming out again a few minutes later.

Halfway home on the bus, she changed her mind and
switched to the route for the theatre district. She felt too
antsy to lie around the flat. She would rather go early
to work and rope someone into reading lines with her.

Might as well earn a few goodwill points with Bennett while she was at a loose end.

She was relieved to find only a few tourists outside the side door of the Metronome. She paused for autographs and selfies, produced a *Mona Lisa* smile and noncommittal answer in response to questions about Richard, and headed straight for her dressing room. A team of builders were doing spot repairs on the upper floors, and she was grateful to get away from the noise. Her mood was precarious enough without constant hammering and drilling.

Sitting down at her vanity, Lainie checked her watch. Too early for Meghan to arrive yet. She wondered if Margaret was around.

She had been sitting there for less than thirty seconds when the door opened again without warning. "Before you chuck that at my head," Will said, nodding at the powder compact she held in her hand, "hear me out."

Lainie's fingers tightened until her knuckles bleached white. "Get out."

"No." Will's face was pale. He leaned back against the door as if anticipating her next move. "Listen."

"*You* listen." Lainie rose to her feet, so angry with him she was shaking. "I don't know what you thought you were doing." She let out a half laugh, half sigh. "And I mean that literally. I don't know *what* you thought were going to achieve."

"I don't know either!" Will burst out. He shoved a hand through his usually impeccable hair, and the gesture was so reminiscent of Richard that Lainie caught her breath. "I don't know," he repeated more quietly. He grimaced. "I was pissed. In every meaning of the word. The paps were there, and it just…"

"Slipped out?" Lainie suggested with biting irony.

"Would it help if I said again I was sorry?"

"I'm hardly the one who needs an apology."

"Well, I'm not apologising to bloody Troy!"

Lainie suddenly felt very tired. "No, I didn't expect you would."

Will reached out and touched her arm. "Lainie…"

She pushed his hand aside. "No. It wouldn't help if you said you were sorry, because you aren't. Not really. I can only assume this is exactly what you wanted to happen. I just hope you didn't think I would turn to you for comfort after Richard performed on cue and dropped me like a hot brick."

"I told you," he muttered, flushing. "I wasn't thinking at all."

"That, at least, sounds plausible."

Will's eyes narrowed. "So he's ended it?"

Lainie didn't reply, and he shrugged. "It's for the best."

"Thank you for that unbiased take on the situation," she said sarcastically. "I don't recall asking for a quote from you."

"Lainie, would you just—"

She cut off his exasperated rejoinder. "For the rest of this contract, I will love you and die for you on that stage. But when the curtain comes down, that's it. We have nothing left to say to each other."

A sense of the dramatic wasn't the sole prerogative of the men around here.

She fiercely shook her head when he began to protest. "No. Seriously, how could you? How fucking *dare* you go public with something you *knew* was private and…and hurtful? Not just to him. To me, as well. After everything you've done already. We are so *done*, Will."

He took a few deep breaths. Then he turned abruptly and left, closing the door behind him.

Lainie sank back down on the vanity stool and closed her eyes. For long moments, she just sat. She had been intimate with Will. Not only in bed, but in spending time alone together, in touching, in kissing, in conversation, she had shared part of herself with him. She hadn't loved him, but she had liked him. She'd been attracted to him.

Now that feeling seemed so negligible she could no longer recognise that version of herself. The Lainie of even a few months ago was a stranger past and gone, a girl who'd had no idea how much she was compromising.

The woman she was now knew what she wanted— and she intended to have him. She would pit her personality against his any day.

But he had a right to be seriously pissed. And she knew him. Even on his best day, Richard couldn't be described as charitably forgiving. He wasn't going to make it easy for her.

At noon, she heard the sounds of more cast and crew arriving, but she suspected Richard would make a point of being even later than usual today.

Her surmise was correct—they were already ten minutes into the main stage rehearsal by the time he turned up. He ignored Bennett's tantrum and seamlessly inserted himself into the scene. Lainie watched him out of the corner of her eye as she ran through her dialogue with Chloe. He looked tired. It was one of the few areas in which men were shortchanged by social mores: no camouflaging makeup unless they were in full costume. She had slathered about half a bottle of concealer over her own dark rings.

He was in an absolutely foul mood, as well. Even Bennett seemed mild-mannered by comparison. By the end of the first act and Richard's fourth sarcastic outburst, whispering broke out among the crew. Onstage, Will was tight-lipped, and the usually patient Chloe was beginning to look a bit frazzled around the edges. Lainie remained stoically unmoved, aided by the fact that Richard's temper was never directed at her. He had reverted to his previous habit of ignoring her existence.

With an annoyed look at Richard, Bennett called an intermission. "Do I look like a bleeding nanny to anyone here? If you're going to keep tossing your toys out of the playpen, Troy," he said nastily, "we can find you somewhere else to play."

Richard wiped the sweat from his forehead with the back of his wrist and drained a bottle of water. He didn't bother to acknowledge the dig.

Muttering under his breath, Will brushed past him, and Richard fixed him with a level, chilling stare. He didn't speak, however, and Will continued into the wings with one backwards, slightly uneasy glance.

Chloe played with the ends of her chic pixie cut and looked uncertainly from Lainie to Richard. "Do you want to come and get a coffee with me?" she asked Lainie, who smiled at her.

"Thanks. Maybe later."

Chloe's eyes went to Richard again. He was adjusting the strapping around the handle of his sword with jerky movements. "Okay," she said dubiously, and disappeared in the same direction as Will.

Lainie walked over to Richard's side and deliberately let her arm brush against his shoulder. He clenched his jaw under the thick growth of stubble. "In the interests of my new open-book policy, you should know that I had coffee and shortbread with Jeremy Steinman this morning."

Frosty veneer shattered on the first try. She allowed herself a tiny, satisfied smile when he turned on her. "You did what?" His glare was incredulous. "Where did you meet Steinman?"

"We bumped into each other in the pyjama section of Primark. We're both really into the onesie this year." Lainie rolled her eyes. "I met him in his lounge. When I went to his flat."

"You went to…" Words seemed to fail Richard for a moment. The man had so much to learn about her yet. "How did you even know where he lives?"

"I have my methods, Watson." Steeling her spine against his hostility, Lainie bent down and picked up his spare water bottle. He was big on hydration. Cracking the seal on the lid, she opened it and took a sip. "He was very nice. It's heartening to know that the RSPA doesn't turn all of its members into handsy, middle-aged perverts. I can stop worrying about your future."

Richard firmly removed the water bottle from her grip. "Get your own drink. Why did you call on Steinman?"

"To tell him about his VP's idea of a postprandial nightcap." Lainie flicked a speck of fluff from her jumper. She closed her fist when she saw that her fingers were unsteady. "And to provide you with a character reference in case he was under the impression that you're an impatient, irresponsible, sarky git. Which is only partly true."

"We *are* in a chipper mood today." The observation was cold.

"Why wouldn't I be?" Lainie's smile was nothing less than the raising of a metaphorical blade. Pure challenge. And no one was seeing through it to the insidious little ribbon of fear underneath. Because she was a damn good actress. Even Richard had said so, in a roundabout, somewhat half-assed way. "You were totally right yesterday."

Richard's eyes had narrowed. He merely raised an eyebrow in response, conceding no further advantage.

"You have no *idea* what you've let yourself in for."

Bennett came slamming back into the stalls from the administration offices, and she turned to resume her position on the stage. "By the way," she said, looking over her shoulder, "you were also *wrong* yesterday."

He remained entirely still.

"We've never pretended with each other, you and I."

From Bennett's perspective, the second act rehearsal was as disastrous as the first. Richard had stopped behaving like a first-class grump, but now seemed distracted. For the first time in their entire run, he had to be prompted on a missed line, which at least had the effect of shaking him out of his trance. The prompt received scant appreciation for her help when he scowled fiercely at her.

And the love scene between Lainie and Will, always awkward for at least one of the participants, now had the effect of making everyone in the vicinity uncomfortable, for one reason or another. Will almost kissed Lainie's chin instead of her mouth; his eyes kept straying to the dark, dangerous presence over her shoulder. Richard's hand tightened around his tankard with such force that the handle cracked and a grip had to run for a spare. Chloe's gaze kept darting anxiously between the three of them.

It was with utter disgust that Bennett called an end to the run-through. "But don't think you're going *any-where*. And get me a coffee," he snapped at Margaret, who rolled her eyes as she walked away. "We'll have an understudy rehearsal of the second act, so we can all compare performances and wonder why the fuck the four of you are receiving principal pay. At three o'clock, we'll take another stab at the final four scenes. Endeavour to make them less of a travesty. Tonight's audience paid to see a Bennett production, not a free-for-all at the local kindergarten."

Lainie followed Chloe into the wings, grateful to get out from under the lights and away from Bennett's critical eye for a while. It was uncomfortable, having her relationship dynamics witnessed and dissected by most of her coworkers.

Will tried to speak to her again, but she pulled her arm free of his grip. Richard stalked past them without even a sidelong glance.

She went back to her dressing room. She needed to gather her defences, raid her chocolate stash and get her act together. They couldn't behave like that onstage tonight. Professional standards didn't need to go out the window with her relationship status.

In a ridiculous flash of hope, her breath caught when someone knocked on the door. Sanity returned quickly. Richard was not going to seek her out right now for anything less than a civil emergency, and he wouldn't politely knock under any circumstances.

"Come in." If it was Will, she was letting fly with her powder compact this time.

The door opened and Lynette Stern came in. She surveyed Lainie where she sat sprawled in front of her vanity table, then sat down on the armchair and helped herself to a few chocolates. "We seem to have our first hiccup."

Lainie rescued the remaining chocolates before Lynette could eat all the strawberry creams. She made a pile of her particular favourites on the table. She was not having a good day. The prospect of comfort sex was exceedingly slim, so she was going to require her full quota of chocolate.

"No offence, but I don't recall agreeing to a ménage. 'We' is Richard and me. And *we* stopped being PR property quite some time ago. And I don't think he views the situation quite that lightly."

"And how exactly did the 'situation,' as you put it, arise?" Lynette warily bit the corner from a chocolate and peered into its interior. "Richard is far too wily to bleat to the press about his father. I was unaware of that particular blip in his history. He doesn't seem to have made a habit of sharing confidences over a cuppa. Logic would thus condemn you as the weak link."

Okay, not exactly a morale boost, but hard to dispute.

"It was my fault, yes." There was no point in mentioning Will's involvement. It still came down to her, and she didn't really want anything to do with him at the moment. She sighed. "How bad is it?"

"It's unfortunate. If it had been a less controversial suicide," Lynette said, with quite appalling callousness,

"I could easily have worked it to Richard's advantage. Father commits suicide due to mother acting like a tart. Sympathy abounds."

"Enjoying sex doesn't make you a tart," Lainie said. "I merely mention."

Lynette ignored the interruption. "However, nobody likes a dirty politician. People aren't all that fond of the politicians who *don't* fiddle with the public funds."

Lainie accidentally squashed a wrapped caramel in her clenched fist. "Has that got out?"

Bloody Richard. Always right.

"Sketchy allusions to dirty dealing. No specifics. Someone's been digging, but most of the records were sealed by a previous government. The press have got enough to run with, but nothing they can actually pin down."

She bit hard on her lower lip. "Exactly how bad *is* this for Richard?"

"The effect on his career should be minimal. Most people expect there to be a few skeletons in the Troy closet. Right now, he's the smouldering, brooding half of the West End's golden couple. The average blog reader isn't that interested in twenty-year-old gossip. They'd rather speculate on what goes on behind closed doors when you disappear into his mansion flat."

Lainie didn't take much comfort from the assurances. She could hear the giant looming *but*. She was almost afraid to ask. "What about the RSPA chair?"

"Too early to tell, but I've been poking my nose into a few nests, and little birds inform me that he's still Jeremy Steinman's favourite candidate. Steinman has a weighty influence. Nor would it help the committee if they openly punished the son for the father's sins.

It's fairly widely known in administrative circles that Richard doesn't share his father's prejudices." Lynette hesitated. "I should warn you, though, that when I left Richard five minutes ago, he was taking a call from a ministerial secretary about the conference next month. First impression—not looking good."

"Oh, fuck."

"I understand the sentiment." Lynette unwrapped another chocolate. "So I'll excuse your French."

"*Merci beaucoup*," Lainie snapped as she stomped toward the door, "but I didn't say *merde*."

What a shit of a day.

She tracked down Richard in a corridor outside the greenroom, which was still reverberating with noise from the builders' drills. He had just ended a call and was sliding his phone into his back pocket.

"What did they say?" She anxiously scanned his face, trying to read something into the bland mockery, searching for a trace of the shiver-inducing feelings she had caught lurking there recently. "They haven't dropped you from the conference, have they?"

"They have." His voice was remote. "It's understandable. The Ministry wants to keep media attention focused on their agenda. Not on the resounding irony of Franklin Troy's son waving a banner for increased cultural funding, after the father manipulated the system to line his own pocket. And made such a tremendously poor job of it, too."

Absently, she reached out and gripped a handful of his jumper. And hopefully a bit of accidental chest hair; otherwise, she wasn't thrilled about the visible flinch. "What can I do?"

"You can't do anything." He shrugged. "We turn the page and move on."

His indifference would have been harder to handle if it hadn't been for the look in his eyes. For the first time in his adult life, Richard Troy's acting ability was letting him down with a thump. Lainie caught her breath.

Before she could respond, a callboy stuck his head out of the greenroom door and politely delivered Bennett's order to return to the stage.

"Er, as soon as possible," the kid said, glancing uncomfortably between them. "Like, *now*, really."

Richard started to move past her and she caught his arm, ignoring his impatient glance. "This isn't over," she said warningly.

He gave her another long, tumultuous look before he turned abruptly and walked away.

Bennett foiled any further attempts at reconciliation that afternoon by turning completely neurotic. He refused to let any of the cast out of his sight, and started demanding peer critiques, as if they were doing group exercises back at drama school. If it wasn't for the fact that he was far too self-absorbed to care about his minions' sex lives, Lainie would have suspected him of deliberate troublemaking. For the last hour before they had to report to makeup and wardrobe, he forced Richard and Chloe to sit in the audience and observe the "total lack of chemistry" between her and Will. Richard sat with his legs stretched out in front of him, one ankle crossed the other. When Bennett requested constructive criticism of the love scene, he turned a stare on the director that could have whittled the edges from a diamond.

It wasn't the strongest performance of the run, but

they made it through the evening without incident. Lainie intended to tackle Richard again after the curtain call, but was ambushed backstage by Victoria and a couple of her friends, whom she'd completely forgotten were coming. She wouldn't have minded so much if it had been Sarah, but Vicky wasn't shy about expressing unsought and usually unwelcome opinions.

"Where's Richard?" Vicky looked around the dressing room and peered under the vanity table. As if they'd been interrupted midtryst and he might be crouching naked under there.

Lainie drew on every remaining scrap of patience. "He's gone home." Damn it.

Her sister-in-law checked her watch and exchanged knowing glances with the other women. "He doesn't hang around, does he?"

"He has an early meeting tomorrow," she lied stiffly, but the attempt at deflection only resulted in more arch smiles.

"Oh," said Vicky. *Another one bites the dust*, said her expression.

Lainie smiled serenely at her brother's ever so slightly unfortunate choice of wife.

Inwardly, she curled into a ball and reached glumly for the ice cream spoon.

RICHARD WAS WOKEN at nine o'clock by his phone, after lying awake until almost five. The first thing that registered on a conscious level was the faint scent of perfume. His vision was bleary; his eyes felt red and gritty from lack of sleep.

Red. He'd always associated his father with the colour red. The redness of rage. The red bloom of whisky. The red stain of blood.

Of shame.

Red. Lainie's hair, smooth and silky around his fingers. He clenched his jaw as he stared up at the ceiling.

Everything was temporary. It didn't last—the bad.

Apparently the good was equally short-lived.

Without looking at the phone, he reached out and grabbed it from the side table.

"Yes?" His tone didn't encourage loquacity. He was going to be running on caffeine and obstinacy today.

"Richard? It's Greg. Were we supposed to meet this morning? I'm outside your front door, but there's no answer."

Fuck. Richard threw off the bedcovers and reached for the trousers he'd left on the floor. "I slept in. Sorry. Two minutes."

When he opened the front door, his assistant was holding a briefcase in one hand and a tray of coffees and bakery bags in the other. The daily papers were wedged under his elbow. Richard looked at the disposable cups and his mouth curved. "Expect a Christmas bonus. I'll have a shower and meet you in the study."

They were halfway through a stack of financial grant contracts, and Greg Worth had doubled the size of his impending bonus by not mentioning the morning tabloids, when the doorbell rang. The document Richard was holding creased under the pressure of his grip.

Greg glanced at him. "I'll get it, shall I?"

"Thanks." He tried to concentrate on the contract, but the words swam into illegible nonsense. He threw it down on the desk in disgust, and turned to wait for her.

Lainie came in ahead of Greg, offering his assistant

a polite smile when the other man bowed out, closing the door behind him.

"Good morning." Her voice was quiet.

Richard noted the heaviness around her eyes, which she'd tried to hide with makeup. Her hair was in a long, thick plait over one shoulder, and she was wearing a woollen bobble hat. Probably hand-knitted by Rachel Graham. There had been a basket of wool and knitting needles at her parents' house. Lainie came from the sort of family where people made things for each other, gifted things simply because they wanted to.

The two of them were worlds apart.

"Good morning." He sat down on the edge of the desk and nodded toward a leather chair. "Do you want to sit?"

Lainie's air of trepidation was rapidly dissolving into more familiar sparks. "No." The line of her pretty mouth was mutinous. "I want you to stop treating me like I'm here to audit your taxes."

He surveyed her. "If you were here to audit my taxes, I would have offered you a coffee."

A flush rose up her neck, and the urge to follow it with his lips was a sharp twist in his gut.

She inhaled deeply, visibly gathering her patience. She jerked her chin toward the closed door. "Was that your assistant?"

"Yes."

"He was very polite. You haven't told him, then?" She looked at him pointedly. "That you think we've broken up?"

She could dig in with her fingers and push his buttons like no one else, and she knew it, but he ignored the bait. "It's none of his business. He's my assistant, not my psychologist."

She started to reply, then paused. "Do you *have* a psychologist?"

"On and off since I was fourteen." He shrugged. "I was okay with any suggestion that minimised the chances of turning into my father." He lifted an eyebrow at the curious look on her face. "What? You disapprove?"

"No. Not at all. I was just thinking that I don't give you enough credit."

Unsettled, he moved irritably and dislodged a morning newspaper from the pile on the desk.

Lainie looked down where it had fallen. "Is there… more today?"

There inevitably would be. The media was relentless. They would wring any profitable topic dry. "I haven't looked."

She pulled hard on the end of her plait. "I had a call from a reporter this morning. Wanting to know if I'm standing by you in your time of trouble—" she seemed barely able to get it out "—or ratting on the sinking ship. His actual words. He's left three more messages since."

A pulse of fury penetrated the cold, bleak feeling in his chest. "What's his name?"

"Anthony…something."

"Not Sutcliffe?"

"That's it. Do you know him?"

"He usually works for the *London Arts Quarterly*. They don't scavenge for cheap sensationalism. He must be freelancing. I'll deal with it. He won't be harassing you again."

She came closer to him, reaching out to touch his

arm. He looked down at her fingers. He wanted to hold them. He wanted them tangled in his hair, flirting with his lower lip, stroking his back, running down his chest.

He needed her to leave.

HE WAS DISTANCING himself again. She could almost see his features icing over, after that protective reflex when she'd mentioned the stalker reporter.

"Richard…" God, she didn't know what to say. She'd still been so *determined* when she woke up this morning. So insensitive, really. She'd thought she could come here and *make* him forgive her.

She'd been prepared for his usual armour, the frosty shell and snotty comments. She hadn't expected him to look so…tired.

"I'm sorry." She held his arm tighter, and he didn't push her away this time. He didn't do anything. "You know I'm sorry. I would never hurt you on purpose. You *know* that. I realise you don't always listen when people speak, but you at least know me as well as that by now."

"Lainie—"

"What can I do?" She bit her lip, hard. "Seriously, what can I do? I can't… I can't just *undo* it. I can't stop them writing about it."

"Do you think that's what matters?" The words seemed to have been pulled from Richard with force. He bent down and picked up the paper, jerking it open. There was a large article on the third page with an appropriately lurid headline: Richard Troy Recalls Finding Father's Body. "Factually incorrect, as usual. By sheer chance, I wasn't the one who found him. It was a Monday. When I was home from school, I was expected to report to my father's study on Monday afternoons to discuss what I'd achieved in the previous week. And what I could do better during the next." His lip curled. "I was late. I got caught up at a friend's house. The house-keeper found him. Screamed the place down like some bit part from *Midsomer Murders*."

She was horrified. "Did he *intend* for you to find him?"

"No. It just wouldn't have occurred to him. I doubt he gave me a second thought that day." Richard sat down on the desk again.

How could he be so *calm* about that? He should be outraged.

He deserved so much better.

"I'm ashamed of him." There was no heat in the statement. "Not because of the suicide, but for every-thing he did before that. Everything he was. It's shame-ful." He met her gaze. "But I'm doing my best to ensure he doesn't have a lasting impact. Not on me. Not on anyone. The press can say what they like. They can dig out the truth—they can make up something more sale-able. If anything, it'll probably give my career a boost. An interesting dark past. Finally—the reason why he's such a bastard."

"But—"

"But it came from *you*." He shook his head before she could interrupt. "I know. I know you didn't do it on purpose, Tig."

At the sound of that *stupid* nickname, Lainie's throat constricted. She felt a burning sensation at the back of her eyes and swiped her thumb across her lashes.

"I still feel like I got shafted. By my lover, my best friend and my family, all at once." His mouth twisted. "All you."

Oh God. This was the problem with falling head over heels for a spectacularly good actor. He had a way with words that could cut her off at the knees.

"I trusted you. Against my better judgement."

Ouch.

The room was so quiet that she thought she could hear the sound of her own heartbeat.

"However this started—" Richard was grim "—I can't be your rebound relationship."

"Rebound…?" she repeated blankly.

"Farmer."

"Uh, has nothing to do with this."

"Doesn't he?"

"No. He doesn't." His face didn't change. He didn't believe her. Maybe didn't *want* to believe her. "Do I throw your exes in *your* face all the damn time? What, am I just never going to be allowed to forget that mistake?"

"Do you want to forget about it?" Dark cynicism.

Lainie folded her arms, as much in need of comfort as to express her frustration. "I had." She spoke slowly. "I almost had forgotten about the whole thing. I was too busy being happy."

She sought for the right words. They were there, but she couldn't say them. Not right now. "God. You've kind of got me over a barrel here." She looked at the floor. "There are things I was going to say, and now I can't, or they'd turn into bargaining chips. Like I'm just using them to get you to forgive me. If you even believed me." She lifted her head, met the intensity of his gaze. "I won't cheapen my feelings like that. They're worth more than that."

That caused a flicker of expression, but the cynicism

was still deeply engrained when he spoke. "Sounds like a cop-out."

Right.

She stood up straighter. "I'm going now." She held up her hand with her thumb and forefinger an inch apart. "Because you're *this* close to pissing me off. And I don't want to have more things to apologise for later."

She turned at the door. He was still and watchful. "But I wouldn't breathe too easy. This is not me giving up on us." It was a vow. "I won't turn my back on you."

She wasn't even tempted to cry on the Tube. She was beyond that. Fortunately, it wasn't too full and she was able to find a seat. The exhaustion was a constant tug at her mind and muscles.

She couldn't think. It was as if she was standing at a crossroads. Her life could go one of two ways from this point, and she didn't dare visualise the dark route, in case it was encouraged into existence. The words teased at the recesses of her mind: *What does my future look like, if he can't get past this?*

An elderly woman took a seat opposite her. She was carrying a mesh bag filled with cans of cat food, her hair was sticking straight out and her black trousers were covered with pet hair.

Lainie chose not to interpret that as a bad omen.

RICHARD DISMISSED GREG early after Lainie flounced out, plait flying, almost crackling with indignation and determination. He sat in the study for a long time, thinking. In a totally misguided move, he went so far as to smoke one of the cigars on the desk.

It was totally rank, did nothing to help clarify his thoughts, and he felt sick for the rest of the morning.

But by the time he left for the Metronome, his coat buttoned up to his throat against the cold, he was finally being honest with himself.

ELEVEN

London Celebrity @LondonCelebrity. 3h
*Emergency services called to the
Metronome Theatre.
We're investigating live at the scene.*

"No. No." BENNETT THREW down a wad of papers in disgust. He had abandoned his seat in the stalls and was pacing up and down on the stage, to the visible annoyance of Richard and disconcertion of Will. He gripped violently at what little remained of his hair. Lainie could see where the rest of it must have gone. "Troy and Farmer, get out. Cool off in your dressing rooms. Take a bit of time to reflect. See if they're hiring at Waitrose. Lainie and Chloe—ten-minute break, then get back here for another run-through of scene four."

Lainie exchanged speaking glances with Chloe. She thought they'd been doing fairly well this time. Bennett was obviously not in a mood to agree.

Will put a hand on the edge of the stage and jumped into the orchestra pit—presumably to have a word with someone, not out of sheer frustration with their director. Bennett was turning into the West End's answer to Big Brother. Every time she turned around, he was there, watching, carping and criticising. They had all been run ragged from the moment they'd entered the theatre.

She finally summoned the courage to look at Rich-

ard. She had been a blatant coward for the past ninety
minutes, not in the mood to sustain another encounter with the Ice Man. To her surprise, he was looking
back at her. And the *way* he was looking at her kindled
a cautious spark of optimism. Deep, searching intent.
She couldn't read exactly what he was feeling, but he
was letting himself feel *something*. That was a step up
from this morning.

He tossed his sword aside and started to walk toward her. Dispensing with the lethal weapon. Also a
good sign.

Lainie checked to make sure Bennett was otherwise
occupied, and met Richard halfway. She could smell the
faint scent of his cologne—deep, spicy and masculine.
There seemed to be new creases around his eyes and
mouth. She wanted to put her arms around him.

Unsure whether he would let her hold him or if he'd
just chuck her into the orchestra pit with Will, she refrained.

"Lainie—"

She interrupted him, spoke quickly to get the words
out before he frosted over again or said something to
provoke her. "Look, I just want you to know. When Will
broke up with me—" she rolled her eyes "—well, *in-
directly* broke up with me, I was embarrassed. I didn't
know about Crystalle. Other people did. A lot of people. I felt stupid, and really naïve, and…and *small*. But
I was no more upset about losing Will, as a person, than
I was about my first boyfriend at school." She winced.
"Less, probably. I was a very emo teenager."

"Lainie, you don't have to—"

"Yes. I do. For a very short amount of time, Will
made me feel like I was worth nothing. I won't have him

doing the same thing to you. Especially since *you've*
made me feel like *me* again."

The fierceness in Richard's eyes gentled. He touched
her then, lightly, his palm lifting to cradle her cheek,
and her own eyes stung.

"Richard." It was Margaret, looking harassed. "Sorry
to interrupt. I need a word about the new set change."

His fingers tightened, unintentionally biting into her
jaw before he released her. He blew out a breath, tearing his gaze from her to acknowledge Margaret. "Yes.
What is it?"

Aware of the hint of curiosity in Margaret's side-
glance, and in desperate need of some fresh air, Lainie
went out the back door by the props room. It opened
into a bleak little side alley, lined with discarded ciga-
rette butts and crisp packets, but it was quiet. The wind
whipped through her loose hair and down the front of
her jumper. She crossed her arms and bounced a few
times at the knees, trying to keep warm. And almost
leapt out of her new ankle boots when the door banged
open behind her.

The familiar scent and feel of Richard's cashmere
coat thumped over her shoulders.

"If you have to stand out here in five-degree weather,
put on a bloody coat." He spun her around, jerked up
her chin and kissed her hard on the mouth. "Bennett's
blown his fuse again." His breath was warm against her
cold lips as he spoke. "Your presence is required." He
looked into her eyes. "We'll talk later."

He left her flushed, breathless and definitely not
cold.

As kisses went, it wouldn't make her personal top
ten. For one thing, there was still an edge of temper

under the surface, and angry snogging didn't really rev her engine the way it seemed to for vintage romance heroines. He'd also caught her by surprise, and she'd bitten her tongue.

But, for the first time all day, she was smiling when she returned to the marginal warmth of the back hallway.

With Richard and Will effectively banished to the naughty step, the atmosphere onstage was a lot more relaxed. However, by the time she and Chloe had run through the same scene four times, to scant appreciation from Bennett, Lainie was equally ready to take refuge downstairs.

"You despise her!" Bennett sounded as if he was at the end of his rope. He gestured at Chloe in exasperation. "This is sheer bloody vengeance, ladies, not a frigging tea party."

Casual sexism was rampant in the workplace.

Lainie frowned, Chloe put a sassy hand on her hip— and an ancient, supposedly defunct gas pipe exploded in the greenroom.

The actual blast wasn't that alarming. It sounded more like a large car backfiring than anything else. There was a moment of blank surprise.

The tremendous *crack* and crash that followed ten seconds later shook the stage. The Metronome's excellent acoustics carried the deafening rumble clear to the cheap seats in the back. It was as if an express train had taken a wrong turn off the Piccadilly line and rammed straight through the theatre. Lainie put out a hand and grabbed at the nearest support, which happened to be Chloe's shoulder.

In the intense quiet of the aftermath, she heard a faint crackling and spitting sound through the wings.

Then the shouting began.

"What the hell was that?" The bemused question was spoken right near her ear. She wouldn't otherwise have made out the distinct words above the rising clamour.

Bennett's deep bellow proved useful for once. His voice cut through the chaos like a guiding foghorn in the mist. "Everybody *out*. Front exit. Gather in the street. Carson—roll call."

"But—what's happened?" Chloe sounded bewildered.

The back of the stage seemed to be full of people in work overalls, jostling aside other people holding clipboards and phones.

"Chloe. Lainie." Margaret was there again, her face pale, her arms outstretched to herd them down into the stalls.

"*Jesus Christ*." Someone spoke from the wings. "The floor's caved in."

A pause. An authoritative, rapid-fire question: "How many people were down there?"

"Troy and Farmer, for sure. Maybe others. I don't know. I'm sorry. I don't know."

The floor of the greenroom was the ceiling of the principal dressing rooms.

Lainie acted on autopilot. She was physically unaware of her feet as she began to walk forward, toward the wings, toward Richard. In her strangely calm mind, it seemed perfectly logical that she could just reach through the hole in the floor and pluck him out.

"*Lainie*." Chloe was grabbing at her elbow. A masculine hand was closing around her upper arm.

Why was nobody going in there?

And she didn't seem to be getting anywhere. She was going backwards. Literally. Even when she was outside on the street, the cold wind biting against her cheeks, she didn't realise how hard she was struggling.

It had happened too quickly. Her mind couldn't catch up with her instincts. Which were urging her to go. Back. Inside.

Tourists were looking at her. People were talking to her. Bill, the props master, was hugging her, which seemed a bit inappropriate. She kicked him, with vague violence, and he yelped.

"If you see a posh prick in a silk shirt in there," he said to someone, in his strong Geordie accent, "tell him to get his arse out here and deal with his own bloody woman."

Obviously, it was ridiculous. She wasn't Lara Croft. She would probably end up falling headfirst into the basement. Intellectually, she knew that. *Intellectually*, she was aware that other people, including Will, could also be inside. Under that floor.

She had no emotional reserves to focus on anyone except Richard.

She really hadn't known that she loved him this much.

People in uniform were streaming into the Metronome. They didn't have tickets.

She had *admired* that death trap. It had seemed to be full of...to be full of romantic ghosts.

She started to shake. She couldn't breathe.

Richard was probably buried under a pile of bricks, and she was having her first ever panic attack, in the middle of a busy London road.

A camera flashed, and she winced.

"Lainie?" Chloe's face appeared right in front of her own, nightmarishly close. The whole thing was a nightmare. And Chloe was almost forty years old, and had no lines on her face at all.

What was up with that?

Lainie wasn't even thirty, and she already had permanent stress creases in her forehead. Probably crow's-feet as well, after today.

Sanity began to return—and with it, crushing horror.

"Oh God," she whispered. "Oh God. Chloe."

Chloe took her hands and gripped them tightly. Her voice was calm and cool as she proved herself once and for all the mother of a teenager, used to hysterics. "They'll be fine, Lainie." She gave Lainie's hands a single, forceful shake. "Keep it together. They'll be fine."

Lainie's attention returned to the façade of the theatre. It looked so innocent. If she raised her gaze above street level, where emergency services personnel were gathering in a buzzing cluster, like the epicentre of a beehive, it looked like any other day.

She was afraid to even blink, in case her whole world came crashing down when she closed her eyes.

IT WAS A MEASURE of how bad the past couple of days had been, that when Richard's dressing room collapsed around him in a dusty pile of rubble, his primary reaction was irritation.

His Wi-Fi connection had kept timing out, which a few seconds earlier had seemed like the pinnacle on the mountain of crap he'd been dealing with for the past forty-odd hours. He was halfway out the door, in search of a stronger signal, when everything went to hell. It was an implosion rather than an explosion. The room literally seemed to buckle, folding in on itself like something out of *The Matrix* before it shattered.

He ended up on his knees, his eyes wet and stinging with grit, the ground quivering beneath him. Strangely, he was most aware of the hiss of an old-fashioned exposed lightbulb as it swayed and flickered from a broken beam. It was nearly impossible to see anything in the gloom, and difficult to breathe in the dense air.

He struggled to his feet, but had to bend at the waist. What was left of the ceiling in the hallway had lowered to proportions that even fifteenth-century cottage-dwellers would have found claustrophobic. The electrics were just barely hanging in there, but most of the lights had shattered.

What the everlasting fuck...

Richard could hear his own breaths, loud and rough in the stillness. He could hear nothing from the floors above. It was horrifically eerie. He didn't know how much of this section of the theatre was still standing. He couldn't think about that, couldn't think about Lainie, or he would lose his mind.

He braced one hand against the far wall, then snatched it back as he felt the stones move. Rubble had spilled over the length of the hallway, blocking the way to the north stairs. His dressing room, to his left, was scrap metal and broken mortar. There was only one way to go.

He tripped and stumbled several times in the dim light. It was slow progress as he inched forward, wary of each careful step as the building shuddered around him. Dust clogged his nose, and he took a glancing blow to the shoulder from falling stone.

He'd once done an independent film set in a bombed hotel during the Second World War, and the staging had not been entirely dissimilar. It was a lot less enjoyable without the cameras and crew.

He crawled over a pile of bricks, got his first glimpse of stronger light and realised that the south hallway was intact. If he hadn't already been on his knees, he would have dropped down in gratitude.

Behind him came a low, rumbling, metallic groan, as if the Metronome was in its dying throes and wasn't going to go out quietly.

It almost drowned out the faint cry for help. He so nearly didn't hear him.

Richard froze, listening, his eyes fixed on dingy, beautifully solid walls and floorboards, every instinct of self-preservation urging him forward. He turned his head, looked at the shivering wreckage. It was going to come down.

Oh, *hell*.

Despite the mess they'd made post-collapse, the walls had been thin. He'd heard the sounds of an iPad game next door, and it hadn't been that long ago. Fifteen minutes at most. He was on his feet again. He took a step back.

"Farmer." His voice echoed down into the depths of the ruined corridor.

A faint scuffling noise in the distance, unmistakable this time.

The Metronome might have the structural stability of Jenga blocks, but it didn't have man-size rats scrabbling in the walls.

All he could think of in that moment was Lainie's

face. The look in her eyes when she'd told him about her sister.

The prospect of telling her that she'd lost someone else.

Because *she* was all right. She had to be. Any other outcome was totally unacceptable.

He went back.

Moving as quickly as possible, trying to keep his weight away from the fragile remains of the walls, he retraced every slow, painful step.

When he found where the other dressing room door should be—and was not—he swallowed on a nauseated wave of dread.

"Farmer?" he said again, sharply. It sounded shockingly loud, and startled his brain back into some sense of normality. "Will!"

A strange sound, between a moan and a gasp. He fought his way through the heavier wreckage in his path. Something sliced into his foot, but he ignored the pain from the shallow cut.

He found his castmate under a wooden beam. The gods continued to shine on Wonder Boy, he was relieved to see. The light at this end was so weak that the vacuous Ken doll face was a white blur.

"You all right?" Richard bent at his side and tested the weight of the beam, trying to see if Will was actually trapped or if he was just shocked into immobility. He felt around the side of the beam, hoping it wasn't supporting anything essential, because it was going to have to move. It was wedging the other man's leg against the far wall. "Farmer. For the first and hopefully only time, I'm going to need you to talk to me."

"What?" Will sounded dazed. His voice was hoarse. "What happened?"

"In the immortal words of Radiohead, 'go and tell the king that the sky is falling in.'" Richard got down on his haunches and braced himself. "Taking a reckless guess, the builders really cocked up in the greenroom. On the count of three, move your right leg back toward your chest. One...two...*three*!"

He heaved the end of the beam upward, just about dislocating his own shoulder in the process, and Will shoved himself free. Richard hauled him the rest of his way to his feet. They were bent over like a couple of elderly golfers, both of them far too tall for what was now basically a hole in the ground.

Inevitably, because Richard was reaping all sorts of cosmic payback for his past sins today, the other man began to panic.

"Oh God," he said, and the words rose in pitch. "Oh-GodOhGodOhGod."

"Not to be insensitive to your religious needs," Richard said sarcastically, "but if you let me know when you're finished praying, perhaps we could get going. I'd prefer to be out of here when the rest of this comes down."

"Oh God." Will had turned into a broken record. And a bloody annoying one, at that. Presumably, the foot-stamping was a nervous tic, but it was a poor idea in a structurally unsound space. It was seriously beyond him what Lainie had ever seen in the guy in the first place. "Oh God, we're trapped. Nobody knows we're down here."

Richard gave him a shove to get him moving. "First of all, *everybody* knows we're down here. You haven't left a room quietly since you passed out drunk at the wrap party for *Fields of Justice* in 2010. Watch your head."

Will turned and grabbed his arm, his fingers biting into Richard's wrist. "Do you think this is *funny*, you arsehole?"

"I don't get my kicks from having you rub up against me in the dark, no. Would you back the fuck off? We're not *that* short on space."

"We're fucking *buried alive*. How the fuck do you think we'll get out of here? The whole thing could come crashing down." He was almost hyperventilating. "Jesus. I'm going to die with *you*. What a fucking joke."

"*Or* we could just keep moving down into the completely intact south hallway and use the old fire escape."

Silence.

"Oh." After a pause, Will said lamely, "I've hurt my leg."

"Is it broken?"

"No."

"Then if you think I'm carrying you, you're mistaken."

In the end, he did have to get far too close for comfort. Will was dragging his leg and their pace was too slow. Dust and debris was falling far more rapidly now. Richard pulled Will's arm over his shoulder and took the brunt of his weight.

"Just move," he gritted out, ignoring the whinging protests that ensued. His nerves were a taut wire, ready to snap at the slightest provocation.

"But—"

"*Shut up.*"

His muscles were burning when they finally crossed

the boundary into relative safety, the adrenaline firing off electrical impulses that made him twitch and jump like water on hot steel. The defunct fire escape had been boarded over. Richard leaned against the wall to catch his breath. It felt reassuringly solid against his back.

"You knew the way was clear." Will suddenly looked up from his half crouch on the floor. He seemed to have regained some of his wits, which was fortunate. He didn't have many to spare. His expression was odd. "You must have—You were already out."

Richard closed his eyes on a wave of exhaustion.

"Did you actually come back for me?"

"Farmer. Seriously. Just shut up." Gathering the last of his strength, he started to pull at the boards. He was banking on the wood and nails being as decrepit as the rest of the Metronome. One piece broke away and he tossed it aside.

Will belatedly got up to help. As they worked side by side, in cooperation for probably the last time, he spoke without looking at Richard. "She didn't love me, you know."

Richard clenched his teeth. He viciously yanked down another board.

"I hurt her, and I'm sorry. But she didn't love me." Will's lips were a thin line. "I can see the way she looks at you." He threw down a jagged scrap of wood. "Just— start looking back."

Richard turned his head. Will's face was etched with a mixture of annoyance and resignation.

"It's all there. Just look at her."

IT TOOK FIFTEEN MINUTES for someone to remember the existence of the old fire escape. Their overall disaster response had been a bit of a fail. If the show must go on, Bennett would probably start doing fire and earthquake drills, which might not be a bad idea.

The entire company was in panic mode, and for some people it was a slight anticlimax when the tragic victims suddenly ambled out from the side alley. Will was hobbling on one foot, propped up between the two firemen who had found them breaking down the boarded-up door. Richard was also limping, but walked without assistance. There was a small smear of blood on his forehead. Both men were filthy and dishevelled. Otherwise, they looked fine.

Lainie's knees almost gave out.

Through jostling crowds and swimming vision, she met Richard's gaze, and saw the intensity of his relief. Silently, they stared across the chaos at one another.

Then he had the barefaced nerve to *wink* at her, picking a really bad time to become flirty, and avoided a punch on the nose only through distance.

They were taken away in an ambulance while she was still stuck behind the police barrier. Chloe drove her to the hospital in her red vintage Morris. She felt sick in the car and impatient with the delays. They were stuck in traffic for almost forty-five minutes. Her hands shook as they circled the block over and over again, trying to find a parking space. She wished she could just pull an *I Dream of Jeannie* and blink straight to Richard's side.

They bumped into Margaret in the hospital foyer.

"Everyone's fine," she told them, relief heavy in her voice. "All safe and accounted for. We were worried about Sally, one of the interns, but they found her on Tottenham Court Road. Thirty percent off American-brand makeup at Space NK," she added sardonically.

"And Bob's on form. He's already contacted our lawyers about litigation." She squeezed Lainie's arm. "Richard and Will are okay. Minor bumps and bruises."

Lainie nodded tightly. She was going to need to see that for herself, within touching range.

However, when she marched up to a nurses' station and asked to see her boyfriend, she somehow ended up in Will's ward. The gossip magazines in the staffroom must be out-of-date.

She stayed anyway, for a few minutes. In hindsight, not caring if her former boyfriend was flattened like a pancake as long as her new boyfriend emerged intact was pretty bad.

"Yeah, I'm all right." Will's voice was raspy, and his leg was elevated and bandaged, but overall he looked quite pleased with himself. He'd been out of the ER for ten minutes and a smitten fan had already sent a shiny Get Well Soon balloon to his room.

The animation drained out of his face when he admitted, "Thanks to Troy." Slowly, he said, "He came back for me. He could have got out straightaway."

God. Richard.

"He *is* okay?" Lainie was desperate for reassurance.

"Oh, he's fine. He's a heroic *dick*, but he's fine." He grimaced. "You'd better warn him I'm going to thank him in person, properly."

"You might want to wait a while." Her halfhearted smile was wobbly. "His body has probably had enough shocks for one day."

"You haven't seen him yet?"

"No, I—No."

Will watched her. "You should go. He'll be wondering where you are."

"I know." Lainie looked back at him. "Will, I…" She sighed. "Do you need anything?"

"Yeah." He grimaced. "But I don't really know what to do with it when I get it. Do I?"

She was silent, and he shrugged and lifted his phone. "I'll be fine. You know me. Never short of company."

"Oh, I know." She poured him a glass of water before she left the ward and went—finally—in search of Richard.

She found him in a single room—naturally, Richard Troy would never be expected to bunk up in a mixed ward with the hoi polloi. Lynette Stern, Alexander Bennett and Bob Carson all stood around his bed, in deep discussion about the extent of the damage backstage and whether it would require a complete relocation of the play. Richard, naked to at least the waist and covered with smudges of dust and dirt, looked exhausted and cross.

Their eyes met. With a muffled sound—and completely ignoring the audience by the window—Lainie launched herself straight onto the bed and into his arms. They closed around her, his hold brutally tight. Her face shoved into his neck, and she breathed in the strong musty smell that completely eliminated his usual comforting scent.

Richard's hand came up to cradle the back of her head. "Shut the door behind you," he said to the others. Through her tears, Lainie choked on a relieved snort and elbowed him. Sounding as if he was rolling his eyes, he added, "Please."

Lynette hid a smile and ushered out the still-arguing Bennett and Bob. Lainie increased the strength of her hug, and Richard smoothed his palm over her tangled hair. "About time you made an appearance." His deep, velvety actor's voice was temporarily a dust-shredded ruin. "I was going to give you three more minutes and then come looking for you."

"You probably shouldn't be walking around," she said to his rough cheek, her eyes closed.

"My limbs are intact and functioning. No thanks to Farmer's bruised knee and all fifteen stone of the rest of him." A tearing cough contracted Richard's chest, and she touched his bare ribs.

"It's not going to help if you come down with pneumonia. Don't tell me the nurses were so desperate for a look at your pecs they didn't give you a gown."

It was Richard's turn to snort. "I'm not sharing a backless nightie with five hundred previous occupants."

Typical. Lainie couldn't help smiling at that, but she still had to stop herself from clutching him again, just to feel him there, reassuringly solid.

Her fingers curled in his chest hair. "Are you naked under there?" She took a sneaky peek under the sheet. He was wearing boxer briefs. He also had nice thighs. She rubbed one affectionately, and he pressed an open-mouthed kiss to the side of her neck.

"Will's fine." Lainie's own voice was still husky with tears. "Thanks to you." She swallowed. "But if the theatre ever explodes again, don't let the roof drop on your head. I swear to God, Richard, if you do this to me again, I'll throw a fit that will make Sadie Foster look like frigging Pollyanna."

Richard's eyes were fixed on her face. He slowly played with a strand of hair under her ear, tickling her throat with it.

"I thought you were going to die."

He pressed her palm flat against his chest, where his heart beat in a strong, regular rhythm. His thumb caught the moisture under her lashes before it had a chance to fall. "Don't cry, Tig," he said quietly, which only made her more hopelessly teary. "You might finish me off completely."

"Don't even joke about it, you insensitive bastard," she said, pushing at him. "Richard."

"I was worried about you too." He shook his head. "*Worried*. I was losing my mind."

"Ditto. I was ready to charge in there and dig you out with my bare hands. Have you seen the film *Diamonds Are Forever*?"

"Probably."

"In the finale, Tiffany Case tries to shoot a gun to save the day and falls straight off the side of an oil rig. Every time I watch it, I want to smack the crap out of her." Lainie exhaled, disgusted. "Well, in a crisis? That's me. Trying to save Bond's arse and toppling off an oil rig. I completely lost it. Chloe, by the way? Voice of reason. It's totally demoralizing. Soothe me."

She was rewarded for her legitimately embarrassing inability to cope by the lightening of Richard's expression. A twinkle came into his eyes.

"Wanted to dive in and save me, did you, Tig?"

"Yes, I did. And don't look so smug about it." Lainie leaned her chin against his shoulder, her smiling fading. "Will says you saved his life."

"I doubt it. He would have stopped wringing his hands and got to his feet eventually. He can't be completely useless."

Her arm tightened around his ribs. "Were you scared?"

"Are you joking? I was scared shitless." He sifted

his fingers through her hair. "I fully expected the walls to come down completely before we got out of there. Christ, I was even scared for Farmer. Although that was mostly for your sake."

"What do you mean?"

His fingertips ran along her lips, absently petting. "I suddenly remembered the way you looked when you talked about Hannah." His voice was grim. "I didn't want you to lose someone else you cared about."

Lainie took a shaky breath. "You risked your own life to help Will…for me."

"Well, for Farmer himself as a borderline human being," Richard said mockingly, "but yes. Also for you." He obviously couldn't believe his own fallibility.

"Because…" She hesitated. "Because you think I… care about Will?"

Which she did, in a very platonic, mostly nostalgic way, but Richard was suggesting something more than that.

"I heard what you said." He pulled on her earlobe, gently chastising. "I do actually listen when you speak. But—you do care about Farmer." He was matter-of-fact, but his finger tightened around a loop of her hair, accidentally giving it a painful tug. "I realised that a long time ago. I suppose that's why I reacted so badly on Sunday night."

Sunday night—God, was it only *two days ago* that everything had fallen apart so spectacularly?

"You had the right to react badly. It was really shitty, what I did. Will might have blabbed, but it *was* my fault he was able to."

"I'm not denying I would have been angry no matter who you told, but I doubt I would have left you

on your doorstep if it had been someone else. Anyone
else." Richard grimaced. "I was jealous. Of Will fucking Farmer. It doesn't get much lower than that."

Lainie shook her head. "You don't need to be jealous of anyone. What I feel for you and how I felt about
Will—it's not even on the same planet."

There was still a definite hint of doubt when he said,
"You wouldn't sleep with a man if you didn't care about
him. That might be gratifying in light of recent activities—" he lifted a brow "—but less so in relation to
events of a few months ago."

"As of a few days ago, I would no longer sleep with
a man I didn't *love*." She touched the ashy black curls
at his hairline. "I know what I would be missing now."

Richard stilled. "Love?"

She put her lips to the corner of his in a feathery kiss.
"You're the most irritating man I've ever met, Troy. And
I love you like you wouldn't believe."

He stayed motionless while she trailed leisurely, affectionate kisses over his brow and the bridge of his
nose, giving him time to take that in. Then he gripped
her face between his hands, so tightly that it hurt, and
took her mouth in a fierce, shatteringly possessive kiss.
They sat curled together for long minutes, noses touching, lips millimetres apart, their breaths mingling.

"Are you telling me," he said at last, in a low, rough
murmur, "that I dragged his sorry carcass all the way
through that building for no reason at all?"

Her smile lit up her eyes. "If it makes you feel any
better, your good deed today probably cancelled out
an entire year's worth of bad behaviour. Firmly back
on Santa's nice list." She held his gaze, needing him to
understand. "Richard. What you said about me being

on the rebound. No. Just—no. Really, *really* no." She wrinkled her nose. "Will's not so bad. But my relationship with him? A pretty mediocre dress rehearsal before I fucking *killed* it on opening night."

Richard finally smiled at that. He slid his hand to the back of her head, tangling his fingers in her hair. "Yeah?"

Solemnly, she sketched a cross over her heart.

"All right, then," he said softly, and she slipped her arms around his neck, hugging him tight again.

Eventually, he pulled back and lifted her chin with a gentle nudge of his knuckle. "You know you're the only person I've ever loved."

Lainie curled her fingers into a ball to hide their shaking. She tucked her hand behind the bulky breadth of his shoulder.

"I think I knew when you tried to leave an imprint of your face on the Metronome stage. I definitely should have known when I found you struggling with Westfield. I could have throttled him with his pretentious bloody cravat." He kissed the arch of her cheekbone. "Last night, I was looking for any excuse not to care."

"And now?"

"Now I will grudgingly agree. I've never been so lucky in my life."

EPILOGUE

COOL LIPS PRESSED behind her ear. Warm fingertips caressed a path down her sternum, coming to rest in the hollow between her breasts. Lainie threaded strands of smooth blond hair through her knuckles, thought about what she wanted for dinner, and waited for the kiss. It didn't come. The masculine six-pack hovering over her recumbent form had gone rigid.

"Cut!" snapped Gillian Keene, their director. She leaned back in her chair. "For God's sake."

Lainie arched her back and turned her head, trying to locate the problem. Her expression of carefully tutored desire melted into a wide smile. Richard, leaning against the wall, was scaring the nonexistent pants off her costar with nothing more than a steady stare. His gaze transferred to her, and the icy blue eyes warmed with affection.

Mark Forster spoke without looking up from the screen where he was monitoring the incoming footage. "That's it. Troy, you're banned from the set when we're doing intimate shots. Women are supposed to be falling in vicarious love during this scene, not wondering if the intimidated hero is going to lose control of his bladder. Take ten!"

Lainie sat up in the four-poster bed and looked with amused apology at Harry Brent, heartthrob of the small screen and of no personal interest to her whatsoever. "His reputation is really quite exaggerated," she lied.

Harry cast another unsettled glance at Richard, who was talking to Mark but still had one eye on the bed. "I don't think I believe you. And I'd prefer to be wearing more than a flesh-coloured sock when I find out."

Lainie grinned as he scuttled away. She threw back the bedcovers and got up, pulling on her cardigan over the old-fashioned shift she was wearing. She padded across to Richard, taking his outstretched hands and letting him pull her in against his body. "All hail the King of Scotland," she said. "In all his ill-fated, sociopathic glory. Or is it the presidential gavel rather than the royal sceptre today?"

Richard held her hands behind his back, keeping her close to him. "Rehearsal this morning, committee meeting this afternoon. Both equally trying to my temper, although I believe there may have been more blatant idiocy and disrespect for authority in the boardroom than in the castle."

"Sounds like you're well in need of a long weekend away, then."

Richard bent and dropped a kiss on the corner of her mouth before she could protest. "Not in the workplace. I know. Call it a special occasion."

"Hmm." She couldn't help smiling. She couldn't *stop* smiling. "No last-minute delays? No late protests from Harlan Powell that His Majesty's presence can't be spared for a few days?"

"It can't, of course, but they'll just have to stumble on without me." Richard stole a kiss full on her mouth, and followed it up with a nip of her earlobe. "I have more important matters to attend to. And shall do so with the greatest pleasure." He nuzzled her lightly with his nose. "Besides, he was suitably impressed that we chose Scotland. Puts it down to research for the role."

Lainie halted in her sneaky exploration of the small of his back. "I hope not. I don't really see us as the Macbeths."

"No. They got on fairly well until the regicide."

"Beatrice and Benedick, maybe. With more bickering. And fewer rhyming couplets."

He released her wrists to cup her face. "God, I love you."

Lainie lifted her hands and laid them over his, linking their fingers. "Do you?"

"More today than yesterday." He tilted her chin up with his thumbs. "More now than an hour ago. By the time I die at ninety of a sex-induced heart attack, I expect I'll love you in a way I can't even comprehend."

Oh...

He really did it very, *very* well. She tightened her grip on him. "I think that's the most romantic thing I've ever heard." She paused. "What play was that from?"

"*Richard III*," said her own Richard, without missing a beat. "To his own reflection in the mirror. Didn't make the final cut."

Lainie started to laugh. The sound was purely happy, and it made him smile. "You know what, Richard? You're all right."

"As I said, Tig, I don't half mind you either."

She looked steadily up at him. "So, you're ready for this?"

His smile grew confident and wicked. "Lay on, Macduff."

London Celebrity @LondonCelebrity. now
Surprise elopement!
A rep for Richard Troy and Elaine Graham confirms that the "very happy" couple tied the knot at Gretna Green this morning.

* * * * *

ACKNOWLEDGMENTS

MY SINCERE THANKS to my editor, Deborah Nemeth, and all the team at Carina Press for their friendly welcome, unwavering patience and sheer hard work!

And without the support of my family and friends (near, far and online), this book might have remained just a handful of vague ideas about a temperamental actor. Thank you—I love you all.

ABOUT THE AUTHOR

LUCY PARKER LIVES in the gorgeous Central Otago region of New Zealand, where she feels lucky every day to look out at mountains, lakes and vineyards. She has a degree in art history, loves museums and art galleries, and doodles unrecognizable flowers when she has writer's block.

When she's not writing, working or sleeping, she happily tackles the towering pile of to-be-read books that never gets any smaller. Thankfully, there's always another story waiting.

Her interest in romantic fiction began with a preteen viewing of Jane Austen's *Pride and Prejudice* (Firth-style), which prompted her to read the book as well. A family friend introduced her to Georgette Heyer, and the rest was history.

She loves to talk to other readers and writers, and you can find her on Twitter, www.lucyparkerfiction.com.

REQUEST YOUR FREE BOOKS!

2 FREE NOVELS
FROM THE ROMANCE COLLECTION,
PLUS 2 FREE GIFTS!

YES! Please send me 2 FREE novels from the Romance Collection and my 2 FREE gifts (gifts are worth about $10). After receiving them, if I don't wish to receive any more books, I can return the shipping statement marked "cancel." If I don't cancel, I will receive 4 brand-new novels every month and be billed just $6.49 per book in the U.S. or $6.99 per book in Canada. That's a savings of at least 18% off the cover price. It's quite a bargain! Shipping and handling is just 50¢ per book in the U.S. and 75¢ per book in Canada.* I understand that accepting the 2 free books and gifts places me under no obligation to buy anything. I can always return a shipment and cancel at any time. Even if I never buy another book, the two free books and gifts are mine to keep forever.

194/394 MDN GH4D

Name	(PLEASE PRINT)
Address	Apt. #
City	State/Prov.	Zip/Postal Code

Signature (if under 18, a parent or guardian must sign)

Mail to the **Reader Service:**
IN U.S.A.: P.O. Box 1867, Buffalo, NY 14240-1867
IN CANADA: P.O. Box 609, Fort Erie, Ontario L2A 5X3

Want to try 2 free books from another line?
Call 1-800-873-8635 or visit www.ReaderService.com.

*Terms and prices subject to change without notice. Prices do not include applicable taxes. Sales tax applicable in N.Y. Canadian residents will be charged applicable taxes. Offer not valid in Quebec. This offer is limited to one order per household. Not valid for current subscribers to the Romance Collection or the Romance/Suspense Collection. All orders subject to credit approval. Credit or debit balances in a customer's account(s) may be offset by any other outstanding balance owed by or to the customer. Please allow 4 to 6 weeks for delivery. Offer available while quantities last.

Your Privacy—The Reader Service is committed to protecting your privacy. Our Privacy Policy is available online at www.ReaderService.com or upon request from the Reader Service.

We make a portion of our mailing list available to reputable third parties that offer products we believe may interest you. If you prefer that we not exchange your name with third parties, or if you wish to clarify or modify your communication preferences, please visit us at www.ReaderService.com/consumerschoice or write to us at Reader Service Preference Service, P.O. Box 9062, Buffalo, NY 14240-9062. Include your complete name and address.

ROM15R

REQUEST YOUR FREE BOOKS!
2 FREE NOVELS PLUS 2 FREE GIFTS!

HARLEQUIN®

Blaze

red-hot reads!

REQUEST YOUR FREE BOOKS!
2 FREE NOVELS PLUS 2 FREE GIFTS!

HARLEQUIN®

Desire

ALWAYS POWERFUL, PASSIONATE AND PROVOCATIVE

YES! Please send me 2 FREE Harlequin® Desire novels and my 2 FREE gifts (gifts are worth about $10). After receiving them, if I don't wish to receive any more books, I can return the shipping statement marked "cancel." If I don't cancel, I will receive 6 brand-new novels every month and be billed just $4.55 per book in the U.S. or $5.24 per book in Canada. That's a savings of at least 13% off the cover price! It's quite a bargain! Shipping and handling is just 50¢ per book in the U.S. and 75¢ per book in Canada.* I understand that accepting the 2 free books and gifts places me under no obligation to buy anything. I can always return a shipment and cancel at any time. Even if I never buy another book, the two free books and gifts are mine to keep forever.

225/326 HDN GH2P

Name _____ (PLEASE PRINT) _____

Address _____ Apt. # ____

City _____ State/Prov. _____ Zip/Postal Code _____

Signature (if under 18, a parent or guardian must sign)

Mail to the **Reader Service:**
IN U.S.A.: P.O. Box 1867, Buffalo, NY 14240-1867
IN CANADA: P.O. Box 609, Fort Erie, Ontario L2A 5X3

Want to try two free books from another line?
Call 1-800-873-8635 or visit www.ReaderService.com.

* Terms and prices subject to change without notice. Prices do not include applicable taxes. Sales tax applicable in N.Y. Canadian residents will be charged applicable taxes. Offer not valid in Quebec. This offer is limited to one order per household. Not valid for current subscribers to Harlequin Desire books. All orders subject to credit approval. Credit or debit balances in a customer's account(s) may be offset by any other outstanding balance owed by or to the customer. Please allow 4 to 6 weeks for delivery. Offer available while quantities last.

Your Privacy—The Reader Service is committed to protecting your privacy. Our Privacy Policy is available online at www.ReaderService.com or upon request from the Reader Service.

We make a portion of our mailing list available to reputable third parties that offer products we believe may interest you. If you prefer that we not exchange your name with third parties, or if you wish to clarify or modify your communication preferences, please visit us at www.ReaderService.com/consumerchoice or write to us at Reader Service Preference Service, P.O. Box 9062, Buffalo, NY 14240-9062. Include your complete name and address.

HDI5

REQUEST YOUR FREE BOOKS!
2 FREE NOVELS PLUS 2 FREE GIFTS!

⊞ HARLEQUIN®

SPECIAL EDITION
Life, Love & Family

REQUEST YOUR FREE BOOKS!

♦HARLEQUIN

Presents®

2 FREE NOVELS PLUS
2 FREE GIFTS!

PASSION GUARANTEED SEDUCTION

YES! Please send me 2 FREE Harlequin Presents® novels and my 2 FREE gifts (gifts are worth about $10). After receiving them, if I don't wish to receive any more books, I can return the shipping statement marked "cancel." If I don't cancel, I will receive 6 brand-new novels every month and be billed just $4.30 per book in the U.S. or $5.24 per book in Canada. That's a saving of at least 13% off the cover price! It's quite a bargain! Shipping and handling is just 50¢ per book in the U.S. and 75¢ per book in Canada.* I understand that accepting the 2 free books and gifts places me under no obligation to buy anything. I can always return a shipment and cancel at any time. Even if I never buy another book, the two free books and gifts are mine to keep forever.

106/306 HDN GHRP

Name _____
 (PLEASE PRINT)

Address _____ Apt. # _____

City _____ State/Prov. _____ Zip/Postal Code _____

Signature (if under 18, a parent or guardian must sign) _____

Mail to the **Reader Service:**
IN U.S.A.: P.O. Box 1867, Buffalo, NY 14240-1867
IN CANADA: P.O. Box 609, Fort Erie, Ontario L2A 5X3

**Are you a current subscriber to Harlequin Presents® books
and want to receive the larger-print edition?
Call 1-800-873-8635 or visit www.ReaderService.com.**

* Terms and prices subject to change without notice. Prices do not include applicable taxes. Sales tax applicable in N.Y. Canadian residents will be charged applicable taxes. Offer not valid in Quebec. This offer is limited to one order per household. Not valid for current subscribers to Harlequin Presents books. All orders subject to credit approval. Credit or debit balances in a customer's account(s) may be offset by any other outstanding balance owed by or to the customer. Please allow 4 to 6 weeks for delivery. Offer available while quantities last.

Your Privacy—The Reader Service is committed to protecting your privacy. Our Privacy Policy is available online at www.ReaderService.com or upon request from the Reader Service.

We make a portion of our mailing list available to reputable third parties that offer products we believe may interest you. If you prefer that we not exchange your name with third parties, or if you wish to clarify or modify your communication preferences, please visit us at www.ReaderService.com/consumerschoice or write to us at Reader Service Preference Service, P.O. Box 9062, Buffalo, NY 14240-9062. Include your complete name and address.

HP15

REQUEST YOUR FREE BOOKS!
2 FREE NOVELS PLUS 2 FREE GIFTS!

ⓗ HARLEQUIN®

Western Romance

ROMANCE THE ALL-AMERICAN WAY!

YES! Please send me 2 FREE Harlequin® Western Romance novels and my 2 FREE gifts (gifts are worth about \$10). After receiving them, if I don't wish to receive any more books, I can return the shipping statement marked "cancel." If I don't cancel, I will receive 4 brand-new novels every month and be billed just \$4.74 per book in the U.S. or \$5.49 per book in Canada. That's a savings of at least 12% off the cover price! It's quite a bargain! Shipping and handling is just 50¢ per book in the U.S. and 75¢ per book in Canada.* I understand that accepting the 2 free books and gifts places me under no obligation to buy anything. I can always return a shipment and cancel at any time. Even if I never buy another book, the two free books and gifts are mine to keep forever.

154/354 HDN GJ5V

Name _____ (PLEASE PRINT)

Address _____ Apt. #

City _____ State/Prov. _____ Zip/Postal Code

Signature (if under 18, a parent or guardian must sign)

Mail to the **Reader Service:**
IN U.S.A.: P.O. Box 1867, Buffalo, NY 14240-1867
IN CANADA: P.O. Box 609, Fort Erie, Ontario L2A 5X3

Want to try two free books from another line?
Call 1-800-873-8635 or visit www.ReaderService.com.

* Terms and prices subject to change without notice. Prices do not include applicable taxes. Sales tax applicable in N.Y. Canadian residents will be charged applicable taxes. Offer not valid in Quebec. This offer is limited to one order per household. Not valid for current subscribers to Harlequin Western Romance books. All orders subject to credit approval. Credit or debit balances in a customer's account(s) may be offset by any other outstanding balance owed by or to the customer. Please allow 4 to 6 weeks for delivery. Offer available while quantities last.

Your Privacy—The Reader Service is committed to protecting your privacy. Our Privacy Policy is available online at www.ReaderService.com or upon request from the Reader Service.

We make a portion of our mailing list available to reputable third parties that offer products we believe may interest you. If you prefer that we not exchange your name with third parties, or if you wish to clarify or modify your communication preferences, please visit us at www.ReaderService.com/consumerschoice or write to us at Reader Service Preference Service, P.O. Box 9062, Buffalo, NY 14240-9062. Include your complete name and address.

HWR16

READERSERVICE.COM

Manage your account online!

- Review your order history
- Manage your payments
- Update your address

We've designed the
Reader Service website
just for you.

Enjoy all the features!

- Discover new series available to you, and read excerpts from any series.
- Respond to mailings and special monthly offers.
- Connect with favorite authors at the blog.
- Browse the Bonus Bucks catalog and online-only exculsives.
- Share your feedback.

Visit us at:

ReaderService.com